CW01653963

Love Lottie

Mel Higgins

Dedicated to everyone who has a dream.

Dream big.

Keep chasing.

Never give up.

Love Lottie

Introduction

<u>2020</u>

The gentle breeze tickled the man's face as he stood leaning heavily on his cane. His roughened black leather jacket protecting him from goosebumps gathering on his skin. Beside him stood his daughter who had said nothing since their arrival at the cemetery. Her olive skin was hidden under layers as she carefully placed a bouquet of flowers amongst many others in all the colours of the rainbow. He asked his daughter to read the messages attached to them, he thought some names would be recognisable but only a few rang a bell.

Rest in peace Charlotte from everyone at Penzance Library x

May you shine as bright as the brightest star, love you always Mum. Love Nancy, and Dennis XXXX

Gonna miss you Nan, say hi to Grandad for me, see you one day. Noah xx

Thank you for being my inspiration, I hope you and Dad are sitting in your favourite chairs or are laying in the sun, young again in the allotment. Sarah, Ollie, and Matilda xxxxxx

The book club won't be the same without you lovely, Margret and the gang x

We may have lost you, but your voice will always be heard through your stories, Meg, and Jimmy xx

You have always been one of the bravest women I have known, you are my best friend, and I am going to miss you every single day, Mum, love Florence, and Stuart xxxxxx

Love you Mum, thank you for always being our rock, Arthur. xxxx

At the end of the rainbow, we will all meet again, lots of love William and Elsie xxx

"We were too late," the man stuttered, gazing at the black inscription written on the marble headstone.

Charlotte Florence Hollister
Wife, Mum, and Grandma
1941 – 2020

"She'll know we're here," the woman softly said linking her arm to her dad's. He had wanted to make the trip as soon as he heard the news of the woman's passing. They had avoided seeing her when she lived, so the feeling of betrayal was strong in her thoughts, but she couldn't let her old man down, knowing what it meant to him.

"At least she isn't alone." Above her name was another, Charlotte's companion in death.

Henry John Hollister
Husband, Dad, and Granddad
1941 – 2018

"He always was the one who took better care of her. Took me a long time to admit it but he was the right man for her. Could you write the message on the card for the flowers for me, sweetheart, I didn't want it to get wet in that shower."

His daughter pulled out the white floral card that her dad had carefully hidden in her coat pocket protecting it from the rain when they left the florists, now with the sun creeping behind a moving dark cloud making a clearing of pure blue she prepared to write it with a new pen her dad bought from the airport especially for this purpose.

"What shall I write?"

"Write: Charlotte we are sorry we didn't come sooner; the right time just never came. We watched you from afar and cheered every success. We hope one day we will all be able to meet and forgive the years between us that have passed. Fly high angel. Love always, Joe and Betty xxx"

1950s

Cathleen

Chapter One

September 1958

The baby cried all night, as if she knew she had been separated from her mother. Nobody was able to soothe her, she was screaming at the top of her lungs right into the dark night, the sound bouncing off the walls, keeping everyone in the Ridley household awake. Cathleen and her husband, Rupert, were staying at her parents' house in Durham to help with the new-born, who had been a surprise for them all. She and her mum, Mavis, had been taking turns to try and comfort the baby.

"This is wrong; we should take her back to the hospital," Frank, Cathleen's dad, suggested. "She needs her ma."

"Her mother is a child, Frank. Our child. How can we allow our 16-year-old daughter, who believes running away from home is the answer to not getting what she wants, to look after a baby."

"I know Pet, but she will have us to support her. I think the decision to take her was too rash. The poor bairn is still none the wiser, man. What will she think when she wakes up?"

"She will thank us. Maybe not straight away, but she will eventually realise that we have taken her for her own good. She is a clever girl, our Charlotte. She is going to make something of herself. She wants to be living it up in London as a writer, not changing nappies. You know as well as I do that motherhood is not what she has always dreamt of."

"Not that we know of," Cathleen interrupted.

"What do you mean by that?" Mavis asked irritably.

"I mean, Charlotte hadn't dreamt of motherhood. Yes, she has always dreamt of London and writing but since Nan died, she's never mentioned it. How do we know that she doesn't dream of motherhood now?"

"Because she is sixteen years old, Cathleen. That is why."

"She's always been great with Peter, and we don't know what she has wanted recently. How do we not know that during the time she was carrying this little one, she didn't long for the day she could meet her, long to be a mam?"

As Cathleen rocked the little one, she thought back to how she felt when she had carried a child, she remembered the sheer excitement of growing her baby only to be faced with shattered dreams when she lost her child, making her long for motherhood twice as much.

"Cathleen is right, we should take the baby back and ask Charlotte ourselves. Only that way can we know if what we are doing is the right thing," Frank tried to tell his wife.

"God damn it!" Mavis shouted before bursting into tears. Frank rushed over to comfort her at the dining table. "How could she be so foolish?" she cried. "Where did we go wrong, Frank? She was such a clever girl. She did well at school, she had a job, she had friends, and helped Mr Flint at the allotments. What happened?"

"Joe Hollister is what happened, Pet, we are not to blame," Frank said, as he rocked his wife back and forth in his arms matching the motions that Cathleen was making with the baby. "She was doing fine until she got involved with him, she was making progress, I began to believe she was moving forward from the loss of your ma. He corrupted her, encouraged her to leave home then dumped her back 'ere once he had ruined her. He is probably with some other poor lass now. Don't you worry Mave, we can sort this out together. We will bring Charlotte home and if she wants to keep the baby, we will support her, if not then we can consider bringing her up ourselves maybe that way Charlotte can get on with her life but still know the bairn."

"We can help Charlotte together, Mam," Cathleen said with hope. "We can do anything as a family."

"Cathleen is right Pet, if we can get through a war and last year worried sick over the bairn, we can get through this."

"Whatever will the neighbours think?" Mavis mumbled.

"Fuck the neighbours," Frank replied, making Cathleen giggle.

Once Cathleen managed to convince her parents to try and get some sleep, she sunk into the couch with her niece in her arms, who was sleeping at last. Cathleen watched her with awe as she stroked her brown hair and tiny fingers.

"You're perfect," she whispered.

Her husband Rupert, was on the late shift at the factory he worked at. Normally she would be home alone now, watching the arrows on the clock tick by until he would arrive back. Clock watching was not on the agenda now, for she had something far more beautiful to watch. Cathleen imagined what her baby would have looked like, would they have had dark hair like herself and her sister or would their hair have been fair like her husbands. Losing her unborn child had been the worst pain she had ever encountered and one she wouldn't have wished on her worst enemy, let alone her little sister.

"Your mammy has got herself into a pickle, Baby Girl. She gave us all a fright when she ran away with that naughty boy next door. Your grandad and nana tried to split them up because they knew he was a bad egg. She used to be with a much nicer boy you know, your Uncle Henry, but for some unknown reason your mammy had a change of heart. I heard that your uncle is who helped deliver you into this world, maybe that is why your mammy got poorly. Don't you worry though, Baby Girl, everything is going to be alright now that you're both home, where you belong."

Mavis gently shook Cathleen awake removing her granddaughter from her arms. Cathleen was instructed to get some proper sleep, as she wrapped the baby up in one of Cathleen's younger brothers old baby blankets.

"We are going to the hospital to see Charlotte, hopefully she is awake now."

As her parents prepared to leave, someone called at the door, a sleepy Rupert answered it, still in his work clothes, having dropped off in the chair opposite Cathleen. He returned to the front room carrying a white crib, Henry following behind. The young boy looked as exhausted as she felt, Cathleen observed. His face was full of worry as he carried in a leather holdall.

"Clothes for Betty," Henry informed them all. "I thought she would need them as well as somewhere comfortable to sleep."

"Thank you, Henry, that was very thoughtful of you," Mavis said.

"I am sorry about Lottie; I did everything by the book I swear," Henry explained, reaching out to stroke the baby's cheek. "I would never do anything to hurt either of them, I am not like my brother."

"We know that Son, but you and your dad failed to let us know Charlotte was home. This could have been prevented," Frank said sternly as he fastened up his coat.

"I'm sorry, Frank, Lottie was adamant we wouldn't. She wanted to tell you both in her own time. We both tried to convince her, we knew you would find out eventually. I promise nothing like this will happen again, I will do the right thing by both Lottie and Betty and look after them both."

"You needn't worry yourself; my daughter and granddaughter will be just fine here with us."

"It is no worry at all, I love Lottie and I assure you that I will work hard and provide for them b-."

"Provide for them! Henry, you needn't do such things. No one is expecting you to step into your brother's shoes," Mavis said in surprise.

"My brother's shoes are far too small for me, Mavis. I asked Lottie to marry me, and she agreed. I promise I'll be both a good husband and a good dad to Betty. You have my word."

The room was stunned to hear Henry's declaration of love and marriage, Frank started to laugh which displeased the youngest Hollister brother. Cathleen found his declaration very sweet despite the surprise.

"This is ridiculous," Mavis laughed. "You're just a child, marriage is a very serious thing. It's a commitment made before God."

"It's out of the question. You do not have our blessing." Frank took the bags from Henry. "Thank you for bringing along the things for the baby."

"Betty, her name is Betty Florence Hollister. I love your daughter, please do not look at me in the same way you do my brother."

"If I remember rightly, your brother declared his love for Charlotte and his love was so true that he got her in the family way and then left her for dust. So please, Henry, do not be so surprised when we tell you that the answer is no. You will not marry her; in fact, I don't want you anywhere near either of them. Do you hear me Lad?"

Henry's fists clenched, Rupert was quick to step in and guide him towards the exit before anyone ended up hurt. It took some shoves to get him to leave, his feet wouldn't move, as though they were glued to the carpet. He glared at Frank wordlessly as though a glare alone could fight his corner. When Henry left everything began to shift.

"What is she playing at?" Mavis shouted, handing a tearful Betty to Cathleen. "What is it with those boys that attracts her to them, she is just going back and forth like a–"

"Don't say it Mam," Cathleen quickly said before Mavis said something she'd later regret.

"First, she couldn't stand either of them, always complaining. Courting Henry was one thing, Joe was another, but then to go back to Henry—agreeing to marry the boy after giving birth to his brother's child. Does she have no dignity?"

"Maybe she realised she loved Henry more. He did treat her better, he was respectful. Is he such a bad catch for Charlotte? If he can love her after everything she did to him, then it must be true, mustn't it?" Cathleen looked at her husband for support, but his only reply was an unconvincing smile.

"If Betty could see us now. What a mess our children have become." Mavis looked up at the ceiling with her eyes tightly shut as she spoke of her best friend, Betty Hollister. "None of this would have happened if you had stayed with us."

"Rupert," Frank who had said nothing since Henry's departure till then was scribbling on the back of the morning post. "Ring Albert, tell him to come as soon as possible. Say it is an emergency."

Cathleen's obedient husband left without hesitation.

"Dad, why are you fetching Uncle Albert?" Cathleen felt anxious as she asked. Uncle Albert was Mavis' brother who lived in Mayfair. Frank had never invited Albert to Durham before—not since before the war that was. He believed her uncle was above himself with his fancy car and big London house, when before the war they had got on swimmingly.

Frank delivered his plan as though it was the only choice they had. "Charlotte is going to go to London. There Albert and Emily will look after her; we will keep Betty here."

"No Dad!" Cathleen gasped.

Frank put up his hand to silence her. "She can stay there and start again. She has never been the same since Florence died. If we allow her to come home, she is going to go straight round to that lad and what if she runs away again? What if she ends up in the family way once again? Then she will have two mouths to feed. Henry's wage is not going to stretch to feed a family of four."

"Walter will surely up his wages, Mam tell him." Cathleen clutched Betty a little tighter to protect the young child from the plan her grandad was making to separate her from her mother.

"You were right yesterday, Mavis, Charlotte is far too young for all of this. She is not mature enough; she can't even make her mind up which bloody boyfriend she wants."

"Joe left her!" Cathleen shouted.

"Your dad is right, Cathleen, I know it is hard to hear but it's true," Mavis said, trying to comfort her, but Cathleen pulled away. "Charlotte is too impulsive. We are giving back her life this way. She will be happy in London. All she ever wished for was to be there. Now she can be. Getting away from here and those Hollister boys will be the best thing for her. She has just been through childbirth, what if she doesn't really love Henry like she thinks she does. Should she ruin her whole life for him?"

"Stop! Henry is not a bad lad. Stop concentrating on him. What about Betty? She needs her mam. How can you just make this choice without Charlotte? How can you send her across the country away from her baby? It isn't right!"

"She committed a sin, Cathleen! A good catholic girl like yourself must know that. Now we are going to fix it." Using her faith was a low blow, Cathleen thought, shocked at Mavis. "Please see that what we are doing is for the benefit of your sister and Betty."

"You're both wrong."

There was nothing more Cathleen could do to convince her parents they were making a big mistake. They left the house shortly after their dispute, stating they would inform the hospital of their decision. Rupert returned from the phone box; her Uncle Albert was on his way to Durham. The plan had been made; it was being put into place, all the while her little sister was lying in a hospital bed with no idea just how much her life had changed—again. Regrettably, a part of Cathleen hoped that her sister did not open her eyes again, she did not wish for her to feel the pain that comes with having to say goodbye to a child. When Cathleen had lost her own baby, she had the love and support of her husband; Rupert had been by her side through it all. Who would Charlotte have? Yes, she loved London, but that was when they had their nan. Now the house belonged to her Uncle Albert and his wife, Emily, who no one liked, and the feeling was clearly mutual. What could they do to support her? Their uncle was a kind man, but he kept his feelings close to his chest. There was William, their cousin, but he spent the week at boarding school. He and Charlotte had grown up quite close, but they had spoken very little lately. Charlotte had not taken the news of their Nana Florence's death well; she had gone through a rollercoaster of emotions. She cut everyone off for a while until it looked as though she had made a breakthrough—her relationship with Henry grew and she had seemed like herself once more. So, it was a shock to find that she had suddenly took a U-turn—out of nowhere she started to stay out all night, not turn up to work for weeks, and left Henry mortified as she turned all her attention and time to his older brother, Joe. Whatever was going through her sister's head during her grief didn't matter anymore. What mattered now was what would happen during her next round of grief and what future both Charlotte and her new-born have.

"Betty," Cathleen said aloud, peering at the baby who was now snuggly settled into her crib.

"Excuse me," Rupert said, as he rubbed his eyes whilst sat across from her.

"Betty. Henry said that was her name. Named after her own nana. Betty Hollister was the loveliest woman, those boys were always running her riot, but she had the patience of a saint."

"So must your sister."

"Rupert!" Cathleen exclaimed. "Charlotte was a bit lost that is all. If Nana had never died, she would have left here and not looked back, not for Henry or Joe. Little Betty here doesn't deserve to be motherless down to ill judgement. She is so innocent."

As Cathleen watched the small torso of the little one move as she breathed, her eyes became blurry with tears.

"Come on now." Rupert was quickly by her side. "Betty has the gift of not being able to remember any of this. She has no idea what is happening."

Betty looked up with huge blue eyes, looking back at the two faces peering over her cot.

"I have no idea what my parents' plan is for her," Cathleen cried. "It's not right, Rupert. Not for her or Charlotte. How is she going to feel when they tell her that she is to leave without her daughter?"

Rupert pulled his wife into his arms hushing her as her crying grew louder; Betty began to stir irritably. "If she is anything like her big sister then she will be strong and will get through it."

Betty's cries reached a higher volume than Cathleen's, so Rupert tended to her as Cathleen dried her face with her skirt. He carefully lifted Betty out of her crib and gently swayed her back and forth in his arms humming lullabies around the front room. Cathleen's heart could have burst observing her husband with the precious child in his arms. Rupert would make a great dad; she had always known this. He was a natural with children and the care he gave her would surely only be amplified with a child of their own. As Betty's cries began to calm, he noticed Cathleen's gaze and smiled. They had spoken about having children for as long as they had been together, they had hoped by now to have had one, but God had not gifted them with any just yet. It would happen, they told each other, one day they would have their own.

Walter Hollister made his first visit at 11am. He shuffled on the doorstep as he kindly asked Cathleen if he would be able to see his granddaughter. Walter had been like an uncle to Cathleen when she was growing up next door to him. He had signed up for the war with her dad and they had fought side by side. When they both returned, neither of them were the men they'd been when they'd left the lanes. While her dad cried over glasses of whiskey and war songs, Walter sat up straight and didn't say a word, as if he had not been away at all. His shoulders however were slumped, and his head was low as he waited for Cathleen's permission. Cathleen allowed the kind man in, after all it was not his fault his son had disgraced her sister, he had at least done well with one of them. Rupert passed baby Betty to Walter who eagerly reached out for his granddaughter thanking them for allowing him to see her.

"She has my Betty's eyes," he said, clearing his throat.

Betty rested peacefully in his arms as he praised her over and over, clearly the besotted grandad. Rupert made a round of tea and Cathleen felt herself feeling all the more nervous as time passed awaiting her parents to return home.

"I imagine Frank blames me for all of this. Joe he—he has done many things I don't approve of, but I know he cared about your sister. I am not saying what he did was right, it wasn't, but he had his reasons and when you speak to Charlotte, she will tell you."

"No one is blaming you, Walter," Cathleen partially lied.

"I will do my bit by her; she may not have her da, but she will have me and Henry. Both of them will have our support."

Cathleen quickly glanced at Rupert, somewhere on the road her uncle was driving towards them to be asked to take Charlotte back to London with him—without Baby Betty. Support and Charlotte's future lay in his hands.

"I know I'll have to speak to your da about this, but you know we have more room over at ours for the two of them. Henry is happy staying on the sofa. Makes a little more sense seeing as you have Little Peter here. Plus, your ma and da would only be next door."

Walter's suggestion sounded perfect, Cathleen thought, he presented a way for Betty and Charlotte to both be home surrounded by everyone that cared about them. He gave the perfect solution to enable Charlotte to live with her daughter, but with Henry also around, Cathleen knew her parents would never allow it. Cathleen pictured Christmas with the two families celebrating together just like they always had before everything changed. Betty could be the one to bring everyone together again. She pictured them all giving the little one chocolate eggs after a trip to church at Easter, all sat around the front room; or birthday parties dancing the night away, Little Peter twirling his little niece as they both perform for the grownups. As sweet as the future could be imagined, it was not to be.

"My Uncle Albert is on his way to Durham now, Walter, Charlotte is going to be staying in London once she is well enough to leave hospital."

Walter raised his eyebrows. "London, well I suppose living with your uncle will be a great opportunity for them. Betty could have things we could only have dreamt of giving you all as kids. I have the van; we could still visit, and I don't mind if anyone would like a lift down there. We are family after all. Henry will be sad to hear this but maybe it would do them a little good."

"He wants to marry her," Rupert brought up.

"Yes, well. Charlotte is very special to Henry; he believes he loves her. He would do anything for her, but time apart may be a good test, they are very young after all."

"A good test for what exactly, to test their love? Are you trying to say that my sister doesn't love Henry?"

"Charlotte's young, they both are. Marriage is a big commitment. They both need to know they are doing it for all the right reasons, that's all I am saying," Walter said with a smile.

Cathleen did not feel totally convinced but didn't bother fighting her sister's corner; she could not blame Walter for such assumptions. She broke Henry's heart and only gave him a second thought when Joe left her. Perhaps Walter was correct in believing Charlotte was not in love with Henry, she was just sixteen and very emotional after all.

"Yes, marriage is a big commitment," Rupert agreed.

"I have more things next door, a pram and such. I will bring them over later." Walter turned his attention back to Betty. "I hope you're not going to be visiting me talking all la de da, we need to keep some Geordie roots in you," he chuckled. "Granda will come and visit you all the time."

"Walter, Betty is not going to London," Cathleen informed the besotted grandad. "Just Charlotte."

Just saying the words out loud did not sound right. The look of confusion on Walter's face told her that it wasn't right. It wasn't natural. It didn't make any sense. Just looking around the room, there were people who would be willing to keep Charlotte on track.

"She is leaving Betty here. I don't understand, is Charlotte abandoning her?" Walter asked.

Cathleen shook her head. "Not at all. She—Charlotte doesn't know. No one has spoken to her yet. My parents believe it is best; they are giving her a second chance."

"But Betty, no ma, no da. What is to become of her? It isn't right, Charlotte has had a tough time but she's a strong lass. I've seen it with me own eyes these past few weeks."

"Maybe after a little while in London, Mavis and Frank will change their mind," Rupert suggested. "Some time down there could be good for some recuperation for Charlotte."

Walter was quiet for the remainder of his visit, his attention purely on the baby, before making his excuses to leave only just missing Mavis and Frank's return from the hospital. They both looked grave, collapsing onto the couch still in their coats. Rupert made himself useful in the kitchen with another round of cuppas. With some probing, Cathleen's parents informed her they told the hospital of their plans for Charlotte, along with plans to have Betty put up for adoption, shocking Cathleen to the core. The hospital agreed it was for the best and they would contact social services on their behalf. Charlotte would not see Betty, nor is she to have any visits from Henry.

"He's banned," Frank added.

Cathleen thought they would all rally round to bring Betty up, but Mavis and Frank said Betty would be better off with a new family, one that can give her everything she needs, a stable family away from bad blood and a big mess. Life with the Ridley's would be confusing for her, they said exhaustedly.

"She deserves better," Mavis said. "Is my brother on his way, Rupert?"

"Yes, Mavis. He left right away; we should expect him by teatime." Rupert placed a fresh cup of tea in front of everyone on the coffee table. "Any news on Charlotte while you were there?"

"She is awake now, the doctor said," Mavis said without a hint of happiness at the news, none at all Cathleen noticed.

"How is she? Is she okay? Can I visit?" Cathleen asked.

"The doctor said she will be fine," Mavis said reaching for her tea.

"You didn't see her?" Cathleen asked. "Why? She needs you, Mam. She's just had a baby; she's just had emergency care. She will be wondering what is going on. She will be asking after Betty. Why didn't you see her? Dad?"

"We will Pet, we will. It was just…I don't know…it was too hard to tell her. The doctor said he would do it for us," Frank said, looking at the floor as Cathleen gasped in horror at her parents' cowardice.

They had left her when she needed them the most. They let an unknown stranger in a white coat declare the news to their daughter that her child was being taken away from her. Rage grew inside her, tears erupted out of her eyes, yet she was speechless. Cathleen did not know what to say. The room fell silent, even Betty was careful not to make a sound as her future was decided for her. Cathleen wanted to reach for her coat and visit her sister herself but when the thought came to her of having to hold the dainty girl whose belly would still be protruding—her pain for her child overwhelming—when it came to the crunch, what would she say? How could she console her? Cathleen had always wanted what was best for Charlotte, she always felt it her responsibility to keep her in line as a child, to make sure she grew up to be charitable and a good Catholic. They were not an affectionate family, the war made sure of that. When they won on the battlefield the fight was not yet over, it had continued at home. It was a fight to keep everyone going, it was a fight to stop her dad from losing it completely, it was a fight to face each day that was fought gratefully. It had been a fight to let Charlotte, who had never met her dad before and had been told countless times of the exciting times to come with the loveable man, know that she was loved even though no one had the heart to show it any longer. Now as Charlotte lay in torment in her hospital bed, the fight had come to an end. They had all truly given up.

The front door almost came off its hinges as it blasted open, interrupting the heart wrenching silence of a shameful family. Cathleen had never seen Henry so angry in all her life, he did not wait for an invitation, he did not come in to make peace. The boy was hot headed, he looked like a bull released into a ring. Frank was the first to stand up ready to take on the bull who was not intimidated at all by the veteran.

"You're making a big mistake!" he shouted pointing to Frank. "You can't take her to London. That isn't what she wants!"

"Son, this is none of your concern," Frank said calmly.

"This is all of my concern; you have no idea what you're doing. Lottie wants to be here; she wants to be with Betty. This will destroy her," Henry shouted despite the cries from Baby Betty who managed to grab a quick glance from the outraged teenager. "She loves her," he cried, signalling to the bundle who was being swiftly removed from the heated room by Rupert who looked slightly pleased at the excuse to leave.

"Henry. Just leave," Frank said. "Before I do something I regret, I have had it up to here with today and you fucking Hollister lads. None of you are good enough for my daughter, none of you are good enough for my granddaughter. The only way to free them from your family is to send them away!"

"You're wrong!" Henry was now in Frank's face, Cathleen panicked at the consequences of his actions.

"Lottie needs to be able to come home and be the great mam she is going to be. She doesn't want the London life anymore, please listen to me. You're making a mistake; Lottie wants her baby and her family here in Durham."

"Henry, Darling, please just go home," Mavis said calmly.

"You. You're her mam. How can you do this Mavis? How can you just send her away without asking her?" Henry asked, rounding on Mavis. "My mam will be looking down at you in disgust. Never would she have thrown her kids out, she would have made you see sense and done the right thing by Lottie because she was a real mam, you are pathetic!" he shouted, before receiving a thud from Frank, Mavis cried, and Cathleen gasped rooted to the couch, worried what home truths may come her way next.

Henry spat blood onto the carpet, then stood up straight as though unfazed by the punch. "She is going to hate you; you do realise that. All of you. She is going to hate you all forever. What you're doing is not for Charlotte or Betty, it is because you're ashamed; ashamed that you all did such a shit job, that she ran far away from here the first chance she could. You don't blame Joe for all of this, you blame yourselves and you want her gone so you don't have to face what you did."

"This is all your fucking brother's fault, now get out my house. Now!" Frank yelled, red in the face.

Henry laughed. "No, this is your fault. You can't control her forever. I will marry her Frank, and I will fix this mess. Mavis, you have a spot of blood on your carpet here, I do hope it washes out." Henry left the terrace house with as much noise as he'd arrived, as he slammed the front door behind him.

"You are banned from seeing her at the hospital too!" Frank shouted after him.

Cathleen felt shaken by the visit, she was not one for drinking. Apart from the sip of wine she took at mass, nothing passed her lips but right then a large strong glass of her dad's whiskey was tempting.

"Henry's right, this is a mess," she said.

"Once she is in London, things will fall into place," Mavis said unconvincingly.

When Cathleen's uncle arrived and learnt of the plan he was outraged. Albert could see no sense in the whole thing. He agreed with Cathleen about how damaging it was to send Charlotte to stay with him without her having any say. He was disgusted that his sister had dragged him all the way from London to ask such a huge favour that would have him rip a mother from her new-born baby as simply as removing a doll from a little girl. Albert found their idea appalling and wanted nothing to do with it, leaving to book himself into a local hotel.

"I'll speak to him tomorrow," Mavis stated after her brother made his leave. He was not on the same page at all. "Cathleen could you please call your brother in from the lane. I'm going to fill him a bath."

Chapter Two

September 1958

The family fell into a routine at the terrace house with Baby Betty, with Cathleen taking the reins and being the most available for the cherub. Walter had passed on Betty's pram, allowing Cathleen to take her out for walks. She knew the fresh air would do them good, yet found herself avoiding people. The community was small, and Cathleen knew many of the locals, having grown up there her whole life. The church had been her domain most of the time, where she got to know many people in her village. Cathleen worried when sweet elderly woman peeped into the pram to see the baby, she grew nervous as she spotted neighbours approaching her. She wished they wouldn't because once the joy of seeing Betty passed, the questions then followed. Whose baby was it? Was it hers? Was she a nanny? Babysitting? And in all honesty Cathleen had been left stumped on what to say. Should she admit Betty was her niece, should she lie and pretend she was doing a favour for a friend for the day? The truth never did manage to pass her lips, she felt mortified telling people that her teenage little sister had a child out of wedlock, embarrassed that the father was the one known for being brought home in the back of a police car, but the worst part was what she should say if they asked what happened next—she knew she would never be able to tell them that her sister had been sent away and the baby would also be taken. She found herself feeling angry at Charlotte, as it was all her fault for putting the pressure on her. Why couldn't she have just stuck with Henry, they were lovely together? They shared picnics and went on walks. She had a job at the library—she loved books, why was it not enough? Why did she have to ruin everything for herself, and why was Cathleen picking up the pieces now? Avoiding people like the plague as though she had committed the sin. As Cathleen decided that enough fresh air was had, she turned around to head back. She spotted outside the corner shop an old fellow, Mr Flint. She knew him as a gentle man, a family friend even, yet she crossed the road to avoid conversation. He was the last person she needed to be interrogated by and he surely would, for he was very fond of Charlotte. Mr Flint lived alone and was known as a strange man to those who did not know him. He spent his days in his allotment, neglecting his home. Yellow nets hung on the window, weeds grew from every gap around his front door, his hair was long, and his clothes were often worn and covered in dirt, yet his heart was bright and big. He first crossed paths with Cathleen's sister when she had to help Mr Flint at his home every Saturday. At first, she detested it, she moaned about the smell, moaned about the mess, however she didn't stop attending. She continued to visit him, often up to three times a week, sometimes more, for the next five years. A friendship grew and bloomed just like the flowers they planted together. Cathleen was pleased with Charlotte's love for him, it was like one would have for a grandad or in some ways a dad even. The allotment was not only Mr Flint's haven but also Charlotte's. Mr Flint knew everything about Charlotte and Joe's relationship, including the baby. Henry had become his right-hand man in recent years so it would come as no surprise if he had been updated on recent events. A discussion Cathleen did not want to have.

As the week went by, the kitchen turned into a military operation of boiling water, making up formula, cooling the bottle, feeding the baby, sterilising the bottle. The fire guard was covered in tiny garments drying by the warmth. The front room doubled up as a bedroom for Cathleen, Rupert, and Betty. The crib neatly tucked into the corner by the window so she could watch the world go by. To enter the house, you had to open the front door carefully, so you did not hit the pram as there was nowhere else to keep it.

"Why don't we leave it outside?" Rupert asked, which was perfectly reasonable.

"It's cold outside, what if it rains?" Cathleen replied, when the reality was that having the pram inside did not tell everyone on the outside that a baby was there.

Not only had the front room turned into a place for Betty to sleep soundly, to feed in the arms of a loved one, to open her eyes and curiously see her temporary world and shriek until her needs were met, it had also become the room of devastating conversations.

Uncle Albert for one had returned after Mavis begged him to. It had taken a lot of persuasion from Mavis and Frank, the words passed between the three of them, sometimes turned heated. Cathleen knew her uncle did not agree with it all, her mam however did not give up; she pleaded with her brother until he finally agreed to take Charlotte with him to London, on the condition that they reach out to her. No one had visited Charlotte yet, who lay alone each night in her ward. No one had it in them to tell her what was happening. Once Albert took her with him, she would be alright her parents repeated over and over. She would be in London—she loves London, and she will be able to start again and follow her dream of being an author. Although Mavis agreed, they were all aware that she would not visit her daughter.

"I will go and pop next door then, I believe Charlotte's belongings can be found there. She will be needing them," Albert said, stretching his legs.

"Thank you for this Albert. It means a lot," Frank said, reaching out a hand.

Albert looked at it and left it hanging in the air, just as Charlotte had been left hanging with no answers. "I will write," he said.

Cathleen showed her uncle to the door, quietly shoving a note in his hand before he could get away. "Please give this to her or put it in her case."

Uncle Albert looked at Cathleen with saddened eyes. He sighed as he placed the note into a deep coat pocket. "I really thought you would have at least gone to see her. My mother would really be deeply disappointed by all of this."

Cathleen was left speechless as her uncle walked away, proceeding to knock on the Hollister's door for what could only be yet another devastating conversation. Walter had not yet been told of the preparations to have Betty adopted. As far as he was aware only Charlotte was leaving and his granddaughter was staying put. The war brewing between the two families, who were once united in everything, was surely about to blow up even further. She had been avoiding the family, waiting until she knew they were at work before setting off on walks. Feelings were heightened for everyone, especially Henry who had made several appearances since his feud with Frank. He was not pleased by the ban put on him at the hospital, stopping him from seeing Charlotte. They had to begin locking the door behind them to stop him from barging in, in a rage. Cathleen could see the hurt the whole ordeal was causing him. He just wanted to see her—at least someone did. Walter had asked to see Betty but was met with a refusal from her dad which was met with more quarrelling. It had begun to dawn on Cathleen that perhaps allowing Betty to be adopted by a loving family was for the best; the origins she has are not at peace, and she will forever be in the middle of the two. Having Betty adopted led to the second devastating conversation in the front room, when a social worker arrived to discuss the matter. She was a plump lady in a pink floral dress and an extremely thick knitted yellow cardigan. On the outside she looked like the kind of woman who was there to help them all and give Betty the very best, like some sort of social fairy godmother. However, as she got comfortable and took out a file and a pen and slipped on her glasses, it quickly became very serious and as quick as a swish from a magic wand the social fairy godmother was replaced with the baby police.

"Let's get this started shall we. I have spoken to the hospital and have been informed that your daughter, Charlotte Ridley, will not be keeping the infant she gave birth to, given that she is unmarried and only sixteen this is quite necessary," she said in a matter-of-fact tone. "How old is the infant?"

"She is nine days old," Mavis replied, her voice scratchy, her arms wrapped tightly around her granddaughter.

"You know, if Charlotte had been placed in a mother and baby home this could have been arranged much sooner. It is also much more practical for the family, I find you can all get on with your lives undisturbed while mother is taken care of elsewhere in private. That way she can return home and get on with her life as it was before." No one said anything to the social worker as she looked around the front room with an odd expression. "Is there a reason you decided to do things this way?"

Frank cleared his throat before replying, "We didn't know she was in the family way."

"Hmm, yes this can happen. Teenage mothers can be so secretive yet so naive to believe they won't have to let the cat out the bag at some point. When will mother be returning home?"

"She won't be returning here; she is going to live with her uncle in Mayfair," Mavis informed her.

"Mayfair, my, my. High five to uncle. At least you have made a good decision there, some girls have fantasies that they will be able to look after the children on their own, having no idea how impossible that would be."

"Why?" Cathleen asked.

"Why what?"

"Why would it be impossible? What if Charlotte did want to look after her own child. What if she had a family to support her?"

"Cathleen," Mavis whispered through gritted teeth.

"No Mam, I want to know."

"If the family were willing to help bring up the child, then yes that is a possibility, however you need to think of other things that will affect Charlotte. Imagine she is home with mum and dad helping. What happens to her future? How will she feel when she is rejected from society? Will she be able to earn her own keep some day? Will any gentleman wish to marry a woman who has a bastard? These things can all amount to a very difficult and unsatisfactory life. One I am happy to hear has been prevented." The woman smiled and began to scribble away on her sheets of paper. "Where was baby born?"

Frank sighed, putting his head into his hands. The woman waited patiently waiting for a simple response from anyone. "Here?" she guessed.

"No, she was born in the allotment," Frank said.

"An allotment?"

"In the shed. She had her in the shed at the allotment," Mavis said without eye contact. "It's a well-kept, erm, shed," she added.

"Hmm, and father?"

"Gone," Frank let her know. "We won't be hearing from him."

"Typical. Ran a mile, I guess. Fatherhood is no job for a boy," she told them. "The majority of our cases are very much like this." Her pen waved back and forth as she added more information. "Right, so the infant will be taken to a home, where she will stay until she is adopted. Like I said earlier, if she had been placed in a mother and baby establishment then a new family could have already been placed. Until then she will be taken care of by the sisterhood." The plump woman put away her belongings in a navy handbag. "I best be off as I have a driver waiting for me outside."

To everyone's surprise she walked over to Mavis with her arms outstretched. It took a second for them to realise that she was waiting for Betty to be handed over.

"Now?" Mavis asked in shock. "You want to take her now?"

"There is no time like the present, Mrs Ridley."

"But you have only just met us. Do you not need to know anything else? You don't even know her name." Cathleen felt herself panic.

"Whatever you have been calling her will not be her name, you do know that. Her parents will decide on a name for her. Now please, Mrs Ridley, hand over the infant."

"Don't you need anything? Like her clothes. Don't you need to know how much formula she's drinking? How long she sleeps for?" Cathleen was hovering so close to her mam, prepared to lunge for Betty if the social lady came too close.

"Cathleen, Pet, I'm sure the sisters know how to take good care of Betty," Frank softly said.

Cathleen's heart grew heavy as she looked down at the sweet child she had lost sleep over for the past week. She had taken her under her wing and fallen in love with her niece. The constant circle of crying, changing, feeding, winding, soothing; she had never complained once. While Rupert worked and her parents stressed over her sister, while appearing to be normal for her little brother, Peter, she had loved nothing more than being the primary carer to Betty.

"Why don't we have her?" Rupert who had sat quietly at the dining table suddenly said. All eyes were on the blonde factory worker. "Cathleen and I, could we adopt Betty?" he asked the social worker.

"Well, erm. Are you married?"

"Yes," Rupert replied.

"Do you have jobs? Have your own stability? A suitable home?"

"Yes, to all."

Cathleen couldn't believe what her husband was suggesting. Not once had having Betty for themselves ever crossed her mind nor had it been brought up in any conversations between them. It was a complete shock and she found herself suddenly filled with hope that keeping Betty could be a possibility.

"Do you have children of your own?" asked the social worker, breaking Cathleen's thoughts.

"Sadly no, my wife and I have had difficulties," Rupert struggled to say, Cathleen caught his glistening eyes. "This week, however, I have watched Cathleen take care of Betty as though she were her own. She would be a wonderful mother and we have grown quite fond of the child. If it would be possible to adopt Betty ourselves, you can be assured that she will be loved and provided for."

Rupert moved closer to the group and placed a comforting hand on Cathleen's shoulder, which she grabbed in her own immediately.

"Well, with the right paperwork this could happen. I will need to see your home to check the suitability. You know, you really are a complicated family. I will be in touch."

Frank Sinatra's deep voice played *All the Way* on the gramophone quietly as Cathleen settled Betty into her crib, collapsing beside her husband on her parent's couch, falling perfectly into his embrace. He kissed the top of her head, leaning his cheek against her brunette hair. The evening had been full of discussions since the social worker left. Rupert's sudden suggestion of adoption had thrown everyone. Mavis and Frank hadn't particularly liked the energy from the social worker and having to hand over their granddaughter appeared to have been harder than Mavis had anticipated, yet they were not a hundred percent sold on the idea of Cathleen bringing Betty up. The issues they raised were of course Charlotte. Would it be harder to learn that her sister was adopting her child rather than a stranger, or a relief that she was remaining with her family? They thought it might be too confusing for Betty.

"I know how much being a mother means to you, Darling, but don't you think adopting Betty may be a little complicated?" Mavis had asked during the debate.

"She is our flesh and blood, Mam. She belongs with us, and you and Dad get to still be in her life."

Cathleen and Rupert had planned to return to their flat in Newcastle with Betty, making it all feel slightly surreal—they had so much to do. A nursery for one; Rupert's parents were yet to meet the little one; and Cathleen would have to stop working as a receptionist as she was needed at home now.

"Can you believe that we are going to be parents if everything goes well? You will be a dad." Cathleen couldn't help but smile at the thought.

"And you will be a mam, Betty is going to be very lucky to have you." Rupert stroked her arms tenderly as they spoke of what lay ahead for them and their plans to finally be a family. Amidst the excitement Cathleen hadn't forgotten that as they prepared to take Betty with them to hopefully her new home where they would begin their new chapter, her sister would be, mourning for the child Cathleen was planning a future with. Mavis had insisted she go straight to London without stopping home, it would be too upsetting she had said.

"Henry is probably right. She will hate us all, but in time I hope she will see that everything we have done is for her own good."

Charlotte would soon learn that she wasn't going to be reunited with her baby and the thought of Charlotte's pain crushed her—guilt consumed her until Betty stirred and Cathleen was immediately aroused from her thoughts to tend to the child who needed her, and truth be told, Cathleen needed her too.

Chapter Three

January 1959

They were now parents—Cathleen and Rupert. They had a daughter, Betty Theresa Brown. Out of respect to the kind woman that Cathleen had been fond of, the name Betty had stuck, which had pleased Mavis no end. Cathleen and Rupert had dived into parenthood headfirst, their quiet little flat had become a little girl's castle overnight. Betty was showered with love from both Cathleen and Rupert's parents, although when Cathleen's mother-in-law held Betty for the first time she did turn and say, "one day you will have your own." Which in the moment of overwhelming feelings had hurt her a little. The comment reminded her that Betty was not her child, but her sister's child, and it also took her back to the harrowing moments when she had lost her own. Cathleen loved being a mother, she loved all the little things like having her all to herself on the night feeds, bringing her into the living area where a stream of light escaped the curtains from the streetlamp, giving them the only light they needed. She loved the funny noises Betty made when having a bath in the kitchen sink, her legs kicking furiously. She loved the smell of her when she was all fresh in her night wear. When Rupert returned home her heart would skip a beat as he asked where his girls were, planting a kiss on both of their cheeks.

"You have blossomed since becoming a mam," Rupert would tell her.

However, the bubble they had created in the early weeks of adopting Betty began to pop as reality began to set in. Bringing up your niece as your own child in a world where too many think it unforgivable and wrong had its setbacks. So much so that the visits to see family in Durham had become a dreaded thing. Cathleen found herself making excuses to not visit her parents when they invited them to the usual Sunday lunch and morning visit to church. When her mam invited her round for a catch up her insides coiled at the idea. Her childhood home and the church that had meant everything to her had now become a thing of nightmares.

"It's home, we can't expect our parents to do all the travelling whenever they want to see us or spend time with Betty. The church is ours; you mustn't let others bully you, Cathleen."

But she did, she had allowed them to, because she did not yet know how to fight back. Whenever she went home, if she bumped into Henry she was met with dirty stares and mean comments. Her parents had learnt to ignore the boy, but Cathleen felt vulnerable to his words, sometimes she even felt like she deserved them. She had taken her sister's child after all. In church she felt like everyone was staring at them, it didn't take long for people to find out about Charlotte being sent away after giving birth. Some people made kind comments, telling the new parents that what they were doing was admiral, while others called it *the robbing of a child*. Then there was Walter who only wished to be a part of his granddaughter's life, while part of Cathleen felt sorry for the man who had just as much right to know Betty as any of her other grandparents, another part of her began to wish he would disappear. Walter was a reminder that her little family made up of Ridley's and Brown's also had another line—Hollister's. For Walter to play a part in Betty's life meant she would grow up knowing Cathleen was a fraud—that she was not her real mother. The thought was enough to frighten her more than anything else could. Ever since Betty had come into her life, Cathleen had stayed by her side and the love she felt for her was real, it was stronger than the love of an aunt, it was the love of a mother. A mother who would do anything to ensure that Betty knew this to be true. Whenever Walter peered into the pram or asked to hold Betty she wanted to scream *go away*. Walter was the figure who would give it all away, he was the man holding the pin that could pop their bubble. He was the main reason Cathleen's visits to Durham began to lessen, bringing great concern to Rupert. They lived in Newcastle only because it was closer to the factory where Rupert worked—their families, Rupert's old school friends, and their church family were all back in Durham.

"Surely, you want Betty to be brought up around the people we love and care about?" Rupert asked one Sunday morning when Cathleen refused to go to Durham for the third week in a row.

"Of course, but do we need to go every week? Maybe we could have our parents here for Sunday lunch. Going back and forth with Betty isn't helpful with all the things we need to pack every time we leave the house. We could invite some friends round for dinner some time too, and there is a beautiful church down the road we could join. We have a baby now; it is much easier here in Newcastle."

"You want us to start going to a new church? We have gone to St. Mary's for over twenty years Cathleen," Rupert uttered in surprise. "I know what you're doing, you're hiding."

Cathleen felt her face flush red. "I am not hiding; it is just more convenient."

"You're hiding from Walter, you're hiding from Henry, and you're hiding from anyone else that has anything negative to say. You can't please everyone Cath. If we never took Betty in, another family would have adopted her, she was never going to be Charlotte's regardless. People are too stubborn to see this. Your parents decided your sister's fate and we chose Betty's because we love her, and we knew what was best for her."

"I know you're right Rupert, I do, but I can't help feel like being around everyone who's against us will push Betty away from us too."

"We are her parents, regardless of what anyone says or who is in her life. She is going to learn the truth about everything someday and when that happens, she will still have us, and we will still be a family just as we are now."

To his delight Rupert won and within the hour they were dressed in their fine clothes standing in a cold pew amongst their parents and little Peter, who was holding back tears for he had been caught by Frank wiping snot on the back page of the hymn book. The six-year-old hid his face behind Mavis' skirt for the whole of the service no matter how many times he was told to sit properly. Peter had begun to show signs of mischief lately, he was always being punished at school for disturbing lessons, and he began venturing too far on his bike so he couldn't hear his mam call him when it was time to go back in. Cathleen felt guilty that she didn't make enough time for her little brother, believing his change of character was down to the disappearance of Charlotte. It was Charlotte that he had enjoyed spending most his time with; she'd read to him every night since the day he was born, and they shared a love of stories and adventures, she often took him to the library and to school. She tended to all his needs like a second mother. Peter had endless love for Charlotte, when she first left home to elope with Joe, Peter couldn't understand it, he asked for her over and over. Mavis loved Peter of course, just as she loved them all, but there was no hiding that she was not an affectionate mother. Having felt that growing up, Charlotte had made sure Peter had all the affection he needed, without his sister he began to cling to Mavis; desperate for that hole that Charlotte left open to be filled once more. With Betty napping in Cathleen's arms the weight of her making her arms numb, she thought, as Father John read a sermon, of all the ways she was going to ensure her daughter never felt an ounce of desperate love.

After the service they retreated from the cold stone building to an even frostier street—the sky looked as though it was ready for snowfall. The church goers didn't take long to rush back to their warm fires. Cathleen was eager to return to her own fireside but knew she had to endure lunch at her parents' first, after Rupert and his mother finished their conversation with Father John that was. Cathleen huddled in the doorway wrapping Betty up tighter in her blanket, keeping her free from the chill with only her face on show. As she spotted Walter, Henry, and old Mr Flint heading her way, she wished Rupert would cut his conversation shorter.

"Cathleen, hello Pet," Walter said cheerily, approaching her. "How is this little lass?"

The atmosphere was all but peaceful in the house of God. Out of the corner of her eye Cathleen could see the watchful eyes of Mavis and Frank from the courtyard.

Henry took a glance at Betty before walking away sourly, "I'll see ya at the house Da."

Mr Flint followed Henry without a second glance at Cathleen or Betty, and diverted the looks of her parents as he passed them outside. When Mr Flint first saw Cathleen at church with Baby Betty, he took one look at the baby before his eyes filled with tears and he turned around and left. He no longer said a word to anyone, he only spoke to Henry and Walter. Mr Flint had once been an honoured guest to the Ridley's, he had become an adopted family member. He had attended Cathleen and Rupert's wedding and was very fond of her late nan. So many ties had been lost when Charlotte became involved with Joe Hollister, whatever relationship they believed to have had, it was made at a cost to all. Yet Cathleen could not regret her sister's love life any longer for it had brought Betty into her life.

"She's great," Cathleen said forcing a smile.

"Are you weaning her yet?" he asked curiously.

Walter always asked all sorts of questions. He wanted to know everything about Betty. What songs does she like? What did Santa bring her? Did she like his gift? Is she smiling yet? Is she rolling yet? All the things a woman might ask. She knew he meant no harm, but she found the whole thing infuriating which she knew made her an awful person. Rupert was always so calm and relaxed about the whole thing. It never seemed to bother him at all that Betty would grow up to learn that she had another dad somewhere, a biological one, the thought of her daughter one day learning the truth terrified her. Although Betty was legally theirs, her true heritage made her feel like they were pretending to be a family. When they were in Newcastle, she didn't feel like this; she could shut their front door and it was just the three of them, no one else. The Hollisters and the haters didn't matter anymore because they could no longer do any harm.

"Cathleen! Sorry Walter, can I have my wife for a moment?" Rupert placed an arm around Cathleen guiding her towards Father John.

"Of course, I'll speak to you next week," Walter said, nodding, though his face looked displeased.

"Thought I would save you," Rupert whispered. "You looked like he asked you something terrible."

"He asked if she was weaning yet."

"Oh my, how dare he," Rupert gasped.

"You're not funny, Rupert."

After lunch, the conversation took a nasty turn from Easter plans to a letter from Uncle Albert. Cathleen and Mavis were sat at the dining table when she showed Cathleen her latest letter from him.

"I got it yesterday, have a read," Mavis said, handing her the neatly written parchment with a black logo of The American Eagle Hotel stamped on the top.

Dear sister,

I write to you not only as Charlotte's uncle but as your brother. I am deeply concerned for my niece. She continues to work shifts at the hotel—something I still do not agree with, but Emily would only allow her to stay, as you know, if she paid her own way. I am hopeful that the time away from the house occupies her mind well, as well as the time she is spending with William when he is home. I am thankful that she has her cousin here for I believe being in this big house with just me and Emily would have certainly drove her mad by now.

I still believe this all to be far from beneficial to Charlotte. She looks as though she has lost a lot of weight and tends to always look pale and worn out. I think you should reconsider all of this and allow me to bring her home where she belongs.

Can you remember that feeling you felt during the war, when Mother told you to stay in Durham because she felt London was too dangerous for you to come with the children? Can you remember how it felt to be separated from Frank? If I remember rightly, you were miserable, now imagine how you would have felt if you woke up one morning and your children had disappeared, taken from you, and all we did to support you was to tell you to move on and start again. You would have crumbled in an instant. Now imagine how your daughter is feeling. Please Mavis, talk it over with Frank. Charlotte needs you both.

I cannot see her recovering from this, her heart is shattered. She walks around this house like a ghost. Only William manages to get any real conversation out of her. Do the right thing, Sister. Not only for Charlotte but for yourself, you could end up losing your own daughter forever. At least write to her, she needs you right now.

Please, Albert.

P.S. let us not forget that in ten months' time Charlotte will be eighteen years old and I will no longer force her to stay here. I imagine she will want answers.

Reading her uncle's letter left Cathleen shocked to the core. She had never considered what would happen once her sister reached the age of adulthood. *I will no longer force her to stay here. I will imagine she will want answers.* Her uncle's words echoed in her mind all evening. He was right, of course, come December she would be able to return home as she pleased, see who she liked. Charlotte would have no power over Betty, but she could go to Henry if she wanted, and if they married, they could possibly remain with Walter next door to her parents. What would happen then? Peter would want to spend time with her, perhaps bridges between Charlotte and her parents could even be made. Cathleen imagined them all together as one big happy family, they were all her sister's family as much as they were her own, but when she positioned her own little family in her happy scenario, she saw Betty and Charlotte getting to know each other, she saw her sister being amazing with her, she saw them bonding and she saw Betty feeling closer to Charlotte as she did her.

"What is it?" Rupert jumped as Cathleen cried out loud in her bed.

"She is going to love her more than me."

"Who is? Who is going to love who more than you?"

"Betty is going to love Charlotte more than me. Charlotte is going to come home one day, and she is going to take her from me," Cathleen cried in distress.

Rupert sighed, bringing Cathleen closer to him so he could comfort her. The top of his pyjamas became damp as Cathleen continued to sob. Rupert tried his best to calm her down, but nothing he said seemed to have been heard, so he made circles on her back with the palm of his hand allowing her to cry it out.

The following week Cathleen pleaded with her husband to allow them to stay in Newcastle. Telling him she had spoken to the priest at their local church who was more than happy to have the three of them attend his service. Their loyalty to St. Mary's spoke volumes and he understood the logistics made more sense for them to take Sunday mass with him instead.

"He said we mustn't feel guilty and hopes in time we will feel at home there," Cathleen added.

Rupert threw down his car keys onto the kitchen counter. Leaning onto it with his head bowed low. "How long are we going to do this Cath?"

Cathleen said nothing as she watched her husband, who looked exhausted. She should suck it up, tell him she was being silly and attend St. Mary's, but she knew in her heart that she couldn't face it. Not again, not anymore.

"Mass is one thing," Rupert continued. "We can work around that, but not going to visit our parents is another. That isn't normal." Rupert sat himself on top of the coffee table opposite Cathleen, taking her hand away from fiddling with her cardigan button and placing it into his own. "Betty is our daughter, Cath, mine and yours. Nothing can break our family apart; she is going to grow up and adore you just as much as I do."

"Charlotte," Cathleen whispered.

"Not even Charlotte, I know this must be difficult for your sister and she may want to see Betty, but we can't let that stop Betty or us from leading a normal life, we can't hide up here forever. I can assure you that Betty will always love you more, you're her mam, even if she does establish a relationship with your sister. What you two have is always going to be stronger. Our little girl was born without a dad, and a mam who was just too young. She needs us, but she needs her family as well, her grandparents and her uncle. Maybe one day that will include Walter, Henry, and Charlotte also, and if it does it won't change anything because you and I will always be her parents."

Cathleen nodded in agreement, while the small button on her husband's cuff found its way into her grasp. "We can go next week, yeah?"

"Okay," Rupert agreed, placing his lips onto her head. "Betty is just months old Cath, and Charlotte is still just seventeen. You need to relax a little, enjoy what we have always wished for."

However many times Rupert tried to convince Cathleen that her troubles were silly, that no one could replace the family unit they were building, Cathleen could not shake the anxious thoughts. She looked at her sweet daughter and imagined all the wonderful things they had to look forward to as a family, but she was burdened with the thought of her sister taking her place in Betty's life. That is before the idea of coming face to face with Charlotte after adopting her child without her say came to her mind. As much as she loved her sister, Cathleen knew she did not particularly want her to come back and be a part of Betty's life. This is why Cathleen called her parents and Rupert's parents, inviting them round to the flat after Sunday service for lunch. She had felt guilty making the call without discussing it with her husband first, but Cathleen knew he would try to talk her out of it. Rupert believed his wife's behaviour would pass once she *got used to everything.* He was adamant they stick to normality. It was easier for him, Joe Hollister was very unlikely to make an appearance to claim his daughter, Rupert would have no one standing in his way as a father figure. Joe was not going to move in with his parents and be part of their family, portraying himself as the best uncle whom Betty will adore, until someone lets the truth slip and Betty comes to realise that he isn't her real dad after all. The more she envisioned the future, the more Cathleen felt repulsed by Durham.

"Why are you cooking Cath?" Rupert asked, entering the kitchen area where Cathleen was rubbing butter over a large chicken for Sunday lunch.

"I'm making lunch," Cathleen said deliberately not making eye contact with her husband.

"My mam is making lunch, you know this."

Cathleen said nothing and placed the chicken in the oven, she could feel Rupert getting closer to her. He placed his hand under her arm pulling her upright to face him.

"What is going on?" he asked, exasperated.

"I'm making lunch," she repeated. "I invited our parents round."

Rupert took in the room properly; the table was set for four, a further three places were set on the coffee table. He looked at Cathleen who once again had gone silent. She didn't know what to say to him, she knew going behind his back was wrong, and she knew how much Durham meant to him, but her lips remained shut. Not even an apology could escape. Letting go of her arm, Rupert left the flat, making Cathleen feel terrible. She should run after him she thought, apologise for making plans without him, but she didn't, instead she began preparing the potatoes.

Cathleen put on a smile as she placed everyone's lunch before them. She sat all Betty's grandparents around the table while she sat with Peter around the coffee table. Rupert had not yet returned home leaving Cathleen baffled at what to tell their guests. In the end she made out that a friend from work needed him to help him fix his car.

"On a Sunday, he could have had his lunch first," Cathleen's mother-in-law tutted. "He did attend church though, didn't he?"

"Yes, Pam, he did."

"I don't know why you didn't just come to St. Mary's," Frank said tucking into his veg.

"You were all missed today," Mavis said, which everyone agreed too.

"It's just easier going to one closer to home with Betty."

"It's not the same though, Father John has known you and Rupert since you were babies," Pam went on. "Please come next week."

"The chicken's lovely Cathleen," Rupert's dad, a quiet man, complimented.

"Thank you."

As the main table discussed the plans for a retirement home being built where the children's park currently was, Cathleen tried to chat to Peter, but not as much as she had hoped to as Betty woke from her nap in a grouchy mood, leaving Cathleen little choice but to tend to her daughter's needs, leaving Peter to eat alone. It was quiet in the nursery with the door closed behind them, Cathleen cuddled Betty on the rocking chair beside her cot. She had woken early from her nap, explaining the frustrated outburst that settled as Cathleen sang to her in the calm little room. The walls were covered in pale pink wallpaper and decorated with forest animals; it was the first thing they did once Betty came to live with them. All the grandparents and work colleagues had chipped in to gather enough funds for the couple to buy furniture. Resulting in a white cot decorated in little lambs and cherry blossoms and a matching set of draws. The rocking chair had been purchased back when Cathleen had first been with child, she excitedly bought it with dreams of rocking her baby to sleep in it, only for it to be left in an empty room behind the closed door unable to be fulfilled until now. The nursery had felt as much a safe haven to Cathleen as it did to Betty. As Betty dropped back into a peaceful slumber, Cathleen could hear the commotion of Rupert's return. He had never before walked out on her, where he had really gone, she had no idea. She had kept a plate of food for him in the oven which she hoped still tasted as good as it did when fresh. She knew she was in the wrong, but she couldn't help thinking that Rupert just didn't understand. It didn't take long for him to creep into the nursery. The cold chill from his body was felt as he sat on a rug facing her. He sat crossed leg like a schoolboy, his face still looked as young and innocent as when she first began courting him.

"I'm sorry," Cathleen whispered.

"It's okay," he replied, rubbing her leg.

Cathleen gasped as his cold skin came across a hole in her stockings, Rupert retreated apologetically. He moved forward and rested his head against her skirt like a little boy begging for affection from his mother. Cathleen ruffled his blonde locks. They stayed like this for some time until Peter began to shout from the living area.

"Cathleen! I'm finished, can I have some cake now?"

"I'll go," Rupert said in a whisper, before Peter's need for pudding woke Betty.

In the evening, once everyone left with their bellies full, Cathleen and Rupert could talk openly alone.

"I'm so sorry Rupert," Cathleen apologised once more, throwing herself into her husband's arms. "I should have discussed my plans with you first. I was just afraid you would make me go to Durham. I know I said I would act normal, but my mind hasn't stopped thinking, and the very thought of it made me anxious."

Rupert squeezed Cathleen tightly. "I know why you didn't tell me, perhaps I haven't been as understanding as I thought. I can see how upsetting going to Durham is making you and I shouldn't force you to go. I want us to look back on these days with complete joy, not of memories of you a nervous wreck, this isn't good for anyone. Come and sit down."

They sat on the couch, moving aside a baby blanket, toys, and a book Peter had been reading to Betty. Rupert took both Cathleen's hands in his own and clasped them tightly.

"To be honest Cath, I am worried about you, you haven't been yourself for a while. Me and Betty love you, but I fear we are losing you a little."

"You're not losing me, I just…" The tears welled up in her eyes as she didn't know what else to say, without admitting that she did feel like she was losing herself.

"You don't have to explain, I get it. I do." The corner of his lips lifted in a small smile. "I heard the lads talking at work yesterday about scaffolding jobs over in France."

"France!"

"It is only temporary a year or two I think, but I thought I should apply. You and Betty can come of course, I thought being away from everything and everyone might do you some good."

"France," Cathleen repeated. "Where abouts?"

"Paris."

"Paris! Are you sure me and Betty can come too?"

"The accommodation is included, with discount on the rent. What do you think? Do you think you could be happy in Paris?"

"My nan used to tell me stories of her trips to Paris; they always sounded like something out of a fairy-tale. It is a long way from home, but it does sound tempting, Rupert."

Cathleen suddenly felt a charge of energy drive through her…excitement? Relief? She wasn't sure but it felt good. "There will be no one who know us there."

"It will be just us three."

They spoke for hours about what life could be like for them in Paris—walks by the Seine, picnics by the Eiffel Tower. What an experience for them to have as a family, and they would be alone, with no one else involved. Cathleen felt like in France she would be the mam she was always meant to be.

Chapter Four

March 1959

As Rupert pushed open the door to their new apartment, they were lost for words at what greeted them on the other side. It certainly was not what had been expected when picturing what their new French home would be—the glamour of Paris was lost on this small residence. The new apartment consisted of two rooms, a kitchen area with a small wooden table, a grey sofa that had seen better days, and a bedroom. A great iron bed made up the majority of the space topped with a thin mattress and one set of drawers. Once Betty's cot arrived, the floor space would be no wider than four-foot. It smelt damp and cold despite the sun glaring through the windows. Music could be heard from across the hall, showing how thin the walls were.

"No bathroom," Cathleen noted.

"I think I saw a sign for a toilet in the corridor, we must have to share with the other residents on our floor," Rupert replied, grimly inspecting a tin bath tucked up in the corner of the kitchen.

"Lovely," Cathleen replied, taking in her surroundings, it was nothing like their home back in Newcastle which had been spacious and bright. The Paris apartment was dark, cramped, and smelt musty. Cathleen squeezed Betty a little closer to her chest wanting to protect her from the smell.

"I am sure we can turn this place around with a good clean, a lick of paint, and our own belongings once they arrive."

Rupert's optimism was touching, Cathleen thought, whether he believed what he preached or it was said to cheer her up, she didn't know but she had no choice but to hope he was right as there was no turning back. Their place in Newcastle already had new tenants, Rupert had left his old job and was expecting to start his new one in only a week. They had to make it work. They hadn't packed up their furniture, having been told the new apartment was furnished, and the cost to deliver overseas was extortionate, but glancing around at the two new rooms Cathleen wished she had. Their table would not have fit, but one of their sofas would have fitted lovely, as well as their own bed. The hardest items not to bring with them were Betty's; they had agreed to pack her cot and, begrudgingly for Rupert, the rocking chair, however Cathleen now knew it would never fit.

"Come on," Rupert said, interrupting her thoughts. "Let us go and walk around our new local area and get a bite to eat."

No one was happy when they found out about their plans to move to France, Cathleen would even go as far as to say that her parents were utterly devastated; they did their upmost to try and talk her out of it. Once the idea had been put into her head of a new start in another country, Cathleen had become obsessed and was convinced it would be the best thing for the three of them. Once Rupert noticed how upbeat Cathleen's mood had become, he couldn't resist applying for the job, and together they had grown more and more excited for the move and what it would mean for them as a family.

When they arrived, Cathleen couldn't help but worry whether or not they had done the right thing moving away from their parents, their home and security, but upon walking the streets of their new city knowing that they could not bump into anyone they knew; it made Cathleen feel elated and she made mental notes of things she could do to the apartment to make it liveable—fresh bedding, flowers, white paint, new curtains, and a throw for the sofa. It just needed sprucing up as Rupert had said. Their apartment was a twenty-minute walk from the city centre of Paris but had local amenities that were only five minutes from them. The sun shone bright and as Cathleen felt the warmth touch her skin, she held her husband's hand and smiled at him. A smile that told him everything was going to be alright; they were going to be happy, just the three of them. That is all their family needed.

There were three other apartments on Cathleen and Rupert's floor, next door to them were two French brothers who kindly introduced themselves as Frederic and Marcel, they were artists who owned a stall by the River Seine. Opposite them were a family who had moved to France five years previously from Jamaica, Aiden and Cedella, along with their two-year-old son, Cyrille. The family had welcomed them with open arms, inviting them round for dinner to give them a warm welcome to Paris, something they had greatly appreciated. Glimpsing into Aiden and Cedella's home, which was beautifully decorated, and cleverly planned to ensure the maximum space possible, and the way they embraced living in France, gave Cathleen and Rupert even more hope that their life in Paris could be as equally wonderful as their new neighbours. Also, Cathleen had felt as though she may have just made her first friend in Cedella, her warm personality made Cathleen want to spend time with her. She was a tender mother and not afraid to tell her husband when he was in the wrong. Cathleen was thrilled when Cedella invited her and Betty to walk with her and Cyrille to the park the following day. Their third neighbour was an elderly woman with a humped back who walked with the aid of a wooden cane and went by the name of Miss Dupont. Miss Dupont did not have much to say, actually she had nothing at all to say to them, even when they greeted her with a friendly "bonjour", instead she looked the other way and tutted nosily. At first the Brown's couldn't help but take it personally until Cedella reassured Cathleen that the elderly woman was the same with everyone and was leaving to live with her daughter in a matter of weeks, to the delight of the other tenants. As uncomfortable as Miss Dupont made Cathleen feel, it was nothing to how she felt sharing the toilet. The procedure was that everyone brought along their own cut paper, Cathleen liked to keep theirs in a blue purse to hide that she was on her way to the toilet. The most horrifying aspect of it was there being no lock, something Cathleen found alarming, and also confused as to why out of the three men living on their floor no one had added one. Cathleen had put Rupert in charge of this task. On the front of the door was a small sign made out of cardboard attached to a piece of string which was nailed to the door. One side had *vacant* written across it and *occupe* was written on the opposite side. Even with the *occupe* on display Cathleen still tried to keep a foot against the door as much as possible, along with a short prayer that no one will come in straight after her, especially Miss Dupont...and the French brothers...and Aiden.

To return the favour Cathleen and Rupert invited their new friends over to their apartment once a few adjustments were made. The fresh white walls gave the impression of a bigger living area. Colourful flowers bloomed on their two windowsills and on the table, along with photos and trinkets from home.

"What a fantastic job you have done already!" Cedella exclaimed, taking in the crisp walls which still had the whiff of new paint.

The apartment certainly felt much more homely; the foursome chatted over a roast that tasted much like the ones they had back in England, apart from the gravy tasting slightly different. Cathleen couldn't find Bisto gravy in her local shop, so a homemade batch was made instead, which didn't taste as bad as she thought it would. Her guests didn't seem to have any complaints as they helped themselves to seconds.

"How are you finding France?" Aiden asked, as Cathleen placed a sponge cake on the table for pudding.

"It's a charming city, but I fear I will never be able to learn the lingo," Rupert replied, taking a serving of cake for himself.

"Oh, you will be surprised how quickly you pick it up. We were the same when we arrived."

"They are not very friendly are they, the French?" Cathleen asked. "I feel they find me very irritating when I can't understand them."

"Ah yes, they do prefer their own, but they are not all the same, those who served in the war met many people from different continents and can be more warming," Cedella replied.

"That is good to know, would anyone like any coffee?"

"That would be appreciated Cathleen," Aiden smiled.

"Cedella?"

"No thank you Cathleen." Cedella almost giggled with her reply, gazing at Aiden who giggled back.

"Cedella is not much of a coffee drinker at the moment," Aiden said gazing at his wife. "She can't stand the taste."

"We are expecting a baby," Cedella blurted out; her hand placed on her flat stomach with pride.

"Congratulations!" Rupert rejoiced, giving Aiden a manly pat on the back.

Everyone was all smiles, but Cathleen, who tried her best to force a convincing one, felt a pang of pain as her friend shared her happy news. It was wonderful news, a new baby of course it was, but Cathleen felt the green-eyed monster jump into her soul. Cedella had a healthy little boy already, a child she grew within her all the way to birth and now she was lucky enough to be expecting another.

"It will be a winter baby," Cedella went on. "We haven't known long but can't contain our excitement."

"You know how it is," Aiden said to his hosts, his smile still stretching from ear to ear. The expectant father was over the moon. Cathleen remembered seeing Rupert like that, eager to tell all his friends and family that he was going to be a dad.

"If there is one thing I wish for after I have this baby is to look as great as you do after six months Cathleen. The weight has just dropped off you. I am still carrying weight from Cyrille now."

Cathleen and Rupert had agreed to not tell anyone in France that Betty wasn't their biological daughter. Cathleen wanted them to believe she was theirs. The lie was quite easy as they had been with Betty since day one, it was only the pregnancy that had to be made up. The first trimester Cathleen could relate to, the nausea especially, that is how she knew she was expecting. As Cedella turned her attention to Cathleen, pregnancy was the main topic of conversation. Cathleen didn't know what it was like to give birth to a child, to feel a contraction or even a kick. She made a convincing story, though she may not have felt these in real life, but she had thought of them often, dreamt of them, prayed for them.

"She has such beautiful blue eyes," Cedella said looking at Betty who had woken from a nap. "Who does she get them from?"

Rupert who overheard Cedella despite his in-depth conversation with Aiden about football, jumped to her rescue as Cathleen felt the cogs in her brain suddenly stop. "My mam—my mother. She has my mother's eyes."

"So pretty," Cedella beamed, satisfied with Rupert's answer because why wouldn't she be, she had no idea that Pam's eyes were in fact hazel.

"I think tonight went well, I like Aiden and Cedella," Rupert said, jumping into bed beside Cathleen.

"Yes, they are lovely."

"Why do you sound so glum?" Rupert asked.

"Nothing, I'm fine." Cathleen turned off her bedside lamp and turned over away from Rupert, pulling the duvet up to her chin in comfort, allowing the tears to fall quietly onto her pillow without any witnesses.

"We will have our own one day, Cath. I haven't given up hope yet. Maybe now we have made this fresh start in France, it should be our incentive to try again."

"Maybe," Cathleen quietly muttered in the dark. "Good night, Rupert."

Rupert said no more as Cathleen passively shut down the conversation. She felt her husband turn over making them lie with their backs to each other like strangers in the night. Cedella's pregnancy didn't make Cathleen ache for a new baby, Betty had filled that longing gap. It had however reminded her of the pain she had gone through, the feelings of her failing as a mother and a wife, the horror as her child slipped away too early. Cathleen knew her husband still wished to have a child of their own, but the thought terrified her. Rupert didn't have to feel their baby die, she did, and besides it had become impossible to get pregnant again. For Cathleen all hope was gone.

Chapter Five

June 1959

As Cathleen dusted the photos on one of the shelves Rupert had put up to enable more space, she cast a look at the memories of her wedding day, with her anniversary approaching the following month, it was on her mind. It would be their first wedding anniversary celebrated in the city of love. She looked back fondly; the whole day went as perfectly as she had imagined. They were married by Father John in front of all their friends and family with the after party held at her parents' house. Cathleen remembered how it had been quite a squeeze, but everyone had a fantastic evening, she had never wanted it to end, she wished it had never ended, as the people smiling back at her were now all different in some way or no longer walked the earth. Cathleen's dress had belonged to her mam but had been altered with her blessing to bring it a little more up to date, it was a beautiful dress but not the first she had tried on. When Cathleen and Rupert had begun courting, she went to stay with her Nana Florence in London for the summer with Charlotte as they had done every year from a young age. She recalled how hard it was to spend three weeks without Rupert and how they constantly wrote to one another. Charlotte had found it all pathetic, but she was only ten and innocent to the impact a man can have on the heart. On this particular visit Cathleen fell in love with a wedding gown she spotted in a boutique window; her nan lent her a ring and the three of them went in pretending that Cathleen was getting married so she could try on the dress, and several others. The experience had left her knowing that Rupert was the one, she knew she wanted to marry him. Looking at a photo of Charlotte as bridesmaid on her wedding day, she recalled the worry of leaving her behind and how they had stopped up talking the night before the big day, both knowing it was the last time they would share their childhood bedroom together. She had thought of Charlotte often, the sister who unknowingly gifted her the best present of all, unwillingly of course. She wondered if her sister was as okay as can be and hoped that her future would turn out to be everything that she once wished for. She did not detest her sister, she would always love her, but her presence frightened her, the DNA that ran through her daughter matched that of hers. It was the reason Cathleen was happy to keep Charlotte in her past, for the future would be much more complicated otherwise; and as she had thought earlier, they were all very different people now to the folk smiling in her wedding photos.

Cathleen was distracted from her thoughts by a tap at her door. "Madame, sorry to interrupt your day but I have a letter that was posted to me by mistake which I believe is yours," one of her artist neighbours said, passing her an envelope, her mam's handwriting recognised immediately.

"Thank you erm…"

"Frederic," he said, his French accent strong.

"Sorry, I am still learning everyone's names and you and your brother look very alike," Cathleen blushed, embarrassed.

"You do not need to apologise madame, if you need help telling us apart just remember that I am the better looking one," Frederic said seriously, his eyes staring right at her, and his lips made a slight smile.

He was always in loose clothing splattered in paint. He had a small brown moustache above his top lip, his hair was short unlike his brother, whose hair was shoulder length. A noted difference in the two she thought. Cathleen felt her face go an even deeper red.

Frederic burst out laughing. "Madame, I am but playing with you. Good day, English neighbour." With that he retreated to his apartment leaving Cathleen with a feeling of utter confusion.

"French people," she uttered aloud, closing the door behind her. Mavis wrote to Cathleen often keeping her up to date with life back home and vice versa. "We have a letter from Nana, Betty," Cathleen informed the baby, who was feeding herself a banana in her highchair, uninterested in what her mother had to say. Nothing could have prepared Cathleen for the piece of news she read, re-read, and read a third time to make sure she had read it correctly.

Cathleen,

I hope you are sitting down to read this—if not I suggest that you do so, as I do not write with good news.

Your uncle arrived early this morning with William. I knew he had not arrived baring good news from their grave faces. Cathleen, I don't quite know how to put this into words, I am in utter shock and disbelief that writing to you is making me face that this is all very true, and my heart feels as though it has been ripped out of my chest. It is your sister; our Charlotte, she has died in a terrible freak accident. Your uncle said police arrived in the night to inform him that she was gone, just like that, gone forever. It was an old café that caught fire, your uncle cannot explain why she was even there in the first place.

That is not all, we are unable to bring her home and bury her, as there is no body to retrieve. The police said what remains of my daughter is needed for investigation and will be sent to a science lab for experiments. They won't allow us to have her at all, the only thing we have to identify her by is my mother's ring. She has just vanished from existence. Your uncle is going to press for more information.

In the meantime, we are going to be holding a memorial at St. Mary's church next week, please come home Cathleen. It will be a small gathering, but it is the least we can do for her.

Mam.

Cathleen didn't hear Betty starting to cry in her chair, she didn't hear Cedella make her way into the apartment. She couldn't feel the arms that wrapped themselves around her body. She didn't feel the wooden table hit her repeatedly with her shaking arms. She couldn't see anything as her vision blurred. She couldn't hear the screams coming from her own lungs.

"Not so long ago she was in hospital for a head injury, why didn't we listen to her then?" Mavis repeatedly said, over and over again.

Cathleen had not been back in Durham for long, they had jumped on the next available flight home. Cedella had stayed with Cathleen until Rupert had arrived home, showing him the letter from Mavis as Cathleen had not said a word since receiving the news. Quietly the duo packed bags and took care of Betty around her as she rested her tired head on the table, feeling numb to the core. She had been on auto pilot ever since. When their taxi arrived on the familiar street of her childhood home, it felt different. Stepping out, it was silent as though the street itself was in mourning for the little girl who used to race her bike down its cobbled paths and skipped until she hit a new record. A lamp was on in the front room of the Hollister's, she wondered if they knew of the news yet, if Henry's life had yet been spun on its axis.

Despite the warm day, everyone felt cold to the bone, huddled at Mavis and Frank's. Peter wouldn't leave his room and her uncle, who was stopping at a hotel, refused to see anyone until the memorial.

"Why didn't we go and get her, Frank?" Mavis asked. "Albert said she had been drinking, he said she was suffering. We did that to her Frank."

Frank had yet to say a word despite his wife's fretful questions. He was deep in his own horror of thoughts, his head in a whiskey bottle. Rupert had dropped Betty off at his parents, as much as it pained Cathleen to be separated from her daughter for the first time, she knew she was in no state to give her the full care she needed right now nor were those around her able to. The little boy weeping alone above them was proof of this. Rupert, who had not been close to the teenage girl, was grieved as a parent, now a father himself, and also found that like Cathleen there was an immense amount of guilt weighing heavily on his heart. Like everyone, they all felt like they played a part in Charlotte's death.

"I need some fresh air." Cathleen grabbed onto the mantel piece as her head spun having gotten up too fast.

"Do you want me to come with you?" Rupert asked.

"No, please stay. I just need a moment."

Cathleen gasped in fresh air like a baby's first breath as she stepped out into the courtyard, the very courtyard where Charlotte had taken her first steps. She remembered it as if it were only yesterday. It was the spring after her first birthday, her mam was beating the rugs outside on the line while Cathleen was entertaining her with some wooden bricks when Charlotte pulled herself up using a plant pot and took two steps before falling back down. Cathleen had made such a fuss, her mam tried to get her to do it again having missed it and got annoyed with Charlotte when she wouldn't. Cathleen remembered her mam always becoming impatient and easily irritable during the war, she knew she missed her dad and worried when there had been no letters for some time. The chain smoking would begin, a habit Mavis only had when stressed. She would send Cathleen to bed early with the baby, but after the sound of her mam's tears subsided, she would always return to her daughters, apologising, while pulling them onto her lap and allowing them to both sleep in her bed with her. As the war grew longer, her mam had grown harder, and when it was over

Cathleen no longer recognised her parents. As Charlotte grew up the slam of the back gate was often heard with her comings and goings; eager to play in the lane with her friends until she was called in for tea. Charlotte had been popular as a child, much more so than Cathleen, whose majority of her childhood was spoilt by war.

The sound of yelling began to erupt over the dividing wall of the Ridley and Hollister household. The top back window was open giving Cathleen an earshot of the life within. She couldn't make out what was being said, but she recognised the raised voices as belonging to Walter and Henry. The shouting was followed by the sound of smashing and more anger, this went on for easily fifteen minutes. Cathleen had never heard Walter's voice boom before, so he must have been extremely upset. Perhaps they did know about Charlotte, Cathleen thought to herself. She had been out for some time so decided to lock herself in the outside toilet in case anyone came to find her, she wasn't yet prepared to return to everyone's sullen faces. Once hidden behind the wooden door, Cathleen let out a sigh of pain. She had loved her sister dearly and she had never wished for her young death to be the outcome when adopting Betty. She wanted Charlotte to be the greatest children's author ever known, she wanted her to fall in love with a decent man who would look after her, and to live the extravagant life she always dreamt of in London, visiting the theatre, having afternoon tea with new friends and shopping in Harrods. Losing her life in a café fire was not what was meant to happen, neither was Cathleen's baby meant to die, nor her nana Florence meant to pass just before Charlotte was meant to move in with her, or even

Betty Hollister meant to leave her two teenage boys so early.

"Cathleen," Rupert quietly said on the other side of the door. "Are you coming back in, your dad has opened a second bottle and your mam is asking me questions I fear answering?"

"I'll be two minutes," Cathleen reassured her uncomfortable husband. She pulled down the chain for effect knowing full well that Rupert was not fooled by her self-imprisonment.

After Cathleen attempted to tidy herself up and return to the house she heard yet more sounds from the Hollister residence, the shouting had reduced, now entirely replaced with weeping. It had been confirmed; they knew about Charlotte, and Cathleen would bet her own life that the tears were Henry's.

It was a small ceremony, Cathleen, Rupert, and her parents sat on the front pew to the left of the alter along with Peter. Cathleen's Uncle Albert, Auntie Emily, and William sat opposite them on the right side of the alter, the tension between them could be cut with a knife. No words were said between the two, as though they were not family members at all but strangers. Emily made sobbing noises now and then into a small white handkerchief edged in lace, Albert looked down to the floor, his hands clenched together and his face stern. William looked on to the array of photos of Charlotte, ranging from her as a baby to the last photo taken of her at an event held at the library she worked at for some time. Her smile was radiant and confident, looking back at the sad faces of those she once walked alongside. William looked on as though in a deep state of hypnosis, a nasty bump to his head was noticed by Cathleen, tended with two stitches. Cathleen had smiled at her cousin when she first spotted him, it was an awkward smile, not a smile of welcome or happiness but a smile from an older cousin checking in on a cousin she spent every summer with, who she knew was close to her sister. The smile was not reciprocated but simply ignored as his face unlocked from her gaze. The love from her uncle and his family was all but lost, the bond they once shared gone, along with the girl they had all loved. Albert and William blamed them, Cathleen was aware of this without the need of an exchange of words, they believed Charlotte would be alive if it weren't for them, and they were right to think that. Emily had simply stepped into a role of the sad aunt for the purpose of the memorial, she had never got on with Charlotte or any of them for that matter, she loved her husband and her son and no one else.

Work colleagues and Charlotte's best friends, Molly and Carol, sat a few rows behind the family and the last pew to the right was filled with Henry alongside Mr Flint. Cathleen was surprised to see that Walter was not present and wondered if it had anything to do with the row she'd overhead the previous night. Henry's eyes were red and puffy with an expression that looked confused to whether it wished to be angry or utterly devastated. They were last to arrive, Frank had bolted up from his seat when he noticed the young boy, before Mavis grabbed his blazer and pulled him back down to his seat. "Not today," was all she said.

As Father John spoke about Charlotte's life, the church was quiet with the only prominent sound coming from the painful cries from Peter, his cries amplified and the vibrations touching them all. With no coffin to bury it felt like a book had been left unfinished, they had all gathered at St. Mary's, yet Charlotte lay alone miles away, her body disintegrated already, being used without anyone's permission as a science experiment. Cathleen prayed that her sister's soul made it to Durham, she wished she could see the people who had rallied together in her memory. She wished she could hear her thoughts and know that she was loved, that she always had been, and that Betty, their daughter would always be cared for. When Father John closed the ceremony with a hymn, Henry surprised them all by walking down the aisle, he slowly made his way to the alter and to the photos and placed a single red rose beside the most recent picture of Charlotte. No one said a word; every eye was upon him as he made the sentimental gesture to the girl he had once teased up and down the lanes and in the playground, the girl he found comfort in when he lost his mam, the girl he fell in love with, the girl he had forgiven because his heart still had room to love her, the girl he proposed to, the girl whose hand he will never hold in his own again. Cathleen grasped Rupert's hand and he immediately gave it a tight squeeze. As Henry turned away, he gave a small nod to William as he passed him before leaving the church with Mr Flint, who at that point was in a state of mourning.

Cathleen's London relatives left for their southern home immediately after. Mavis already in a state of grief watched on as her brother left without a word, leaving everyone wondering if they would ever be able to reconcile. The few people remaining gathered into the Ridley household for the worst wake Cathleen had ever attended, her sister's now being the third one she had attended. The table of food was barely touched, no one said anything, instead settling into comfy chairs deep in their own thoughts. It came as no surprise when their guests left. Molly and Carol each gave Cathleen and Mavis a hug before escaping the house of misery. They'd been Charlotte's friend since they first started school, all three had been part of each other's lives ever since. It seemed strange seeing the two of them in the front room without Charlotte. Cathleen imagined they were waiting for her to return from Mr Flint's allotment covered in dirt or out in the yard fixing up her bike ready for a bike ride. Cathleen imagined that Rupert's sleeping body beside her was in fact her sister's, the walls were the same colour they had always been, a pale shade of blue, the curtains were the same peach ones they had closed each night. The only difference was the little boy toys scattered across the shelves and floor where there were once books. Earlier when settling into bed, Rupert had made the outrageous suggestion that they should not return to Paris. He thought now they were needed at home with their family more; he believed Charlotte's death was a reminder of how important family was. Cathleen did not agree and had been yearning to return to France since the moment they arrived back in Durham, not just to escape the grief that was felt in every room, every face, and every breath but because France was where they could be something else completely. France was pure, it was untouched by the people that surrounded Cathleen in her hometown. It was a place where she wasn't reminded of her sins. She was just Cathleen Brown, wife to Rupert Brown, mother to Betty Brown. She was not the daughter of a war veteran, she was not the daughter of a wife who put her husband first above any other, she was not the neighbour to an angry young man whose looks could kill, she was not the sister that her brother would happily replace, she was not frightened to walk the streets, she was free, and most of all, while in France she could pretend that she hadn't taken her sisters child and contributed to her ultimate end. She could be someone else, and no one would know any different. Durham had been a big part of her life; she loved growing up here with the church, and she loved her family dearly, but it wasn't enough to keep her here.

1960s

Chapter Six

March 1960

Four months she had held on to her little one, four months the longest time she had ever been able to hold on before, but of course her body wasn't enough to incubate such precious cargo any longer, and at four months Cathleen lost her second child. They had believed this time it would be different; she had felt movement, they had reached further than before, but it wasn't to be. The grief felt different this time; Cathleen felt as though her husband wanted to blame her but couldn't admit it. Instead, Rupert took on more work, he said it was to distract his mind, but she couldn't help feeling abandoned by him, and to make matters worse Cathleen had overlooked a letter Rupert had sent to Pam expressing his deep concerns that he may never have his own child from Cathleen, which had torn her apart even more. Rupert was a good dad to Betty; they were no doubt a family. Betty's kind nature and thriving milestones made them proud parents, yet for Rupert it wasn't quite enough, he still dreamt of a biological child and the fact that Cathleen had failed once more to give him what she was meant to, made her feel like she was no use to her husband at all.

Cedella, who now lived a few streets away in a bigger apartment, was her only true friend in Paris, but with her two sons and a once again blooming belly Cathleen found it hard to find comfort in her. How could Cedella possibly understand? Afterall, she had no problems bearing children—she was as fertile as they come and Cathleen envied her body and what it could achieve, leaving her lonely in her grief. With Rupert working six days a week from dawn till dusk it was just Cathleen and Betty most days, luckily the apartment didn't take long to clean, and she could spend most her time with her daughter who kept her on her toes with her sudden bursts of tantrums. She had Charlotte's stubbornness Cathleen reflected. She remembered her sister as a toddler having a meltdown at the Hollister's, they were having dinner when Charlotte started to scream on her mam's knee flinging her bread onto the floor. Mrs Hollister had a small dog then who was ever so pleased with his luck, everything was rationed in those days. Charlotte had arched her back and wouldn't stop screaming setting Henry off who had bitten his tongue when she had first given an alarming cry. Cathleen had tried to help her mam in calming her down, but nothing seemed to settle her, while Joe had used the opportunity to take an extra slab of butter onto his bread while everyone was fussing. Just as Mavis looked as though she herself may have a meltdown Charlotte stopped, looking around for her bread as though she had been freed from a possession.

With Betty now on two feet it was easier to walk her to the shops to grab their groceries, what with two flights of stairs to their apartment, a buggy was not the most convenient thing to drag up and down. After a pleasant day out in the sunshine, their tea packed in netted drawstring bags, Betty decided now was her moment, a chance to test her mam and her lungs. At the foot of the stairs, refusing to take a step more, Betty crumpled to the floor and screamed, kicking her legs, and ignoring any peace talk or even the bribery of a biscuit. Cathleen was sure those perched on top of the Eiffel Tower would be able to hear her daughter. It was their first public tantrum and Cathleen could feel herself beginning to sweat.

"Come on Darling, Maman needs you to just walk up to our door," Cathleen gently persuaded, knowing better than to be too stern with her, it never worked when she wouldn't come out the bath nor when she couldn't have two cakes for pudding.

"Oh, young lady what is all the noise for?" Frederic asked, entering the lobby. His voice startled Betty who looked up to the face of its owner. "No need to cry on such a beautiful day." He turned his gaze towards Cathleen. "Madam, can I assist you in any way, I have popped back to grab my lunch."

Feeling flustered and on the verge of tears Cathleen was thankful for her neighbour's sudden appearance. "Oui, please. Would you mind taking my shopping up to my door."

"Of course, it would be my pleasure." Frederic took the shopping into his colourful hands freeing Cathleen to scoop Betty off the floor.

"She wanted her maman to carry her, oui?" Frederic asked, as they walked upstairs.

"Oui, I would bring the buggy, but she is too big to pull up the stairs or carry with the shopping now."

"Can you not wait for your husband?"

"He works through the week now; he isn't free until Sundays."

"Perhaps I can help you Madam, if you wish I am free on Wednesdays, I could accompany you and bring the shopping up for you or the er *buggee* or if you just let me know you are heading out, I can look out for your return. I do not mind which you prefer."

"That is very kind of you Frederic, I will bear that in mind."

"You remembered my name, Madam," Frederic smiled.

"Yes, I did, and please call me Cathleen," she said approaching the front door where Frederic placed her shopping.

"Cathleen," he repeated. "What a beautiful name your maman has little girl. All that crying has made her sleepy I think."

"Yes, I'm not surprised," Cathleen replied, adjusting Betty onto her other side.

"You look tired too, *Cathleen.*" Frederic's accent seemed more prominent whenever he said her name. "Children are a gift, but Maman is important too."

Cathleen was taken aback at his gentle words. "Oui," she whispered.

"I will see you on Wednesday, *Cathleen.*"

"Maybe…I never said yes. You might see me. On Wednesday," she replied finding herself startled, Frederic chuckled and headed to his apartment. "Merci, Frederic!" She called after him quickly.

Frederic nodded his head, removing his beret. "No problem at all, *Cathleen.*"

Locked behind her door, Cathleen took a deep breath before putting Betty down for a nap. "*Cathleen*", she mimicked in a French accent as she unpacked the shopping.

"*Maman is important too.*" She couldn't recall anyone telling her this before now. To be a mother had been everything to her, she had felt it was her purpose, to bring up a child and be their everything but no one had told her before now how her welfare was equally as important as the child's would be. She could see his logic. The way things were at present, Frederic's offer to help was both thoughtful and also very much needed. She did not think he needed to come with her but if he could help her out once they reached home then it would make things a lot easier and future tantrums could be prevented.

As Sunday arrived so did the rain, keeping Cathleen and her little family indoors for the day. A day within the small walls was what they all needed, Cathleen believed, it meant they had to spend time together. Cathleen felt guilty and angry at her body for not being able to give Rupert what he so desperately wanted but she wanted him to remember that she, as his wife, was still a value to him, that she needed him, and she was a good wife. Cathleen prepared a traditional roast dinner while Rupert and Betty played with toy animals on the floor, singing hymns that they taught Betty from their days as altar singers at St. Mary's church. They had visited the local church a few times but with it all spoken in French they felt closer to God saying their own prayers and readings at home as a family every Sunday morning. Cathleen used the time to thank God for Betty and pray for the health and happiness of her family. She lit a candle by her sister's photo and prayed for her forgiveness.

In the evening once Betty was put to bed, Rupert opened a bottle of red wine. Having not been big drinkers they had become accustomed to sharing a bottle of wine now and then, how could you not when living in France. They snuggled up together on their couch, the rain battered noisily against their window, even with music playing on the radio it made its presence known, but the sound was somewhat soothing to the couple.

"I'm sorry I haven't been around very much lately," Rupert apologised while stroking Cathleen's arm gently. "I will try and be around more, my boss has noticed me, and I think he wants to keep me on these shifts for a while. It will be good for us in the long run. He thinks we could be here a year longer than planned, so we could maybe afford a bigger apartment next year. Betty could have her own room, we could have a balcony to sit on and you never know, we could be lucky and have a baby." Cathleen's peacefulness was interrupted by Rupert's dream, the pit of her stomach felt dread and nauseous. "I know it will happen for us, why wouldn't God gift us with a child when we are so devoted to him."

Rupert's faith in God struck a chord with Cathleen, perhaps as devoted as they had always been to him, he was no longer pleased with them. Perhaps he did not want them to be devoted to him any longer. Perhaps the day they left Charlotte alone in a hospital bed and took her child, was the day he no longer saw them as his children.

Chapter Seven

May 1960

"Not today, Frederic, merci." Frederic often popped by the apartment to ask if Cathleen needed anything, sometimes it came in handy if all she needed was a loaf of bread or a bottle of milk, but she waited to do her shopping on Wednesday, piling everything onto the buggy handles. Like clockwork Frederic would be waiting for her in the lobby, ready to carry everything up the stairs while Cathleen held Betty or slowly took each step with her if she decided it was a walking day. Frederic had been a blessing to them, especially with Rupert working all the time, as he wasn't around to help with such things. Lately, they had become passing ships in the night, they were separated all day and when they were united, all they both had on their minds was sleep. Sunday had become a sacred day dedicated to the three of them; it had become Cathleen's favourite day of the week; they slotted back into place, and it always felt nice to catch up with her husband.

Cathleen and Betty were taking an afternoon stroll along the River Seine, the sun was bursting on a clear day, shining rays of goodness below. Betty was sticky from a strawberry ice cream, and she walked with one hand on her buggy becoming more independent by the day. With no shopping to heave up the stairs, the buggy was light enough to collapse and carry up, Cathleen liked having the option of allowing her daughter to walk and rest whenever she needed to. Cathleen felt lucky to be able to explore the city with Betty in the good weather. She had received a letter from her mam who was complaining about the rain back home despite it being spring. Rupert never took that into consideration whenever he suggested they return; Betty would be cooped up most days, whereas in France she had the open air and so much richness at her feet.

"Ric! Ric!" Betty called out.

They were walking along the kiosks by the river, some were filled with books that looked decades old, their spines worn and pages turned yellow, some sold vegetables and fruit of every colour, its stalls bright under the sun. Others sold sun hats and souvenirs for tourists to take home. The kiosk that grabbed Betty's attention however was none other than Frederic and his brother Marcel's, their paintings filled every space available in an array of different sizes and settings. Frederic was in the middle of painting a portrait of an elderly couple who were sat on stools holding hands.

"I will be with you in a moment, Ma Chére," Frederic told Betty without looking up from his painting.

"Frederic is busy Betty," Cathleen informed her daughter who was eager to get to the painter.

"He won't be long, come Betty, come and help me with these paints." Marcel reached out for Betty's hand and sat her down on a tall stool, tall enough to reach the kiosk bench. "I need someone clever to help put them away."

With Betty happy to be of help, Cathleen took a peek at some of the paintings for sale, they were not priced very highly she observed, she thought artists sold their work for hundreds, but the ones before her ranged from anything from twenty Franc to fifty. There were paintings of all the famous sites such as the Notre-Dame and Arc de Triomphe, others were simply of the river or the park in different seasons and then there were portraits, Cathleen did not recognise who they were, perhaps famous French people she thought and then there was one she did recognise, it was quite striking. The portrait was of a woman, dark haired and dark eyed. The background was in dark shades of brown and black and she was painted from her head to her torso, wearing white. She did not smile but looked to the side as though deep in thought. Cathleen noticed the portrait had a higher price tag of eighty Franc, she felt herself start to feel rather embarrassed.

"You like it?" Marcel asked, noticing her transfixed look.

"It's me," Cathleen gasped.

"Yes, you make a very good painting. My brother painted three of these, the others sold very quickly."

"Maman!" Betty shouted, pointing to the portrait.

"Cathleen, do you like it?" Frederic asked, once his elderly couple left happy with their finished painting.

"It is erm–"

"You don't like it?" Frederic asked, Cathleen could not help but hear disappointment in his tone. "People love it, you have the presence and the face of an angel, but your eyes are filled with sorrow."

"And that is how you see me? Sad?"

"No, that is not what I am saying."

"That is exactly what you just said, my eyes are filled with sorrow. You know nothing about me Frederic and I did not give you permission to paint me either."

"Cathleen, I did not mean to offend you. I am an artist; I paint the beauty that I see before me as I see it."

"Betty, come on now Darling." Cathleen carried Betty from the stool straight into the buggy for a faster escape.

"Cathleen, please don't be angry with my brother he did not mean any harm," Marcel said in defence of Frederic who was now dealing with another customer. "He does not see you as sad, but as a work of art, a beauty he had to paint."

"Au revoir, Marcel." Cathleen could sense her actions were childish, even as she was storming off from the kiosk.

She was aware that her main cause of anger was not really directed at Frederic for painting her, but for how she had come across to him—how he read her expressions. In his company she was always smiling and pleasant in conversation, how could he see what hid beneath? How could her eyes alone give so much away of the guilt, the grief, and the pain she carried every day. Marcel had said two paintings had already sold, it felt peculiar to her that somewhere in France—or perhaps elsewhere—a portrait of herself stripped to her bare emotions was hung on a stranger's wall or sat on their mantel piece. The stranger unaware of her name or her story, unaware of the secrets she kept and the lies she told. Betty kicked her legs and squealed to get out and back on her feet, but Cathleen ignored her daughter, she ignored the stares, and she did not stop until she closed the door of her apartment and slowly allowed her body to fall to the floor. Betty watched on, bewildered at her behaviour. As Cathleen sat in silence on the floor, Betty wrapped her small arms around her neck and sat on her knee quietly as though she knew it was time for silence.

Cathleen's back felt stiff against the door as she arose from sleep, Betty still in her arms drooling onto her blouse. Looking down at her daughter deep in sleep, Cathleen found herself tearful. She hoped that she would be the best mother that Betty could ever need, not only because she wanted the best for her daughter but because of how she became her mother. To fail would be to fail in vain, but to succeed meant she could not fall at every boulder that tried to stop her in her tracks. She had to be happy, she had to be blessed, and she had to be present every day. If Frederic, a kindly neighbour, could see the cracks then so would Betty.

An envelope was pushed under the apartment door skidding on the hard floor towards Cathleen's tucked knees. It was written to her in the most beautiful handwriting.

Cathleen,

I did not wish to upset you with my paintings. You are right I should have asked for your permission first, for that I am sorry. I am not sorry for what I see however, you are not like other woman I see in Paris with their red lipstick and pretty handbags. You are real, and your humanity shines through. No life is perfect, no one is smiling from dawn till dusk, no one is fulfilled every day. You are a wonderful maman, and I am sure you are a wonderful wife also. I could be wrong, but I sense something is missing in your life or there is an emptiness of some sort or a burden, and this is the reflection that I see in your eyes, in your soul. This is what I captured in my painting; they do not sell because people believe it to just be a painting of a beautiful woman. They sell because other people can feel what they see in you in themselves. If you wish it, I will not paint anymore, and you may keep the one you saw today, but what do I know? I am just your neighbour who helps carry your shopping once a week. I am sorry if I have overstepped the mark.

Please forgive me. Frederic.

Carefully placing Betty onto the couch, Cathleen tiptoed out of the apartment and knocked on Frederic's door. She was pleased to see that it was he who answered and not Marcel for she was feeling rather foolish, and one neighbour to grovel to was enough for her own pride. Still clutching the letter, Cathleen rested her head onto Frederic's chest and felt her body feel at ease as she closed her eyes and felt kind arms wrap around her, pulling her closer to him. He smelt of coffee and cigarettes and his warm arms felt like a soothing blanket.

"I am sorry," she whispered. "You are right and that is why I was angry, but I do not wish to talk about it."

"You do not need to; I do not wish to intrude in your life," Frederic replied, also in a whisper.

"Please pass on my apology to Marcel."

Frederic's body shook as he laughed. "Oh Cathleen, you were but a mouse. Marcel has women speak to him more fiercely than you did quite regularly."

Cathleen felt relieved, pulling away from Frederic's clutches. "Well, I best get back to Betty before she wakes. I will see you on Wednesday."

"Oui, bonne nuit."

"Oh, and Frederic, you can paint me if you like."

"Je vous remercie, Cathleen."

"Good night."

"I saw Cedella yesterday."

"That sounds lovely, did you do anything nice?" Rupert asked over breakfast. Breakfast on a Sunday was the only day of the week they sat to eat it together; in fact, it was sometimes the only day they ate anything together. Rupert was arriving home so late some nights that his tea was left in the oven for him.

"Oh, we just had a small picnic in the park, she said Aiden saw you actually, last Tuesday at the pub down the road."

"He did, did he? I never saw him," Rupert said, cutting up a sausage for Betty.

"I never knew you had time to go to the pub," Cathleen said curiously.

"I sometimes go with some of the lads after work."

"You don't even drink and Cedella said it was at lunch time."

"Well, I would have gone for my lunch then. Jesus, Cathleen, what is this, an interrogation. God, can't a hardworking man go to a pub now and then."

"Rupert!" Cathleen was shocked at his blasphemy. "I was only asking, I don't get to see you that much nowadays, all I was going to suggest is maybe we could meet up now and then and have lunch together."

"Sorry, I am just tired. Yes, of course that sounds like a lovely idea. Perhaps a café, with Betty an all."

"A café sounds lovely."

"Come on then, eat up Sweetheart, it is almost time for prayers," Rupert instructed his daughter.

Cathleen was taken aback with Rupert; she had never heard him speak how he'd just done, and she made a mental note to ask for the Lord to forgive her husband in her prayers.

Chapter Eight

June 1960

The one-year anniversary of losing Charlotte was fast approaching. A letter from her mam reminded her of this, although there had been no need, for how could Cathleen forget such a day? Her parents begged her to visit home for the occasion, but she refused. There was still no coffin, there was still no headstone, or a place for her to rest. Instead, there was a shrine in her parent's front room, photos, flowers, and candles covered a whole sideboard. It was a reminder of their loss, and in Cathleen's eyes, it was not healthy. She had her own photo on her shelf, of course, which she returned to each Sunday during prayer, but she tried to look on with memories of what had been, not what was lost, to help her clear her conscious. As the anniversary approached, she was finding it harder to ignore. The Charlotte who looked back at her was innocent, excited for her future. The last conversation she had with her sister was the day before she ran away. She had popped round for a cup of tea with her mam, Charlotte was getting ready for a shift at the library, she looked well and happy. Cathleen remembered feeling relief because the death of their nan had been hard on her sister. She was in a rush so did not say much, Cathleen had asked her if she had any book recommendations. Charlotte being Charlotte rattled off three novels from the top of her head without hesitation.

She asked Charlotte if she was wearing makeup, Charlotte had said she was wearing just a little as did everyone at work. Cathleen did not think much of it at the time, she was young, and she was proud of her for working hard. Little did she know that she had not been to work for weeks and was secretly meeting up with Joe Hollister. If only she had seen the signs, she thought. Perhaps she could have talked to her, tried to make her see sense that he was no good for her, but no matter how much she thought of a number of what ifs, they all took Betty away from her, making Charlotte's ending inevitable. If given the option to turn back the time, she would still choose having Betty. Even though the thought tore at her morals and filled her with an overpowering rush of guilt. Not seeing much of her husband meant she did not have to pretend that everything was okay when all she wanted to do at present was scream. It was as though her body could not handle all of the emotions, it was confused, there was too many trapped feelings and nowhere for them to go. She often let it out into a cushion when alone, she had told herself that Betty would never see the cracks, not after the ordeal with the portrait of her at Frederic's kiosk. Cedella, who was aware of the approaching anniversary, had left a hamper on her doorstep. The hamper contained sweet treats and essential foods with a little note attached. '*In case you don't feel like going out. Cedella xx.*'

It had slipped her mind that it was a Wednesday until Frederic stood on her doorstep casually in linen brown trousers, a loose beige top and his feet bare.

"I came to see if you were all right, you did not need me today. I can see now that you are definitely not."

Cathleen had known she had been upset but had not realised how transparent she was; before she could send Frederic away, he let himself into the apartment towards the kitchen stove. "We need coffee. Bonjour Ma Chére ."

"Bonjour Ric," Betty replied from the floor, rocking a doll to sleep in its wooden doll sized cradle.

"Sit, Maman," he instructed Cathleen, to which she followed obediently.

There was something about Frederic that made her feel like she could trust him, that he understood her, that he could be the person that she could offload some of her thoughts and feelings to. She could not tell Cedella, for as much as she loved her friend, she was also envious of her and did not wish for her pity. Frederic however, seemed somewhat different, but she did not have it in her to tell him the truth when he sat opposite her and asked what was troubling her. She was frightened he would look at her in the same way people did back at home—with disgust and shame that she could take her sister's child and raise it on her own without her permission, without even a discussion, while she recovered her health all alone. She was scared he would no longer wish to be her friend if he knew she was lying to everyone about Betty being her own biologically, and that her own needs to desperately be a mother had killed Betty's birth mother. Instead, she told him only part of the story. She told him her sister had been staying with family in London when she was killed in a fire. She told him that she had not spoken to her in some time before hand, which made her feel guilty. Frederic listened as she told him about the memorial and how she found it hard to cope with her anniversary or returning home where everywhere is a reminder of her. She told him everything, missing out the parts that could change his view of her.

"Is that your sister?" he asked, pointing to the photo sat behind the candle.

"Oui."

"She looks like you."

"She was better than me," Cathleen admitted.

"Oh. Cathleen. You cannot change the past; your sister will be with your grand-mere now. She will be looking down wanting you to be happy. I didn't know your sister, but from what you have said I am sure she will want you to not forget, but also to not be so sad."

Cathleen appreciated his sweet words; it had been good to talk about Charlotte but in her heart, she believed Charlotte would not wish her happiness, but perhaps the happiness she knew she would wish for Betty had to start with Cathleen and with this maybe even forgiveness could be given from her sister's spirit.

"You should write back to your maman, tell her you will be okay," he said with a smile. "Why not invite her here, to France?"

"My dad will never set foot in France again; he was here during the war. He will not even board a plane, never mind one here."

"Time, Cathleen. Give everything time. One year is not long, he may never come to France, but I believe you will find the courage to go back to England, if not for you then for your Ma Chére ."

"Shhh!" Betty whispered rather loudly. "Baba sleep."

"Sorry Darling," Cathleen whispered, finding it hard not to giggle as Frederic laughed out loud making Betty annoyed with him.

"I better go before your husband returns; I don't want him to think I am up to no good," Frederic teased, clearing away the table.

"You don't need to worry about Rupert, he won't be back until tonight."

"Your husband always works this late?" he asked.

Cathleen nodded. Rupert was aware of Frederic offering to help on Wednesdays with the shopping and had been as thankful with the arrangement as she was, however, she had not told him about the painting, and she knew she would never mention his present visit. It wasn't that she felt like she was doing anything wrong, but on the off chance her husband found her friendship with another man inappropriate. She knew she would be sad to have to end the friendship she'd built with Fredric.

"Well in that case, how about I stay for dinner? I will cook you both a French meal. How does beef bourguignon sound, the way my papa used to make it," Frederic proposed.

"You and your papa can cook?" Cathleen laughed in genuine surprise.

"Cathleen, all good Frenchman can cook. I will pop out and grab the ingredients, you are both going to love it."

The beef bourguignon tasted divine, Frederic made extra so she could put some away for Rupert and not have to cook. She found her neighbour to be exceptionally thoughtful and was pleased she had not gotten hot headed earlier and threw him out as she initially had thought of doing. It was good for the soul to have some company and someone to talk to. She knew she had not told Frederic everything, but perhaps one day she might feel she could. When he headed out to grab the ingredients for his meal, she found herself looking back at herself in the mirror analysing how she looked. She remembered Charlotte putting on lipstick to meet Joe, Cathleen had not been into make-up very much, she saw it as an occasional thing rather than something daily. She looked tired she noted, and older than her twenty-five years. It would be strange for Frederic to return and for her to have a face full of makeup, but she did brush her hair and tied it up into a tight ponytail allowing her jaw line and neck to look better. As Cathleen looked back at herself in the mirror once more when Frederic had left, she questioned if it was wrong for her to make a small difference to her appearance for a man who was not her husband, but for the first time in a while she smiled back at herself recalling how the evening had uplifted her spirits. It had not felt alien having a man cook for her in her own kitchen, she embraced it as she sat back and allowed him to pour her a glass of wine and enjoyed the grown-up conversation while playing with Betty, all the while the preparation of the meal was taken care of. Cathleen hadn't heard Rupert come in from work as she slept off good food and wine. She hoped he enjoyed his tea, and the effort she would pretend she'd put into it.

A week later Cathleen and Betty were returning from a lovely lunch at Cedella's. Three children under the age of three could get hectic and loud at times but it was great to see how well they got on, especially Betty and Cyrille.

Almost arriving to the lobby of the apartment, Cathleen turned around thinking she heard her name being called but shrugged it off when she didn't see anyone she recognised.

"Cathleen!" she heard again. It was definitely her name. She stopped, looking around.

"Cathleen." The voice was louder, closer, and more prominent. "Please, stop Cathleen." The voice also had a distinct accent—an accent that made her heartbeat rapidly increase. An accent that she recognised above all others. It was from the North East of England. A man walked towards her—he was unrecognisable at first. His clothes were shabby and had seen better days, his beard was long and scraggly. It was the black leather jacket and the blue eyes of her daughter's that gave the identity of the man away.

It was Joe Hollister, Betty's real dad.

He stood before her, in Paris, in her haven. Cathleen gripped the handlebars of the buggy tightly and almost ran to the lobby.

"Cathleen. Stop!" Joe shouted.

He was running now, Cathleen noted as she picked up her own speed, fear coursed through her. It couldn't be him, why would Joe be in France? She was seeing it all wrong, perhaps it was the heat, she thought. As much as she wished it were not him, there was no denying it as he stood before her, his hands gripping the sides of the buggy.

"I just want to see her; I mean no harm," he told her looking down at Betty.

Joe gazed at her as though he'd never seen a child before, tears brimmed his eyes. Betty looked up at Cathleen and then back to the stranger before her with confusion. Cathleen pulled the buggy away from his grip.

"Get away from her," she said sternly.

"I don't mean any harm; I just want to see her." Joe raised his hands in defence.

"Well now you've seen her, now get away."

"Cathleen, please."

Cathleen proceeded to step back and ran, not stopping until she was home. Her heart was ready to emerge from her chest, her arms shaking, her head dizzy. She had no idea if Joe had followed her home, she feared he knew where they lived now, down to the very apartment. Her mind filled with scenarios of him returning and stealing Betty, or telling Betty and everyone they knew that he was her real dad. She held Betty closely, scared of letting her go. Cathleen felt desperate for her husband to return, she had vomited twice and felt the foundations around her cave in.

It was past eleven o'clock when Rupert arrived home, Cathleen lunged into his arms knocking him back on his feet.

"What is it? What's happened?" he asked alarmed.

Cathleen pulled herself away from Rupert, she could not look at his face as he came closer to her repeatedly asking what was wrong. She had to tell him about Joe, but she felt sick from the smell of her husband. There was no denying the scent, it was strong and cheap. Her husband was covered in women's perfume. Cathleen knew she had cuddled Frederic once and enjoyed his company, but she knew that did not mean she too smelt of cigarettes. For his scent to linger on her clothes and skin he would have had to be extremely close for some time. A woman had done just this with Rupert, she had been close to him for long enough to leave her scent.

"I saw Joe today," Cathleen said almost casually, sitting on the couch away from the invading smell. "He was outside, he wanted to see Betty."

Rupert bent down to his knees to speak to her, he said words that he believed to be of comfort. He told her it did not matter, that Joe had no rights, and that she should not get herself so worked up. All the while he was talking, his lips moved, but all Cathleen could do was smell his deceit. Surely there was an explanation, she thought. Rupert was a good man, a good Christian. He made his vows to her before God. She had to be wrong, Rupert loved her.

Chapter Nine

June 1960

Thoughts of Rupert's deceit kept Cathleen awake through the night, she tossed and turned, got in and out of bed. Nothing could aid her sleep. She looked at her husband sleeping soundly beside her. His blonde locks and angelic face made Cathleen think of excuses and reasons for him to have woman's perfume on him. Maybe he was sat beside a partner of one of his work mates at the pub. If he got the bus home, he could have been sat beside a woman with an exceptional amount of perfume on. She picked the clothes Rupert had been wearing up off the floor, placing them in the wash basket, out of sight. Whatever Rupert had been up to; he was still her husband and Betty's dad. They had promised to be joined together in matrimony till death do they part. Cathleen thought of all the reasons she had let her husband down; she was hardly prompting him for intimacy, not since she realised, she was in the family way again. She had heard that men had needs and sometimes other woman filled them, they required something new and exciting, but she had never imagined Rupert to be one of them. Rupert also disliked living in France, she knew this, but still insisted they stay—was this along with her struggle to give him a child a reason for him to stray? She didn't know the whole story so did not want to accuse him of anything, instead she decided to say nothing. Their wedding anniversary was in July, and doing something together might give her husband a reminder of their commitment.

It was a Wednesday, and the cupboards were bare, so as much as Cathleen hoped to stay home and wash all Rupert's work clothes with bleach, she had to face the shops. With herself and Betty all dressed in summery floral dresses, they headed out only to be met by Joe sitting on the bottom step of the first flight. He looked as though he was sleeping, his head leaning against the wall. If it wasn't for Betty's humming, they may have managed to sneak past him. Joe immediately stood up facing them, Cathleen had forgotten all about him after Rupert had arrived home the night before. It was as though she had almost dreamt him, but he was very real.

"Cathleen, hear me out. I am not staying in Paris for long, I will be gone in a day or two, I just…I just had to see her again, please."

Cathleen ignored him as she hastily put Betty into her buggy, she believed that if she pretended she couldn't see him then he would vanish, it was wishful thinking of course.

"Cathleen, please. Maybe I could spend the day with her, a couple of hours, anything," he begged, standing in their way. Slowly Joe bent down, putting him head-to-head with Betty, and smiled at her. "Hello there," he gently said.

Betty's hand stretched out and grabbed his beard giving it a small tug, which made her giggle. Joe pretended it hurt, giving the little girl more incentive to do it once more. "Funny face," she laughed pointing to him.

"My name is Joe," he said pointing to himself. "What's your name?"

"Betty."

"Betty," he repeated, clearing his throat. "Pleased to meet you, Betty."

The scene before her was an emotional one, even to Cathleen. Betty took an instant liking to Joe, and he was hiding his emotions, she could tell. Cathleen wanted to manoeuvre the buggy around him hoping to end his first meeting with his daughter, but she found herself frozen to the spot as Betty continued to laugh and chat with the new amusing stranger.

"Has Charlotte seen her?" Joe asked, while pretending to steal Betty's nose. "I know the last time I saw her she was distraught that she was in France."

"You saw Charlotte!" Cathleen gasped. "When?"

"Last year, must have been around April or May time. I was leaving London when she appeared out of nowhere. I don't know where she'd been, but she was upset about Betty." Joe looked up from Betty and added in an almost hiss, "She said you took her."

Cathleen imagined her little sister distraught in London, all the while she had been living a fine life in Paris with Betty—the one thing stopping her sister from being happy.

"It was for the best, for both of them," Cathleen said defensively hiding her guilt at the actions taken after Betty's birth.

Joe smirked. "You're wrong. No one did what was best for Charlotte. Her life is always decided for her, who she can date, who she can love, where she can live, whether she should have her own child. If you all just listen to her, you will see that she's very capable of making her own choices."

"I know my sister," Cathleen said, rage getting the better of her. "I know she did not want to settle down at sixteen in Durham as a single *abandoned* mam."

"She was not abandoned!" Joe yelled standing up, making Betty jump with the sudden change of his tone. "I left to protect her and Betty, I left to give them a better life."

"Well what good did that do?" Cathleen yelled back, leaning over the buggy towards her sister's former lover. "If you had just stayed away from her in the first place, she would still be alive now!"

Joe stepped back stunned. "Alive?" Cathleen, in that moment, realised that Joe had no idea what she was talking about, he'd obviously never returned home to receive the news that Charlotte was gone. "What do you mean alive?"

Cathleen pushed the buggy towards the lobby entrance before her, desperate to feel the air beyond them, desperate to get away but Joe gripped the buggy stopping her from pushing it far.

"What do you mean? TELL ME!" he shouted, making Betty cry, he was angry now, his face twisted, she had heard stories of Joe getting into fights after his mam died. The police were always on his back warning him that his behaviour would have him in prison if he kept it up.

"SHE'S DEAD!" she screamed back. As Joe's grip loosened, Cathleen took the opportunity to leave, not stopping until she was a few streets away from the apartment. She checked on Betty whose little tears were strolling down her cheeks matching hers. "I'm sorry Darling, Maman is so sorry."

Having done her shopping on autopilot and getting Betty an ice cream to cheer her up, Cathleen headed back relieved to see Frederic standing outside finishing a cigarette.

"Ma Chére, did you eat your ice cream or wipe it all over your face?" he chuckled. "You, okay?" he asked Cathleen seriously, looking at her as though he was looking into her brain and pulling out all her thoughts and feelings.

"Of course," Cathleen said displaying a smile. "Let's get this lot in then, oui."

"Oui, mind the homeless man inside."

"Homeless man?" Cathleen asked as her heart changed rhythm.

"Oui, he's been there a while, crying. He will not speak to me. He will probably stay there a while until someone yells at him."

Joe was still there; the homeless man Frederic had mistaken him for, though from the look of him he may in fact be homeless. His eyes were red and his nose running. Cathleen couldn't help but feel sorry for him.

"What happened?" he asked.

Cathleen let out a sigh as Frederic held on to her arm. "You know this man?" he whispered in her ear.

"He is a friend of my sister's."

"Let me have Betty for a little while so you can talk to her friend."

Joe looked at Cathleen anxiously, she didn't want him around Betty, but the look in his eyes at the thought of Frederic taking Betty cut her and her beliefs.

"It's fine, merci."

Cathleen never imagined she would be making tea for Joe Hollister in her apartment in Paris, nor did she ever imagine it would be down to her to inform him of how her sister died. Betty had fallen asleep giving them the opportunity to properly talk about what happened. Joe, like all of them, was left with more questions as he wiped his eyes. Why did they take her body? Why was she out in the middle of the night? What was she doing?

"I went back a few months later, to London. I had left in such a hurry that I hoped to bump into her again and be able to check that she was alright. She told me it was my fault," he cried. "I never wanted to leave her; she knew this. She begged to come with me, but it wouldn't have been right. Look at me, what could I have given them?"

"Why did you leave?"

"I upset someone, someone who had a reputation for pulling people's limbs off. I had to keep them safe, I had to take her home." Joe pulled out a ring from his leather jacket. "Things were great before I messed up, we were happy. I was making good money; we had a nice place with great landlords. They owned a book shop downstairs, Charlotte loved it," he smiled, reminiscing; Cathleen could imagine her sister's delight. "We were excited about the future, for Betty. I was going to marry her, we were gonna be a family. I know your family hate me, but I loved her, I loved her so much." Joe hid his face in his arms on the table and sobbed some more.

Cathleen cried with him, silently in her chair opposite, she had never known anything about her sister's life on the run with Joe. She imagined them sleeping on people's couches, going hungry, but the life Joe had told her about made Cathleen think perhaps her family had got it all wrong.

"Sorry," he said, blowing his nose into a tissue.

"Don't be."

"I guess my family know about all of this."

Cathleen nodded. "Henry took it in the same way as you have, he tried to stop the arrangements we made for her to move to London. He was willing to make an honest woman out of her and look after both of them."

Joe let out a loud sigh. "Yes, my brother the hero. I knew he would look after her, that is why I left her at my dad's. He and Charlotte were close, and we hurt him, I know we did, but I knew he would be there for her." Joe's gaze drifted off to the photo frames, a small smile forming from the corner of his mouth. "That was your wedding day."

"It was," Cathleen replied, surprised he remembered.

"She looks stunning, happy. I remember we snuck a bottle of wine out the back, Henry, Charlotte, and your cousin, Will."

"William?"

"Yeah, he didn't really wanna, but we were making fun of him, so Charlotte convinced him. Your nan caught us, but the legend told us to move somewhere more secretive so we wouldn't get caught."

Cathleen laughed. "I had no idea that ever happened, my nana was not the average nan."

"That's why she adored her so much, she wanted to be just like her."

"Well, I don't think my nan would have made a very good housewife, she would never be caught in a pair of rubber gloves or cooking dinner."

"Oh, she couldn't cook," he laughed. "But neither could I, so I didn't complain."

Cathleen found that talking about Charlotte with someone who knew a side to her that she never experienced was actually comforting. Her sister lost her life young, but she had the experience of love and family. It had all gone terribly wrong for various reasons, but Betty lived on, and Cathleen would bring her up well. Joe stopped for dinner, playing with Betty on the floor all afternoon. It was as though the two had always known each other. She was pleasantly surprised at how he interacted with her, making all the animal noises, and 'feeding' her dolls, he was a natural and Betty loved the attention.

"Do you love her as your own?" he asked.

"I do, with every fibre of my being."

"And Rupert, does he? Is he a good dad?" There was a sadness to Joe's question along with concern for Betty.

"He is and he loves her very much."

Joe nodded, his care was genuine and the way he spoke about her sister, and his care for Betty, made her think of how much time she'd missed with Rupert. The time Charlotte and Joe ran away together to Gateshead sounded almost romantic in some way, more than hers and Rupert's apartment in Paris had felt. Joe made her sister sound like the most important person in his life, while her husband worked at every given opportunity and spent time at the pub afterwards rather than spending time with his wife—time that was already limited. Joe may have been the scoundrel in his teens but the man before her was someone different, she saw a side to him that Charlotte had known, a side no one else had taken the chance to know. Joe left before

Betty's bedtime, with permission to return the following day. Cathleen didn't see much harm in it as he was leaving soon. Betty wouldn't remember him, and she would have done a good deed by someone.

As the time passed and the night grew later and later, Cathleen's eyes grew heavy waiting for Rupert to return home. It was late, the night was dark. He worked as a scaffolder why hadn't she realised before now that this was not a job done in the dark? All the late nights were not keeping him at work, but with her—the woman whose perfume he brought home—the woman that he could be laying naked with as she lay waiting for him, his side of the bed cool and untouched. Cathleen tortured herself with images of infidelity until sleep consumed her.

Joe returned as planned, much to the delight of Betty to have her play mate 'Joe-Joe' return. Cathleen couldn't help but notice that Joe looked unwell. His skin was almost black in some places, his beard was untamed, his hair long, his eyes sunken, and he ate her food as though he was starving. Cathleen was not one to pry or look down on people; the years on the run had not been kind to the young man, but she could offer some assistance. Cathleen offered him a warm bath set up in the bedroom as well as some clean clothes of Rupert's that he had not worn in a long time, with the use of a razor and a pair of scissors.

"Thank you, I appreciate this very much," Joe sincerely said. "Are you sure Rupert will not mind me taking his clothes?"

"Not at all, I can clean your clothes, they will be dried by tomorrow if I hang them from the window."

"Thank you but please leave the jacket."

As Joe freshened up, Cathleen, who could smell Joe's jacket, thought to go over it with a damp cloth taking care of what was left of the leather. Joe used to be seen riding his motorcycle all over the village in the jacket, it seemed he was very attached to it. As Cathleen dabbed over his pocket, she could feel the ring, he carried for her sister. He had wanted to make her his wife, as did Henry, both prepared to make a big commitment to her. Would they have been true to their word? Would they have looked after her? Would they have strayed? And if Charlotte knew about it, would she have put up with it, pretended it wasn't happening? Cathleen knew the answer to this was no. Her sister was stronger than she was, she would have come clean by now, she would have wanted answers, but it was the answers what frightened her the most.

"It's Joe-Joe." Joe had emerged out of the bedroom looking like a new man, confusing Betty no end. Years had been lifted from him and a true twenty-one-year-old stood before them. He was more recognisable to the young man who had previously been her neighbour for most of her life. Although the clothing looked as though he was playing pretend.

"Not my usual look," he admitted. "But they are clean and for that I am grateful."

"You look smart," she said looking at Rupert's cardigan swallow his small frame.

"I will take your word for it." Joe's soft face suddenly hardened as his gaze fell behind Cathleen. "What are you doing?"

Cathleen followed his gaze to the leather jacket on the table. "Oh, I know you didn't want it washed so I just went over it with a damp cloth, you can still wear it." With the summer heat blaring Cathleen couldn't understand how he could comfortably wear the thing but the look on her face began to tell her that this had more to do with being attached to the worn item of clothing.

"I told you to leave it." Joe picked up the jacket muttering the word *'no'* panickily as he opened the pocket with the ring pulling out a folded piece of paper no bigger than a bus ticket. The fabric must have been worn somewhere as one half of the paper was wet, causing it to rip as he opened it up.

"Joe, I am sorry. I did…"

"Thanks for the clothes and the bath," he interrupted making an immediate exit from the apartment.

"Joe-Joe gone," Betty observed.

"Yes Darling, he is."

Whatever the small paper was, Cathleen had destroyed something important, and she felt awful for it.

Chapter Ten

June 1960

Cathleen greeted her husband in the best dress she owned, with a hot meal ready for him to delve into. Her lips pink from a new lipstick she bought earlier and a warm smile as she gave him a welcoming hug.

"This looks lovely," he commented. "Smells good too."

"I thought I would stay up later tonight to ensure you got something fresh rather than reheated and I thought it would be nice to sit up with you, have a little catch up." Cathleen took Rupert's tool bag from him before dishing out a hot steak pie onto his plate.

"I'm sorry I haven't been around much, I stopped on the sofa last night. Seemed a shame to wake you, but this is nice. You look nice."

Nice. Helping an elderly woman across the road is nice, she thought. Betty learning her Ps and Qs was nice. Complimenting your friend's new hair was nice. Joe had called Charlotte stunning, bold as brass.

"Thank you," she replied with a large smile.

"How has Betty been today? You both been up too much?"

Cathleen had not had the time to tell Rupert about Joe's visits, as much as she would have once wanted to tell him everything and have him reassure her that she was doing the right thing; as she watched him eat pie and lie about his own day she decided against it, he wouldn't care anyway, probably thinking it was a fine thing to do. He'd never understood any of her anxiety post adoption.

"We just stopped at home today." Cathleen wished she had added wine to the meal.

As they got ready for bed Cathleen put on a pale pink silky nighty that she had not worn for some time, she had bought it for their honeymoon but had found it a little too revealing. She casually slid into bed beside her husband and watched as his eyes followed her. She acted as though she didn't notice and snuggled into his warm arms. Rupert wrapped his arms tightly around her and planted kisses on her shiny soft lips. The small pecks became stronger, her eyes closed, and she allowed herself to be showered in affection. He loved her, she thought, maybe she got it all wrong after all. The perfume and the late nights, they no longer mattered. He was her husband and each kiss, every touch, sent butterflies fluttering through her body.

Cathleen felt a small kiss on her head as Rupert left for work in the early hours, before Betty would wake Cathleen. She lay there with a real smile, thinking back to the night before where the sheets were left in a sweaty tangle. Having not been intimate with each other in some time, had led them to act as though they were experiencing something new and exciting yet old and comfortable all at the same time. She felt like she was floating in ecstasy when a knock at the door brought her back down to life, Cathleen pulled Rupert's robe over her to protect her modesty from her early caller, whose knocks were increasing in sound.

"I'm coming!" Cathleen unlocked the door and Joe burst into her apartment; his energy as wound up as he had left.

"I'm leaving, I wanted to say goodbye to Betty."

"She's still asleep—Joe." Her old neighbour made his way to the bedroom and planted a gentle kiss onto Betty's cheek, so gentle that she did not so much as stir. Cathleen watched on from the bedroom door, as he stroked her dark locks.

"I'm sorry about yesterday," Cathleen whispered. "I feel awful."

"I'm going to pop back now and then when I can," he replied hushed, Cathleen's apology ignored. "I let Charlotte down by not being there, but I won't let Betty down. I will be in her life one way or another whether you like it or not. You may blame me for leaving her at her most vulnerable but believe me I regret that every single God damn day, but I had no choice. It was your family who wanted to stop us being together in the first place, it was your family who sent her away, and it was *you* who took our child. For someone who lost a baby herself it was a pretty shitty move to make, don't you think? No one ever asked Charlotte what she wanted, if you had all just let us be in the first place and given me a chance to prove myself, we would have been happy. She would be here now, alive, and able to watch her daughter grow. You said you knew your sister, but you didn't, you weren't there to hear the long chats about our growing baby, you didn't witness the excitement on her face when I got down on one knee, you didn't know that she spent some of her days talking to Mrs Gregory about the stories she would write for her child. She was loved and supported, and she would have been a great mother and a great writer, but you took both of those away—you all killed Betty's mam."

Cathleen stood frozen, unable to think of the words to say in response. The hardest part was that he spoke the truth, and the truth hurt. It was on everyone's mind at the memorial, everyone from her uncle to her parents. Cathleen had tried to think herself out of it, she hadn't wanted Charlotte to go to London, she had tried to talk them out of it, but she still abandoned her, she still took her new-born baby. Her actions were the ones that would have left the biggest mark, the largest scars. She loved Betty, she was Cathleen's world and she hated to think that she would grow up to find out the truth. What if she too looked at her the way Joe currently was—with disgust and so much detest.

"Joe-Joe loves you." With another farewell kiss, Joe took himself away from the cot and stopped inches away from Cathleen, she could feel his breath on her face as he spoke. "What would God make of your actions, if I remember rightly one of the commandments is *Thou shalt not steal.* Pass on my message to your husband. I will be back."

Joe's comment had left her stunned; all Cathleen wanted was Rupert. She longed to be back in the safety of his arms. As she slept on the couch waiting for his return home, she woke sometime after four am to find that he was still not home, and she did not expect to see him at all. She screamed into a cushion as the realisation hit that her husband was with someone else, he was holding another woman in his arms with no idea how much he was breaking her heart.

Chapter Eleven

July 1960

July was the month Cathleen would be celebrating her wedding anniversary. Despite not seeing much of her husband and knowing when he didn't return home he was with another woman, she still hoped for the future. She still pictured a future as the three of them. Cathleen held her head high and acted as though everything was normal. When she looked at Rupert, she still saw the boy she met at church, the good man who whisked her off her feet. Maybe the month celebrating their love would remind Rupert of his vows. They had planned to go out to eat at a small café that they'd met up at a few times. Rupert wasn't big on the idea, suggesting that they were not celebrating a big milestone, but with some persuasion he agreed as it would make her happy. Cathleen wondered if everything Rupert did was to make her happy. Adopting Betty—was that just to make her happy or did he really want her? He was a great dad when he was present, but the problem was he wasn't present enough. He didn't particularly enjoy his job, but he kept going and continued to pay the bills; she knew he wished to return to England, but he stayed because she would not leave; not when he had a job there even though she knew he hated it. He did it for her, they were in France for her. To live a life you are not happy with, in order to allow another to live a life they want, is in some way a form of love, isn't it? If, in return, Rupert found affection in other people and happiness in other places, perhaps that was the compromise she believed she had to accept.

Despite this, their marriage was still important to Cathleen, she wanted the day to be perfect, Rupert had managed to get the day off and Cathleen had planned her outfit weeks in advance. It was a Saturday morning and Cathleen had expected to wake up to find Rupert home, having returned home Friday evening. Instead, she woke to find he was not there. Cathleen prepared him an English breakfast and hoped he would return while it was fresh and hot. Then she got dressed in an outfit she had not worn since the early days of their marriage when they used to go out on date nights, along with a pretty dress for Betty. They played dolls for a while, they read books, Cathleen chopped up fruit for snack for Betty. The plan had been to go out for lunch but as the time passed, it was clear that it was no longer possible, and Betty needed feeding. Cathleen had to stop hoping.

They had plans, Cathleen thought angrily as she prepared a romantic dinner for two once Betty was in bed. They had agreed to eat lunch at the café then to take a walk in the city, take in the tourist sights, eat ice cream, and walk hand in hand. It was going to be perfect, and Rupert was going to look at her and remember why he chose her, why he loved her. Cathleen rubbed her eyes unsure whether it was the onions or the pain causing them to grow wet. She wondered where he was and looked forward to hearing his excuse this time. He definitely had the day free; she'd seen him mark it on the calendar herself. Anniversary cards that had arrived early were placed on the shelves, from their parents and friends from back home, a reminder to him whenever he walked through the apartment of the approaching day. Cathleen watched the food boil in the steaming hot water her head in a thunderous cloud, she thought back to how uninterested her husband had been to celebrate their anniversary in the first place; she recalled the nights she slept alone while he was elsewhere, and she felt like a fool when he gave his excuses, actually believing that she was dumb enough to believe them. Cathleen pushed the burning pan off the cooker, spilling boiling water across the counter and burning her arm in the process. She let out a scream, a scream that was not hidden behind a cushion, or held within. The scream was free to be as loud as it desired, as loud as it felt. The release felt good, as did sweeping the set table for two, plates and glasses smashed when they made impact with the floor, cutlery bounced before settling, a knife sliding under the couch, a glass vase shattering into tiny fragments. Cathleen couldn't hear the outcry she was making, only the noise she was making with her hands. She enjoyed the feel of watching everything around her breaking. Cathleen didn't hear Frederic and Marcel enter her apartment, she didn't notice that Betty was also screaming from her cot, only to be consoled by Marcel rocking her in his arms calmly, whispering hushed French words into her ear, nor did she appreciate Frederic holding her back from smashing more of her apartment up. Forcing her to be in his arms. Her arms stood to attention by her sides like a solider as she could no longer move them.

"Cathleen, arrête! Stop please." He pulled her wriggling body in tighter, whispering, "please."

Cathleen's knees gave way and together they slowly headed to the floor, Frederic quickly slid any fragments of glass out of the way. He kept his arms tight around her as she wept in his arms. Cathleen's rage turned to grief as she poured what was left of her soul into Frederic's arms. Her back was against his chest, and he said nothing. She could feel his facial hair on the back of her shoulder as well as his heavy breathing warm on the back of her neck.

"Marcel, could you wet a tea towel for me please in cold water?" Frederic asked, as his brother appeared back in the room, he approached the kitchen area, and the crunch of glass was heard beneath his shoes. Frederic wrapped the tea towel around Cathleen's shiny red arm, she gasped as the cold cotton met her burnt skin. Marcel busied himself finding a sweeping brush to remove the glass and smashed pottery. Cathleen meanwhile closed her eyes, her cries turning to heavy breathing that followed the same pattern and movement as Frederic's.

"We need wine," Marcel suggested. "Maybe two bottles." Marcel left, returning moments later with two bottles of red wine and three wine glasses.

Frederic and Cathleen slowly raised from their position on the floor, joining Marcel at the table, glasses were filled with the red liquid and Cathleen stepped on a fork under the table as she tucked her chair in. The two brothers looked at her with bewildered expressions and Cathleen looked downcast as she took a large gulp of wine.

"Cathleen, what has happened?" Frederic asked.

Cathleen took a deep breath in, urging herself to stay calm.

"Whatever is going on, if you tell us, it will go no further. We will act like priests in the confession box. It will stay confidential," Marcel promised.

Cathleen looked at them both and believed them, and for the first time she felt ready to talk, to really talk. Before she could take anything back and crawl back under the blankets she lived under, she told them everything and they said nothing. They silently listened to her as she told them about her sister running away and getting pregnant with the man Frederic had thought was homeless, she revealed to them that the baby was in fact Betty, and then she told them how the decision to adopt her came about. She told them how she had felt in the aftermath of the adoption and her need to get away leading to their move to Paris, and ultimately the downfall of her sister's life that she now would always carry with her. She told them that she knew Rupert was sleeping with another woman, maybe more than one, she wasn't sure, but she had stayed silent. She told them it was her wedding anniversary, and she was disappointed in her husband for not showing up even though she knew it was all in vain. She told them that she had been brought up to be a good catholic girl, she went to church every Sunday, she sang in the choir, and helped the elderly and the community. She told them she believed she had been abandoned by God and was being punished for her sins. Cathleen poured the last of the red wine into her glass and drank it in one.

"Say what you're thinking," she said.

Marcel cleared his throat and took a glance at his brother whose gaze had not left Cathleen's. "Cathleen, I am not a religious guy, but my grandparents were devout Catholics like yourself. My grand-mere always used to say that if your heart was good then God would forgive you, and I believe your heart is good."

"What happened to your sister," Frederic began, his eyes still locked on Cathleen, whose glistening eyes were apprehensively fixated back. "It was a tragedy; I can see why you might believe yourself to be to blame, but her death does not sit on your shoulders. It was a number of things that happened that were not fair or justified, but what's done is done. You did not set fire to the building she was in. You believed her to be safe in the house of your uncle. You took Betty believing you were doing the right thing for both your daughter and your sister. Your heart was in the right place despite others not agreeing. Guilt cannot undo the past; you have to look at things from the point of view of a lost mother now. Whatever the feelings were between you and your sister before, you both love Betty and you both wish nothing but the best for her. You must provide that, Cathleen. She needs you to do that for her."

Frederic grabbed Cathleen's hand and gave it a tight squeeze, as tears gently flowed down her blotchy cheeks.

"And you are doing a great job," Marcel added to which Frederic agreed. "As for your husband, I hear British marriages are strict but here in France, especially in the city of love, it is normal for married men to have a mistress or two. I have even been with a few married women myself," Marcel said with a grin, as Cathleen's intrigued eyes widened. "The majority of people you see taking romantic strolls are either fresh new love or affairs. A lot of marriages last longer due to this set up of free love. There is a lot of love shared here in Paris, Rupert is one of many."

Another bottle of wine was opened, and the conversation swayed to lighter topics as the French men told Cathleen about their upbringing in the city and how their love of art came from an aunt whose masterpieces inspired them, but as a woman her own art was not appreciated. As Marcel decided to call it a night with the second bottle empty, Cathleen felt lightheaded, and her heart fluttered in gratitude as the brother kissed her cheek good night. Meanwhile Frederic lingered a little longer, the two sat opposite each other and the Frenchman said nothing, but he smiled.

"Stop that," Cathleen blushed.

"I was just thinking about your husband, the fool that he is. Marriages here may not be as they are back in England, Cathleen, but if you were my wife, I would be much suited to a traditional British marriage. If I were lucky enough to be your husband, I would not need to touch any other body but yours."

A smile returned to Frederic's face; one that she felt herself reciprocate; his words had stirred up something in her—a feeling she could not understand. It was cut short and replaced with resentment when Rupert waltzed into the apartment. He observed the small kitchen area, his wife sat with their neighbour in the dimly lit room, the two empty bottles of wine, three glasses, and an ashtray filled with cigarette butts.

"Have I missed a celebration?" he said hanging up his jacket.

"Only your anniversary," Frederic replied. "Cathleen, I bid you good night." Frederic gently lifted Cathleen's hand, giving it a small kiss, before leaving the apartment and giving a small smile to Rupert as he passed him.

"Cathleen, I'm sorry I…"

"Be quiet Rupert!" Cathleen shouted. "I don't want to hear your pathetic excuses any longer, I'm going to bed. Make yourself comfortable on the couch."

As Rupert failed to say anything back, Cathleen felt powerful as she walked away from her husband closing the bedroom door firmly behind her. As she lay her head on the soft pillow, she hoped the couch would cause Rupert discomfort, just as it had each night she had laid there waiting for him. The wine had made her a little hazy and as she drifted into a peaceful slumber, she told herself in the morning if Rupert was still there, she was going to confront him.

Chapter Twelve

July 1962

Two years later it was finally decided that Rupert was to return to England alone, much to his mam's disproval, and they were to be divorced. Their marriage had become tedious ever since Cathleen told Rupert that she knew he had been disloyal. At first, he cried for her forgiveness, he apologised repeatedly until she began to believe he was sorry. He stopped staying out late and returned home to his family and for a few months the apartment was filled with love and laughter. Cedella and Aiden came for dinner often, and Cathleen began to feel lighter and at peace once more. Rupert looked at her how he did when they were younger, when she first caught his attention. However, it didn't take long for the tide to change, by the time the spring of 1961 came around, Rupert returned to his old ways and Cathleen returned to the couch once more. His sudden change from loving husband to adulterer had spun Cathleen's world on its axis once more. On the lonely nights, all she had to do was tap on the door of her good friends Frederic and Marcel. They would pop round with a bottle of wine. Frederic's intimidating stares would often make her feel hot under the collar. Sometimes this led to Cathleen wondering what lay beneath the artist's shirt when thoughts of him came to her at night. Thoughts that she fought to stay away.

By the time, the smell of oranges and roasted chestnuts filled the air, Rupert was once again forgiven and besotted with Cathleen in time for Christmas. Cards from loved ones back in Durham hung on string and the tree was decorated neatly above the height of Betty who hung each of her baubles grouped together on the left side of the tree. They looked like any normal family preparing for the big man's visit. On Christmas Eve Cathleen and Rupert shared a sherry as they carefully wrapped up presents for their daughter, adding a delicate ribbon before leaving them under the tree. Rupert gifted her an eternity ring, promising her that he would love her forever; only for that to be tarnished by the time February arrived, when once again he began to arrive home whenever he pleased. Gone were the days of pretence and excuses. What Rupert was up to was obvious and, in these times, he crashed on the couch as Cathleen cuddled up to Betty, her soft brunette curls tickling her face, with thoughts of her husband's face, ridden with shame. In March 1962, while cleaning the dishes, Rupert arrived home with a slam of the front door. He daringly wrapped his arms around his wife pulling her close to him, smothering her neck in wet kisses. Cathleen felt her body repulse at his touch, the smell of alcohol and cheap perfume was strong.

"Rupert, please, I'm busy," Cathleen said, shrugging him off her.

Rupert laughed, letting go, holding both hands up in the air before falling into a chair. "I'm done, Cathleen. I'm done with this city, this country. It's time we went home."

Cathleen shook her head. "I'm not going anywhere."

"Four years we've been here, four fucking years! That was not the plan, Betty is not French, and we are not French. I can't stand the fucking French!"

"You stand the French enough to fuck every whore you meet," Cathleen calmly stated as she dried a plate.

"Well, some of those whores listen to me, unlike my wife."

"And what is that supposed to mean!" Cathleen shouted, turning to face a man she barely recognised anymore.

"Look at us, Cathleen, where is the love, the promises we made to one another?"

"Are you kidding me? Where is the love? The promises we made to each other. You fucking destroyed those promises, every time you stuck your cock in someone else!" She had never said so many curse words out loud before; but she didn't care who could hear her.

"I only do that because my life is so shit, and you can't see it because you're so obsessed with Betty's heritage! Having her was meant to be the start of something amazing and instead, it turned you into a madwoman who can't see past our daughter's bloodline! I came here for you, and I hate it, but you don't give a shit because it is all about you and what makes you feel better. WHAT ABOUT ME! WHAT ABOUT WHAT I WANT!" he bellowed, thumping his chest. "You're the one who is destroying our marriage, not me. You!"

"How dare you turn this on me, Rupert. For years I have put up with your infidelity and invited you back into our bed with open arms because I love you! If I can forgive that then the least you can do is accept that this is our home now, if you love me enough."

"If I love you enough! I'm still here, aren't I? Doesn't that say enough? I'm still here. You live out your Parisian dream, my love, don't worry about me."

The room fell silent, Rupert fidgeted with a silver lighter in his hand, Cathleen didn't even know he was a smoker. She lowered herself to the seat opposite, feeling exhausted. The only sound came from a small beige mantle clock that had been with them since the day of their wedding, having been bought as a gift by a work colleague of Cathleen's. They had unwrapped the gift back in their flat in Newcastle.

The clock had witnessed the first of many—the first night, the first meals, and first Christmas.

The clock had been the hero of every event they had left the flat in time for.

The clock had listened to sweet promises and hopeful dreams.

The clock had heard the cries of the broken and hurtful words, passed without apologies.

The silence between the couple lasted for days, Rupert returned home each day after his shift and sat at the dining table with a bottle of whiskey until he collapsed into bed. Cathleen hid her tears from her husband, she wanted to comfort him, but held back, not sure whether she had it in her to make things better.

"Are you happy?" Frederic asked her while carrying the food shop up the stairs, despite Betty now being out of a pushchair, Frederic was still there every Wednesday to help. "I don't mean to pry but our walls are thin."

"Are marriages meant to be happy?" Cathleen asked, avoiding the question.

"Maybe not, but do you love Rupert that much that you are happy to accept this as your life. This constant circle of forgiveness and pain. Is this how you pictured your life?" Cathleen ignored her neighbour's questions as she dug out her keys out of her handbag. "Cathleen, all I am trying to say is, we only get one shot at this. If this is what you dream of then so be it, fight for it if that is what you want. Otherwise, put down your swords and let the battle come to a truce. If not for yourselves then for Betty, is this good for her to see? Is this the example you wish her to look up to?"

"That's enough, Frederic," Cathleen snapped.

"I only care," he replied looking hurt.

"Well don't, this is nothing for you to concern yourself with."

Frederic was right, of course, Cathleen admitted to herself, which made it all the harder to hear. She wasn't happy anymore; this was not how she pictured her life, and she did not wish for Betty to grow up believing that a husband should walk in and out of your life whenever it pleased him, nor should she force him into a life he did not wish for.

After many tears, long heart felt discussions, and an idea that was thrown up and down like a yo-yo—July 1962 marked the end of Cathleen and Rupert's marriage. They were tired of trying to make something work that was only hurting them. Rupert did not want to live in France, which he made more than clear, just as Cathleen did not want to live in England. The decision had not been an easy one, but it was the right one.

Chapter Thirteen

September 1962

Within months Cathleen's world had changed, Marcel and Frederic opened a small gallery and asked Cathleen to be a receptionist. Since Rupert had returned to England, she hadn't heard a peep from him, so to be able to make her own money and provide for Betty was a blessing. Cedella helped mind Betty and was proud of Cathleen for pulling her big girl boots on and seizing the day. Working at the gallery meant her French was improving every day. The brothers' work was displayed on the walls, some of which were different versions of Cathleen's face, a favourite of Frederic's, and to her surprise one that also sold quite well. Cathleen felt as though she had a spring in her step. No longer did she wait for the door to open to see what mood her husband would arrive in—loving or guilty—no longer was she followed with thoughts of her husband in bed with another. She was free from his infidelity, free from the invisible shackles that kept her attached to him even though she wasn't happy. Each day was her own, each night was her own, and she was adamant that she and Betty would do just fine without him.

For Betty's birthday, Cathleen held a tea party at the apartment. It was a bit of a squeeze, but it was filled with those who mattered. Frederic and Marcel arrived with arms full of presents, much to Betty's delight. Cedella, Aiden, and their boys added to the gathering. Pink bunting and balloons decorated every wall, a pink cake took centre place on the dining table, and Betty looked adorable in her frilly pink dress. Cathleen had planned all the traditional party games that reminded her of her own childhood, such as pass the parcel and musical statues. The children's biggest competition was Marcel, who joined in the games and took it very seriously. Cathleen could not have coped in Paris without everyone who stood in the room before her. They had become her new family. Rupert returning home was the moment Cathleen realised there was no going back, Paris was now her home. She missed her parents and Peter back in England, but nothing was the same back in Durham.

The party was in full swing when there was a tap at the door.

"I hope no one has ordered a clown, Betty is terrified," Cathleen joked, as the brothers had mentioned earlier that their parents always booked a clown for their birthday parties.

Frederic made a cross sign over his heart. "I did not."

Cathleen wished it had been a clown however when she opened the door to a young man in a leather jacket that she was surprised had not fallen off given its current state.

"Joe!" she exclaimed.

It had been so long since his last visit that she had put Betty's biological father behind her in the hope that as each year went by, he would not return. Marcel and Frederic's ears pricked as they heard mention of Joe, they were aware of his true identity and were instantly in protection mode as Cathleen invited him into the apartment. All eyes were on the new guest, he needed a good haircut as well as a shave.

Cedella put a finger to her nose as he walked by her, he was aware of how he looked, but he had come for one reason and one reason only. The sweet little girl in the pink dress.

"Betty!" he called. Betty gave him a strange look, too young to remember their last meeting. He was a stranger to her, a strange looking one at that. "It's her birthday?" he asked Cathleen, his voice almost a squeak.

"Yes, her fourth."

"I did not know, happy birthday Darling." Joe crouched down so he was level with Betty. "I am sorry that I didn't realise. The next time I come and see you I will bring you a gift, what is it that you like?"

"Dolls," Betty timidly replied.

"Dolls," Joe repeated.

"And ponies."

"Ponies."

"And storybooks."

"You like stories?"

"Oui."

Joe stood back up allowing Betty to return to dancing with her friends, his eyes glistened and Cathleen couldn't help but feel sorry for him. His eyes glanced over at the photo of Charlotte, and the French brothers dropped their gaze. Marcel returned to freezing like a statue once Aiden paused the music and Frederic poured Joe a glass of red wine.

"Thank you," Joe said, scratching his throat.

"I'm Frederic, Cathleen's neighbour." Frederic held out his hand and Joe shook it.

"Pleased to meet you, I'm Joe. Cathleen's old neighbour."

"Joe used to date my sister, Charlotte," Cathleen added for all to hear. "He likes to pop by when he is in France." Aiden and Marcel introduced themselves next.

Cedella ignored the odour and took a plunge, giving Joe a hug. "I am sorry for your loss," she said softly.

Joe's eyes widened, and his body, that had stood in a guarded posture, relaxed a little, returning the hug to the woman who was the first person to ever show him sympathy for the loss of Charlotte. When Joe hung up his jacket, Cedella secretly squirted a few drops of her perfume onto it. It didn't take Joe long to relax, everyone was polite and welcoming, and Betty was soon enough trying to get his attention with a pink party blower and pulling him off his chair to dance with her.

"It's like she can smell his blood," Cathleen whispered to Frederic in the kitchen area. "She is like a magnet to him. She was as a toddler as well."

"He seems harmless," Frederic commented. "He could do with a bath, but I'm not one to judge."

"He is homeless, on the run from some gangster. He is hardly a trustworthy man to be around, and he was vile the last time I saw him."

"But?"

"What do you mean but, but nothing." Cathleen shrugged as she chopped up more cheese.

"But he is good with Ma Chére, and it is clear to see how much she means to him. Every man has his weaknesses."

"Oh yeah and what is yours?" she asked coyly.

Frederic laughed. "Now if I tell, you must promise not to use it against me."

"I promise," Cathleen said, making a cross over her chest.

"You," he said seriously.

Cathleen felt the beat of her heart protrude out of her ears, she felt her face grow hot and had not realised that one of the children had taken the plate of cheese out of her hands. Cathleen did not know what to say, so instead laughed it off giving him a playful slap on his arm.

"You're funny Frederic, let's light the candles!"

As the rest of the guests left the apartment, Frederic lingered behind, Cathleen could see him hovering in the kitchen piling up glasses by the sink. Joe promised Betty that he was going to return soon.

"Tomorrow?" Betty excitedly asked.

"Would you like that?" he asked, leaving his heart open for her reply.

"Yes! Come tomorrow. Maman, can Joe come back tomorrow?" Betty asked, pulling on Cathleen's hand.

"Of course," Cathleen replied, which left Joe with a smile plastered across his face.

Frederic carried on clearing away, allowing Cathleen to get an overexcited Betty to bed. She spoke fondly about her party as Cathleen brushed her hair, putting it into two little plaits. Everything had to be pink for Betty at the moment; pink pyjamas, pink bedsheets, and snuggles with a pink bunny in her bed. She read her the gingerbread man twice, a copy her parents sent from England along with a few others the previous Christmas. She knew Betty's love for books came from Charlotte, as soon as Betty had first come across stories she had fallen in love. Sometimes when she read to her daughter, she imagined her sister sitting with them on the bed, listening in and telling Cathleen to do the voices better. As Cathleen waited for Betty to eventually stop wiggling and sitting up to tell her, 'one more thing,' she thought back to when she was young and how books were never of as great an importance to her as they were to Charlotte and Peter; they got that from their nan. The Bible or a prayer book were the only books Cathleen took real joy from. She wondered how much of her Betty would inherit. If Charlotte got her love of books from her nan and Frederic got his love of painting from his aunt maybe there was hope that in her arms was a mini-Cathleen in the making.

The radio played softly as Cathleen re-emerged into the living area, after almost nodding off herself. The apartment was tidy, a red candle flickered on the table alongside two glasses of white wine.

"I thought you were never going to come out," Frederic smiled.

"Sorry, she was hard to settle tonight."

"Sit, you look exhausted Maman." Frederic pulled out a chair for Cathleen and sat beside her. She could feel the cotton of his trousers brush against her bare legs under the table, the simple touch made her stomach flutter. She rested her head on her left hand and looked at the Frenchman who she felt so comfortable around. Frederic took a sip of his wine, his eyes staring so deeply into her own that Cathleen could feel him touch her soul.

"I am proud of you, you handled today very well. I thought for a second, when Joe walked in, that Marcel and I were going to have to drag him out and hide all the plates and glasses from you."

"Ha-ha, very funny. I decided to be mature and not make a scene is all."

"I don't quite understand something Cathleen, if you can accept Joe's company around Betty, why not return home to England where you and Betty can be surrounded by all her family?" Frederic asked.

"Joe comes and goes like the wind; he will be soon forgotten. The memories and people of Durham will always be there like an anchored ship. Reminding me of my lost children, my failed marriage, my dead sister, and all the in-between. I want Betty to be surrounded by love and life, not the misery and regret of those who failed Charlotte. Paris is my home now, there is never going to be a return to England for us."

Frederic's face broke into a smile and a small sigh. "I sometimes wonder if you will ever come knocking on my door asking me to redirect the post. I am sorry for the pain held in your hometown Cathleen, but I am glad to hear that you wish to remain here. I was serious earlier on when I told you, you are my weakness." Frederic moved a little closer to Cathleen, tucking a piece of stray hair behind her ear. "If you ever moved back, I think I would have to follow you."

Cathleen leant her head onto Frederic's hand, which had lingered on her face. "I believe you," she whispered.

Frederic leant over the table a little more, placing his other hand on Cathleen's face resting his forehead against hers. "Believe this too," he whispered as he kissed her mouth ever so gently.

Cathleen accepted the kiss with great ease, and as soon as it had come to an end, she wished for the feel of him once more.

"I believe you," she repeated, this time pulling Frederic by his collar closer to her, they both stood up in unison wanting no space between their bodies. Frederic lowered Cathleen onto the couch and covered her in urgent kisses, from her lips to the top half of her breasts. Cathleen felt a rush of excitement run through her, but felt her body go rigid as Fredric began to unbutton the front of her dress. Frederic noticed and immediately stopped.

"Are you okay? Do you want me to stop?"

"Yes. No. Yes, I am okay, no I do not want you to stop. I am just a little…embarrassed."

Minutes away from making love with Frederic was the wildest experience Cathleen knew, she was about to have intimacy out of wedlock, on the couch with a Frenchman who had talked of many sexual encounters in his past. The only experience Cathleen had was with Rupert, in their bed, and the majority of the time in their nightclothes. However, Frederic put her at ease as he kissed her body slowly with each button he undid, whispering how beautiful she was. Cathleen was taken somewhere she had never been before and once she got a taste of him, she wanted more. Neither of them managed to get much sleep; they were both on a high and desperate for the next fix. Cathleen believed she had seen Frederic's manhood more times already than she'd ever seen Rupert's, as he proudly walked around in the nude to fetch them a glass of water. His body reminded her of a Greek statue and although she was hidden under a thin blanket, whenever Frederic scooped her up with his large hands and her bare skin touched his, she felt every inch the goddess to Frederic as she saw the hunger in his eyes.

When Joe arrived the next day to see Betty, Cathleen felt as though she was floating on cloud nine. He gifted Betty with a stack of French second-hand books that he hoped someone would translate. Cathleen knew he would have starved to buy them so made him a big lunch as well as giving him the use of the tin bath, and some money to get a decent haircut and shave. He wouldn't accept the money at first, but she insisted. Joe was grateful and apologised to Cathleen.

"I spoke out of line the last time I was here. I am sorry."

"There was some element of truth there. I love Betty, Joe. And she has a good life. I know it is not the life that you and Charlotte planned but it is the one she has been dealt."

Joe nodded. "You are doing a great job, she is amazing."

"Thank you, that means a lot."

"I'm never going to agree with what you did."

"I get that."

"But if she can't have Charlotte then I am glad she has you."

They were all sitting on a rug—Cathleen, Joe, and Betty—having 'tea' from little China cups and saucers. Cathleen found it rather amusing to see the northern scallywag pretend to drink from a toy cup that he had moments ago dipped his invisible biscuit into. Joe Hollister had rough edges that much was clear; but like a biscuit, in a tea, he was also a softy. With Frederic at the forefront of her mind, Cathleen wondered how Charlotte felt when being intimate with Joe. They were both younger than she and Rupert had been their first time. She remembered being so nervous and Rupert breathing anxiously above her. Was Charlotte frightened? Did she regret it afterwards? Was Betty made from their first encounter or were there many? Of course, she couldn't ask Joe any of these questions, but it had intrigued her how ballsy her sister had been. Joe walked around like a ticking bomb, but with Betty he was gentle and attentive. Was he gentle and attentive when making love or was he rough and aggressive?

"I have to leave tonight," Joe said interrupting her thoughts. Betty gazed up from feeding one of her dolls with a small metal spoon. "I'll be back as soon as I can," he reassured her. "Are you coping okay without Rupert?"

"Yes, we are coping just fine, we have support around us, and truth be told Rupert is not much of a loss to our lives."

Joe nodded without pressing for more information on Cathleen's estranged husband. "Do you have enough money?"

"Yes, I work at Frederic and Marcel's gallery, they pay me well."

"And you and Frederic—you are serious?"

Cathleen blushed immediately. "What do you mean?"

Joe laughed. "It's obvious there is something going on between you two. I can tell from the way you look at each other."

"Well, if you must know we are new—very new."

"And Betty likes him?"

"She does," Cathleen replied. "They get on very well."

"Good," Joe quietly said. "That's what matters."

Joe stayed to tuck Betty into bed with Cathleen. Betty voted for Joe to be the reader of the night. After one round of The Gingerbread Man and two rounds of The Ugly Duckling, Joe had read bedtime stories to his daughter for the very first time. Cathleen packed his backpack with winter clothes that Rupert left behind, that she had been meaning to donate, as he wished Betty goodnight. He told her he would be back as soon as he could this time, as two years had been far too long. His sweet care towards Betty and the last glance at Charlotte before he left settled Cathleen's thoughts; Joe would have been attentive.

1970s

Chapter Fourteen

March 1973

Paris was cold in the winter months, reminding Cathleen of the times back in Durham when her dad would light the fire and tell them all to huddle round to warm up when they got in from school. Meanwhile her mam would cook something hot and delicious for tea. Cathleen had not returned to Durham since Charlotte's memorial. A part of her missed the old village she grew up in, with its friendly neighbours, rolling hills, and of course St. Mary's Church and Father John. It dawned on her that she hadn't been to church in several years, and Betty was not the slightest bit interested in the Catholic teachings, although that was not for lack of trying. Betty Brown's interests nowadays were playing atrocious music as loudly as she could in her bedroom, hanging out with her long-haired, peace-loving friends who did not all have Cathleen's approval, and leaving her schoolwork to the last minute. Betty was growing up to be wild and independent with dreams of being famous; this worried Cathleen, for Betty could not sing a tune nor act very convincingly— she could see right through her. Then there were the boys. A different one every couple of months knocking on the apartment door claiming to be her boyfriend. She knew Betty sent them up on purpose to get a reaction out of her. They fought often, but whenever the relationships with boys turned sour, it was Cathleen's arms she fell into. Without a shadow of a doubt Charlotte could be witnessed in Betty with the way she thought, and she was not the only one who could see it. Joe Hollister had found his place in Paris permanently in 1965 when given a tip that his predator was dead, leaving him a free man. Durham was a no go for him, the only place he wanted to be was with his daughter. To Cathleen's annoyance he moved in across the hall, into Cedella's old place, leaving him feet away from Betty who had grown close to her Uncle Joe. She idolised him, and Cathleen couldn't deny that he was there for every school performance, every Christmas morning, every swimming competition. He never missed a thing which was great, but his strong relationship with Betty meant sometimes she chose to confide in Joe rather than her. If she was in trouble, she would knock on his door knowing he would take her side because, to Joe, Betty could do no wrong.

Even when they moved to the other side of the Sienne, Betty stormed out of the apartment and hopped on her bike to Joe's after an argument, such as when Cathleen found cigarettes on her. Frederic was the mediator, everyone's peacemaker, the one to say enough is enough and sit everyone down to talk. He changed Cathleen and Betty's life for the better and Cathleen didn't know what she would have done without him by her side. Their relationship had gone from strength to strength, once the papers arrived announcing the end of her marriage to Rupert two years after he left, the two were married quicker than you could say *I do*. Frederic and Marcel's gallery had become increasingly successful enabling the two brothers to open a bigger gallery. The success meant that Frederic and

Cathleen could move out of the small apartment and purchase a larger one with views of the Eiffel Tower, fresh white walls (carefully decorated with Frederic's work), and everyone had their very own room—a luxury to all; the previous living room had been doubling up as a bedroom for the newlyweds for some time. With Marcel living down the road in his bachelor pad, Joe had then moved into Cathleen's old place with his girlfriend, Madeline, and her twin boys, knocking through (illegally) the walls separating the brother's old apartment to enable a bigger space, and renting the two separately.

"Why don't you just rent a bigger place?" Cathleen had asked when witnessing the broken plaster boards cascading everywhere.

"Because the price for both of these is cheaper," Joe replied proudly, a piece of his dodgy personality forever present.

As for his new partner, Cathleen approved of Madeline and despite her ongoing clashes with Joe regarding Betty, they got on well. Madeline's husband, a university professor, had passed away, and Joe, who understood her grief, was a wonderful partner and a fantastic stepdad to the two boys. Early on in their relationship Joe asked Cathleen if he could reveal the truth about him being Betty's biological dad. It had shot a bolt of concern and terror through her initially, but Frederic reminded her that she had confined in him and Marcel before they were a couple, Joe only wished for his partner to know everything, which was only fair. There was something about Madeline that reassured Cathleen that it would go no further than the circle they'd formed.

Mavis still wrote to her daughter often, informing her of news back home. She wrote with joy when Walter and Henry decided to leave the village. She wrote sadly when she witnessed Mr Flint being physically dragged from his home and into a car by two men. Rumour was that the elderly man's hoarding had got out of control, and he was no longer able to take care of himself. His nephew had arranged for him to be put in a care home in Scotland near where he lived. It was no surprise that Mr Flint put up a fight; his home and allotment was all he had. Cathleen thought of how lonely things must have gotten for him once both Charlotte and Henry left. Mavis wrote when Peter decided to sign up to the military. Frank was against the whole idea but there was no stopping him once the idea was planted—he ran with it and on his eighteenth birthday headed straight to the recruitment office. One by one each of the Ridley's children had left to far off places, Charlotte was sent to London, Cathleen ran to Paris, and Peter joined up and left as quickly as he possibly could. Betty often wrote to her grandparents updating them on how she was doing at school, only informing them of the good stuff, of course. Mavis also wrote with great sadness when they decided to move out of their home and into a bungalow down the road. They said the house had grown strange over the years, once everyone had left and new neighbours moved into the Hollister house. Nothing was the same as it had once been, and it no longer felt like home but more like a heavy reminder of what once was. They were worried when they found out Joe Hollister was living in Paris and was in contact with Betty. Frank had even put pen to paper and written his own letter to Cathleen detailing his rage that after everything they did to protect Charlotte and Betty, she had just allowed the monster back in. Mavis wrote back later to tell her that Frank had calmed down but would not be travelling to France for any special event where Joe would be present. The letter had made Cathleen chuckle—Frank and Mavis had only visited them once on her wedding day, and never again. She distinctly remembered her dad stating after a number of whiskeys that he made a vow to never return to France again when he returned home after the war, that he had broken the vow for her, but would be making the same promise to himself on the journey home. Cathleen could no longer deny Joe's presence even though her parents thought differently. Frederic had even suggested telling Betty the truth, but that was a line too far for Cathleen. It would mean she had to also let Betty know she was not her biological mother and the thought of the unravelling of that information made her sick. Charlotte's picture hung in the hallway of the apartment above a small shelf with a candle on that was always lit on special occasions, Joe was normally the one who lit it. He told Betty stories of her *aunt* often, and she always showed great interest in the woman she never knew. When Joe and Betty were in their own bubble sharing stories of the past or whenever Cathleen took her frustration too far leading Betty to storm out to Joe, she secretly feared that if it were Charlotte and Joe bringing her up, they would have done it better. Frederic often saw the pain in her eyes when Betty ran from her and reminded her that she always came back to her maman. Frederic was everything Cathleen didn't realise she needed in her life; he made her feel whole. When he first told her he loved her she knew she felt it too, but felt a pang of guilt that she would never be able to give Frederic a child of his own. To be able to carry and give her husband a child was a burning desire she knew would never be fulfilled, although Frederic was alright with that.

"I already have everything I need; I have the perfect wife and the perfect stepdaughter who I see as my own child. To top it off, I am able to provide for you both." Was what he would always say.

When Cathleen's menopause started a few months back it was bittersweet. Cathleen was saddened that God never gifted her with a biological child, yet relieved that there was no chance of ever going through the pain of losing a baby again. God had different plans for her, her fate was to be Betty's mam, to live in Paris, and marry Frederic. They were why she was here; they were her purpose.

Chapter Fifteen

April 1973

It was Cathleen's day off when out of the blue she received an unexpected parcel from Durham. She was relieved that she was home alone when she ripped open the brown paper and a letter fell onto the table, leaving her with a book in her hands. A children's book. She quickly and curiously scanned the cover that showed two boys and three girls running down a street in bright colours.

"Mischief in the Durham Lanes," she read aloud.

It was then that she noticed in bold blue font at the bottom of the cover the author's name: *Lottie Ridley.* Cathleen felt her heart jump in a different rhythm. A sharp fast one, one that felt as though it would stop at any moment from shock and be the end of her.

"Lottie Ridley," she said aloud. "How?"

Cathleen opened the attached letter noticing her mam's handwriting at once.

Cathleen,

I hope you are well. Me and your dad were in town doing a little window shopping when I spotted this book in the window of a bookshop. I grabbed your dad by the arm and together we went in the shop to see more copies on the shelves, the name on the spine staring at us. Your dad said it's a coincidence, but we all know how special the name Lottie was to Charlotte, what do you think? Am I looking too much into it? Your Uncle Albert is gone now so I can't ask him to go over what happened that night or ask his opinion. Your dad is refusing to believe any of it. I just keep telling myself that there was no body so could there have been a mistake? If you turn to the back of the book, you will see a small description, it mentions she lives in Cornwall with her children. Again, your dad believes this to be proof that it is not our Charlotte, but the name and the title of the book could be her, surely? If so, wouldn't this be a way we could make everything right?

Let me know what you think? Do you believe it could be your sister or am I looking for every sign that could point out that my daughter is alive?

Mam

Cathleen immediately turned to the final page of the book where it stated that Lottie Ridley lived in Cornwall, by the sea, with her three children. It went on to say that *Mischief in the Durham Lanes* was her debut novel. Cathleen couldn't help but see the signs her mam pointed out *Durham, Lottie Ridley, children's author.* It all pointed to her sister, but why would Charlotte move to Cornwall and not have returned to Henry or Betty? Why after all these years had she not made any contact with the family? It didn't make any sense. She found herself almost hoping that it wasn't true because that would mean once word got out that Charlotte was alive her secret about Betty would unravel. If her sister was alive then the news had to stop at the borders of France. If Joe found out, Cathleen knew he would run home to tell Charlotte everything—Madeline or no Madeline.

Mam,

This is a huge shock and I understand your hopefulness that the author may be our Charlotte, however I think Dad may be right. I'm sorry. It was the police that told Uncle Albert she was gone, remember, they gave him Nana's ring, why would they lie? If they made a mistake, it would have been rectified by now. We all know that if Charlotte had survived the fire she would have come home to Henry, not Cornwall. Why would she go there? She knows no one in Cornwall, everyone she's ever loved was in Durham, even Joe is here now, so it isn't like she met up and ran off with him. It just doesn't make any sense. I know you desperately want it to be her, but I think until we know more, we should keep this to ourselves. Don't tell Peter, this will only get his hopes up. If it is Charlotte, then perhaps she wants to be left alone. Many years have gone by and if living by the sea with her family is what she has chosen then that tells you what she thinks of us.

I will be in touch again soon,
Love Cathleen x

Cathleen had never made her way to the post office so hastily. Panic rose in her like bile as she imagined the family reunion of her parents and her sister, which would surely result in a flight to Paris and straight to Betty. Joe would be delighted, of course, and only too pleased to introduce her to their daughter. Naturally, Betty would adore her just as she does Joe and slowly, she would become second to her sister in the eyes of her only child. If it was Charlotte, she had three children, so the book stated, three! Charlotte didn't need Betty, Cathleen needed Betty.

"Cathleen?" Cedella approached the post box. "Are you okay?"

Cathleen realised she was almost hugging the post box, coming out of her trance she realised people were watching. "Let's go and get a coffee." Cedella hooked an arm around Cathleen's and pulled her away from the box.

Cathleen did not tell her what was bothering her. Of course, she had wanted to tell Cedella the truth many times over the years, but she was scared that the mother of three wouldn't understand. Instead, she told her she thought she was going to be sick so held onto the post box for support. As her friend ordered two strong coffees, Cathleen's mind was elsewhere. Picturing Betty embracing Charlotte, wishing that she was her mother; she pictured Joe looking lovingly at her sister, desperately trying not to spill the beans to Betty that they were her biological parents. Would Betty still love her the same? Would she blame her as her parents did? Then Cathleen remembered the memorial they held for Charlotte at St. Mary's; her uncle was stone-faced, there was no way any news given by the police had any glimpse of being a mistake. She was gone, he was told; her body was a mess; only a ring survived. Her dad was right she thought, it was just a coincidence. Charlotte was gone and this author—Lottie Ridley—was living out a life by the sea that their Charlotte would have dreamt of.

Frederic made tea that evening, much to Cathleen's delight because she did not feel up to cooking. With the wine tasting extra good, her husband gave her a sideways glance.

"What is wrong, Mon Ange?" he asked.

"Nothing," she lied, patting his hand trying to reassure him that her lie was true.

Frederic glanced across the table to Betty who shrugged her shoulders unable to speak through the mouthful of food. "I don't believe you," he said with a smile. "Tonight, I will pretend I believe you, please though, Mon Ange, slow down. I only restocked the wine today; you are drinking it like water."

"I'm just dehydrated that's all, I haven't drunk enough today." Her words felt like a betrayal as she saw them bounce off her husband's face.

He simply chuckled which irritated Cathleen with how well he knew her. Betty was in a world of her own, oblivious to the conversation, one hand was being used to shovel food into her mouth in a very unladylike way Cathleen observed, and the other wrote franticly on a piece of homework that was due in the next morning.

Cathleen avoided her husband as much as she could for the rest of the evening, worried just a glance too long would reveal all. She loved Frederic but wanted to keep the contents of her mam's letter to herself. She had thrown away the letter and book in an outdoor bin in town, far out of reach of anyone she knew who would find the letter's contents interesting.

In bed Frederic held Cathleen close and whispered, "whatever the matter is, I am here when you wish to talk, otherwise I hope you will feel able to smile again soon, it pains me to see you so troubled."

Cathleen turned her body around to face her husband, the outline of his body in the dark was familiar as was his kiss as she leant in.

In the week that followed, Cathleen's mood did not improve. She felt sick to the core, nothing she ate stayed down, and she knew she was walking around biting everyone's head off about the silliest of things. Betty took this as a cue to stay in her bedroom and stay out her maman's way, or to eat tea over at Joe's which stung. Frederic's patience grew thinner by the day, but he was tired of asking Cathleen what was wrong with her, knowing her reply would be a lie. She was hurting her family, but her mind was consumed with thoughts of her sister, there was no rest as thoughts of Charlotte taunted her dreams as well. She worried Charlotte would find them all and take Betty away from her.

"Are you coming into work today?" Frederic asked hovering by the bedroom door fully dressed and ready to go as Cathleen lay motionless in bed. "You know I can't help you, Mon Ange, if you don't tell me what is troubling you."

"I will be fine," she mumbled in reply, avoiding his sincere gaze.

"Of course. I will see you tonight." Frederic left for work leaving Cathleen to cry into her pillow.

She wanted to call Frederic back and tell him everything, but she couldn't bring herself to move. The day slipped by in a daze of hazy consciousness and sleep. It wasn't until Frederic came to bed, that she realised the late hour. He silently undressed before slipping in beside her without a word, as sleep found him, tears slipped down Cathleen's cheeks. She didn't need her sister to come and ruin her family, she was doing that all by herself. She lay close to Fredric and wrapped her arm around him, her heart leapt as he stirred taking her hand in his. No one knew if Charlotte was alive, she had to get out of her pit of worry and remind her family just how much they meant to her.

"Are you coming to work today?" Frederic asked the following day, dressed and ready to go.

"Yes, I just need to put my shoes on," she replied, at which Frederic slowly came into the bedroom trying to keep his surprise at bay. "Don't look so shocked." Cathleen smiled as Frederic sat beside her on the bed and planted a gentle kiss on her forehead.

"I will take you out for lunch today, that nice place you like by the Notre Dame."

"Mmm, that sounds perfect."

"Whatever was the matter Mon Ange?" he asked, his face an array of concern.

"Nothing, really. I was just thinking about my sister a lot, that's all. I kept dreaming of her, but they are just dreams. They are not real, and I won't let them get to me any longer."

Frederic nodded. "Well, you look better." He softly outlined Cathleen's face. "In fact, you look good enough to eat."

Cathleen moaned as Fredric proceeded to nibble and kiss from her neck down to her collarbone. "Frederic we will be late for work."

"I won't tell the boss if you don't," he replied cheekily, lowering her onto the bed, eager to make love to her.

Chapter Sixteen

May 1973

"Post, Mon Ange," Frederic said, placing an envelope in front of Cathleen who was sipping coffee and eating a warm croissant. "Has she emerged yet?" he asked, taking a place beside her.

"I doubt we will be seeing our daughter for quite a while; I believe today she will be nursing an almighty hangover," she replied.

"You handled it well when she called you from Joe's. I thought you were going to flip."

"I was on the inside, believe me, but what good would it have done, it's not like she would remember any outburst."

Frederic laughed. "When he said she tried to pee in the bin."

"That's not funny Frederic, she was what we call back home wrecked off her face."

Frederic laughed again, spreading jam onto some bread. Cathleen couldn't help but smile, picking up her post she noticed her mam's handwriting and felt the padded envelope.

"Your maman?" Frederic asked, also recognising the neat scroll. Cathleen nodded. "Looks interesting," Frederic commented, as he watched his wife dissect the envelope as though it may contain an explosion. "Just open it," he chuckled.

Cathleen could feel the worry monster creeping up from behind her as she peeled back the seal on the envelope. Cathleen pulled out a small note from her mam.

'I told you! What shall we do? Mam.'

The note was accompanied by a newspaper clipping which caused Cathleen to gasp as she unfolded it. She dropped the newspaper as though it burnt her skin.

"Cathleen!" Frederic was by her side in seconds. "What is it, is everyone alright?" Frederic picked up the paper.

Cathleen was too shocked to stop him. She could see the photo as her husband scanned the page, there she was, in front of a shop smiling from ear to ear holding a copy of the book she herself had held in her own hands a month ago, surrounded by cheery children. There she was in her early thirties looking well and *alive.*

"I don't understand this, who is this Lottie Ridley?" Frederic quizzed.

"Charlotte, it's Charlotte. My sister," Cathleen cried out.

Frederic proceeded to read the article aloud sitting beside his wife, one hand clutched hers tightly.

"Monday was a great day for children's author Lottie Ridley who celebrated an outstanding reaction to her new novel, 'Mischief in the Durham Lanes'. The debut novel that was released only last month has already been declared a best seller. Children were lucky to meet Lottie at a local bookstore in Cornwall where the author was signing copies of her book. The mum of, Florence, Nancy and Arthur said, "I can't believe how successful my book has been. This is a dream come true and I am already excited about future

novels, I can only hope children will enjoy them too." We wish Lottie all the best for the future. To purchase a copy of 'Mischief in the Durham Lanes', visit all good book shops now."

Frederic carefully put down the paper. "I thought your sister was dead."

"So did I. We all did."

Had it all been a trick, a punishment perhaps that her uncle had played out to give them all what they deserved for taking Betty and sending Charlotte away.

"This is good news? Right?"

"I don't know Frederic," Cathleen cried. "I want to be happy; I do. My sister is alive, and she is doing well, of course, this is better than thinking she died in a fire but…"

"But?"

"Betty. What if she comes for Betty, what if Joe finds out and unites them."

Frederic read the small note from Mavis. "Your maman has mentioned this before?"

Cathleen nodded whipping her eyes. "She sent me the book; we weren't sure if it was her though. Dad thought it was just a coincidence."

"That is what made you so ill," he realised, followed by a heavy sigh. "I wish you could have confided in me Mon Ange; I am sorry that you felt you couldn't."

His comment hurt Cathleen, she hadn't meant to keep things from her husband but that seemed to be what she did best, keeping secrets from those she cared about most.

"I'm sorry," she whispered. "In all honesty Frederic, I was more swayed in the hope that she was not alive than that she might be, and that makes me a terrible person."

"Your sister seems happy Cathleen, she has children. She has her dream job; she has been alive all this time and has not tried to come and find Betty nor contact your parents. Why would she now? We have just found out she is alive, but she has always known. Perhaps you are overthinking things just a little."

"How do we know she hasn't tried; my parents have moved house and how do we know that she hasn't been to Paris looking for Betty. She will know we are here, my uncle would have told her, he cared about her the most. Joe found us pretty easily."

"Joe found you by luck, he wasn't intentionally searching for Betty, he was running for his life. We will have to tell him."

"What? No!" Cathleen shouted.

"Cathleen," Frederic sternly said.

"No! We can't tell Joe. He will tell her where we are, he will probably write to the newspaper, get her address, and tell her. He will tell her everything. We can't tell Joe!"

"Mon Ange, you're not thinking straight. The man walks around with a ring he gave his dead fiancé over a decade ago, like a child carrying their comfort toy. We must tell him it is only fair. He still mourns her death."

"No Frederic, this has to stay between us. I will write to my mam now and tell her to do nothing. This cannot change anything. Charlotte is happy, we can all see and agree that she is living her best life, she doesn't need us. Not any of us."

"If you thought I was dead for years, wouldn't you want to know that I was alive?" Frederic asked looking at Cathleen straight in the eye.

"That's different, you're my husband."

"Love is love, Cathleen. We must tell him; you must tell him."

"No!" Cathleen said removing herself from the table. "Stop Frederic, please. My decision won't change. It wasn't easy taking Betty as my own, I loved my sister, I played a huge part in her upbringing. All I ever wanted was the best for her. I wanted a life for her that was filled with love, but when the opportunity came to become a mum, I took it with open arms. It was me or the orphanage. Charlotte was not an option. My parents took care of that. Now I have had Betty for fourteen years; she is my daughter, I have been there through the sleepless nights, the teething days, and the tantrums, now I am battling the teenage years of her turning up drunk because her friends think it's cool, while I stay awake worried sick. She is my Betty, and nobody is taking that away from me. Nobody."

"And nobody is trying to. Look around you Cathleen, we are all on your side, even Joe kneels down to you. He is happy to be known as her uncle just to be a part of Betty's life. He has never tried to sabotage that, it is all in your head, your obsession with people trying to take Betty away from you has to stop," Frederic declared, rising from his seat following his wife to the balcony doors where she stood for air.

"Obsession!" she shouted, turning on him.

"Yes! Obsession, everything about your life here in Paris has been about Betty and her parentage. You left your family and her family behind in the United Kingdom for fear of even the mention of your sister's name. Here, everyone who loves Betty, you, me, Marcel, Joe, and

Madeline, are all under a sacred oath to not speak the truth because that is how you wish it, and we follow it like obedient soldiers. You are in charge, yet I have watched you weep every New Year's Eve on Charlotte's birthday. I have seen the guilt in your face. Now is the time to make it right. You can clear your conscience and we can all be a part of Betty's life if your sister wishes to seek contact."

Cathleen shook her head violently, everything Frederic was saying was true, she had wept for her sister, she had lit a candle every year without fail, but when the mother of your child has passed away you can mourn their death and feel guilty that they are gone. But when reality kicks in and you find out they are alive, that changes the dynamics completely and her mothering instincts kicked in without much remorse.

"Charlotte has not made contact, Cathleen, Betty is now fourteen," Frederic reminded her, moving closer to his fretful wife. "For Joe, knowing the truth will put his mind at rest, he will be able to move forward with Madeline knowing that Charlotte is okay. The chances of him travelling to this UK town and finding her are as possible as me walking down the street and bumping into an actor. I think…"

"Enough, Fredric! Please just stop! I get it, you think I am irrational; you all do by the sounds of it, but me and Rupert adopted Betty; she is our daughter and as the only present parent, I will decide who knows what. Now let me make this clear, news of Charlotte's life in Cornwall will go no further, she is dead as far as we are concerned. Dead!"

Fredric took a step away from Cathleen, the look of shock teamed with hurt was evident, yet Cathleen stood as still as stone. He placed his hands in the air slowly taking another step further away from her. "I'm sorry, Mon Ange, I clearly took my place as your husband and Betty's beau-pere too far. Maybe you should write to Rupert and see what he can do to console you as I am clearly out of my league."

"No Frederic, I didn't mean that," Cathleen panicked.

Fredric blew his wife a kiss and smiled. "It's okay, you wish no one to know. You wish to lie to Joe forever. Okay. You think you can hide the truth from Betty all her life, I don't know, maybe you can. Okay. You and your family decided Betty's destiny for her, and I have seen it eat away at you over the years. I am not saying go and spill the beans to *your* daughter. All I am suggesting is you let those who are grieving free from their pain, including yourself, but what do I know, ask Rupert. Let's be honest he knows better than anyone how your love for Betty trumps everything and everyone else. I am going to work."

Frederic turned away and left the apartment with a slam of the door. Cathleen was stung by his words. He had never walked away from her before, nor had they really fought come to think of it. He was always the one by her side cheering her on or quietly telling her where she went wrong. Just as he had tried to then, but the difference was that her mind had already been made up before the newspaper article had even reached France. If Charlotte was alive it was going to go unnoticed in her circle. Everything had to go on as it was, everything worked, and it was perfect. Betty had all she needed, Cathleen had all she needed, Joe had all he needed, and Charlotte was happy which was a weight off her shoulders in some respects. She was no longer responsible for ruining her sister's life. Madeline was good for Joe; he was going to propose any day now, she knew it. Why did the past need to interrupt? Cathleen hovered over the newspaper article looking directly at her sister's face once more. The last time she saw those eyes was in her parent's living room. When she left, Cathleen and her mam had hoped her mood meant that things were back on track with Henry, and that she was on the mend from the grief of losing their nan and her silly rondo with Joe Hollister. Of course, he was the very boy she was getting ready to see. Yet the woman in the photo looked somewhat wiser—crowfeet wrinkles arriving on her face, her youth disappearing, yet she looked full of life. She had *three* children, Cathleen thought once again, scanning the photos of the children for any resemblance to Betty; they would after all be her brother and sisters. Their dad was not mentioned she recalled, not in the paper nor in the book. Who was he? She was not married if she still called herself Lottie Ridley, it occurred to her. She sighed heavily thinking maybe nothing had changed and her sister had just fallen for one bad boy after the other. Grabbing a pen off the sideboard, Cathleen flipped over her mam's note and replied.

We are not to do anything. Charlotte is happy, happier than she was when we last knew her whereabouts. She has followed her dreams and that is amazing, look at the photo Mam, she is happy. We hurt her, each one of us placed a scar on her heart and her silence is proof of this. I think it is best to let her be. If she wants us, she will try and find us, especially you and Dad; you have not moved far. Searching for her may open old wounds that she has fought hard to forget, you remember the details of her pain in Uncle Albert's letters. She is a mam now, let us not reopen them for the sake of your grandchildren. She is alive and well let us seek comfort in that. Again, I advise you not to tell Peter, this will take his mind off his duties and lead him to a path of desperation. He is engaged to be married to the lovely Aimee; he too has a wonderful future. I know it is hard Mam, but I think we should let it be, let her be.

Cathleen.

Tucking the note in an envelope Cathleen ran to the post office, breathing heavily whilst waiting in line for a stamp. Only once the stamp was applied and the letter posted through the slit in the post box could Cathleen breathe again. And with that breath, everything became dark, and her legs gave way; her body crashing to the ground.

Chapter Seventeen

May 1973

Cathleen's eyes were stinging from the bright lights—the smell of disinfectant making her nose twitch, as the sound of beeping made her realise, she was not waking up in her own bed. She turned her head to the left to find Fredric clutching her arm in his sweaty hand. He let out a sigh and pulled her hand to his mouth, smothering her in kisses.

"You gave me a fright, Mon Ange," he whispered tearfully.

"What happened, why am I here?"

"You collapsed outside the post office, luckily someone recognised you from the gallery and came to tell me. I ran here with you in my arms myself."

"I collapsed," Cathleen said in surprise, just as a young nurse popped into the small room with a smile.

"Bonjour Madame Lemieux, comment vous sentez-vous?" she asked.

Cathleen nodded. "Fine, I feel fine, just a little tired."

The nurse smiled at Cathleen and then looked to Frederic who smiled back.

"I think she wants you to translate, Frederic," Cathleen guessed.

"Oh, of course. Elle a dit qu'elle était fatigue."

"Oui bien sûr c'est prévu," the nurse said.

"She said that is to be expected," Frederic told Cathleen. To which Cathleen smiled in acknowledgement at the sweet looking nurse.

"Le docteur a dit que votre femme allait bien Monsieur Lemieux. Elle a juste besoin de beaucoup de repos dans son état."

Frederic looked confused Cathleen noticed as he failed to translate to her and continued the conversation.

"Quelle état?"

They both watched as the nurse opened the file she was carrying and read her notes, her eyes scanning the words quickly until she stopped and looked at the pair.

"La grossesse de votre femme monsieur."

"Grossesse!" Frederic said in alarm.

"What is it? Will someone please tell me what is going on. What is wrong with me Frederic?" Cathleen panicked.

The nurse looked stunned as did her husband making her feel like something awful must have made her collapse.

"Je ne comprends pas Monsieur Lemieux. Madame Lemieux a Presque cinq mois de retard. Ne saviez-vous pas?"

"Cinq mois!"

"Five months, you're both saying five months. Frederic what is going to happen in five months, am I ill?" Cathleen looked at her husband desperate for him to fill the gaps in her tragic thoughts.

"No, Mon Ange, you are not ill. Cathleen you are pregnant!" he gasped, with a shocked chuckle.

Cathleen sat back against her pillows and repeated the words her husband had said like a turntable in her mind, each time she repeated them it didn't feel any more real. "Pregnant, are you sure?"

"Almost five months the nurse said," Fredric beamed tightening his grip on Cathleen's arm once more.

"Ask her to double check," she commanded in disbelief. "Tell her I am going through the menopause not pregnancy, I can't be pregnant. I barely have a bump, Frederic."

Cathleen looked down and caressed her stomach gently, she had put on some weight she admitted to herself, but that could happen during the menopause her mam had told her, she also told her that her great aunt went through an early menopause at age thirty, so it wasn't unheard of for Cathleen to have begun it at thirty-seven. Frederic asked the nurse what Cathleen had asked, and she watched their faces as they spoke to one another, the nurse was still smiling, Frederic was holding back a cheshire cat grin, she could tell. He looked at her with an expression she would never forget.

"You are pregnant, Mon Ange, not going through thc menopause. The doctor checked you himself. It is written in your notes."

"Felicitations Madame Lemieux," the nurse cheered as she headed out the room.

"Merci," Cathleen replied.

Almost five months, she was four months away from holding a baby in her arms. Her baby, Frederic's baby. Four months was a long time, she worried. She could easily lose the baby in that time.

"Cathleen, I can see the worry in your eyes. I know this is a shock, a wonderful shock, but a shock all the same. I understand your concern because of your past pregnancies, but you are already five months, and our baby is healthy."

"But I collapsed that can't be a good sign."

"You have been stressing over Betty and your sister, I know Betty is everything to you, and you're frightened of her ever finding out, but like I said this morning, Charlotte has never found you in all this time, why would she now? I think for the sake of our child and your own health it would be best if you try and put this worry about your sister to bed. You are already more than halfway through your pregnancy, the least we can do is try and give them a good, fighting chance."

Cathleen agreed and ran her hand through Frederic's dark hair which was growing grey. "We are not young Frederic."

"Speak for yourself, there is still life left in this forty-year-old, and you a maman again at thirty-seven, I find that sexy."

Cathleen laughed then quickly stopped and cried. "Oh, Frederic I was awful to you earlier. I said things I regret; you are a great pere to Betty. We couldn't wish for anyone better. I am so sorry."

"Hush now, that is all forgotten. If you don't want Joe to know then that is your decision, and I will support that. Right now, all I care about is my wife and our unborn child."

"I never thought I would be able to give you a child."

"I know, and I never saw it as a fault. You have always been perfect to me. I love you Mon Ange."

"I love you too."

Cathleen and Frederic kept the news of the baby to themselves for a short while, only telling Betty and Marcel.

Cathleen also wrote to her parents to tell them the news. Mavis had not replied to her daughter's last letter causing Cathleen to worry about what plans her parents could be making without her. Cathleen was heading over to Cedella's when the post man gave her the letter she had been waiting for. Her parents were what stood between Charlotte and Betty. If they decided to find Charlotte and make amends, then their guilt may lead them to tell her sister exactly where Betty was.

Cathleen,

First off, congratulations on the news of your pregnancy, I have to say it came as a bit of a shock to me and your dad, but life is full of surprises, look at when we realised we were having Peter. We have already been to church to pray that this time God will be kind to you. You deserve this very much; you must relax and take it easy at your age, that is what Pauline over the road advised. Which is why, after much thought, me and your dad have decided to leave things be with our Charlotte. We do not wish to cause any distress to you at this delicate time. What you said was true, Charlotte has always known where we live, she would have come home if she wanted to. She obviously cannot stand any of us, to not even come and see Henry, the man she was meant to have loved, tells us this further. She has wiped her hands of us all and who can blame her. I am nothing but ashamed. I failed her as a parent, that I know. There is comfort in knowing that she fulfilled her dream of becoming an author. We knew she was talented. Did you read the paper? We are so proud, and we are grandparents to more children. We may not know them, but I bet they live a lovely life. Perhaps one day she may come home.

Pass on our congratulations to Frederic.
Mam xxx

Peter was not mentioned in the letter, she wondered if her parents had told him. Putting pen to paper once more she scribbled a quick reply asking them to not tell Peter; he would hunt Charlotte down until he found her.

Chapter Eighteen

September 1973

The first jolt of pain was felt at around three in the morning. Frederic lay sound asleep and Betty's light snores could be heard from across the hallway, but it was in that moment that Cathleen knew it was time—her baby was on the way. They were all shattered from celebrating Betty's fifteenth birthday. *Fifteenth!* Where had the time gone, and was she prepared to start from the beginning again with her new-born. Everyone was eager for the baby to arrive. Although Cathleen had tried to detach herself from the idea that she may actually go full term, as each month grew closer to that possibility, the more she allowed herself to believe and grow an attachment to her bump. Every ounce of discomfort, from heartburn to back pain, she endured with patience, seeing it as a gift. The journey wasn't over yet, there was still the part where she had to give birth and hope that at the end of the experience, she would hold a healthy baby. She had thought about her sister a lot during her pregnancy, knowing now that she had given birth to four children, she was full of questions and knew Charlotte would know the answers. She hadn't been able to ask Cedella too much as she was under the impression Cathleen had given birth to Betty, she played it at times as though she had forgotten a lot with it being so long ago, but the big questions were about the birth. No one had said what she had to prepare for it was as though someone her age was expected to know. She knew a little of what to expect, she knew where the baby was coming from and that she should expect pain but nothing much else. Madeline had been a saviour throughout the last few months having known this was the first time Cathleen had carried this far and was very knowledgeable, but she didn't feel comfortable asking Madeline questions about the actual giving birth part. Charlotte would have been the perfect person to ask. She thought back to Betty's birth fifteen years ago and wondered how Charlotte had felt when she knew she was on her way. Was she frightened? Did she know what to expect? She had given birth in a shed with Henry playing nurse—did he know what to do? Was he helpful? She must have been frightened Cathleen concluded, just sixteen with no medical help, and the only source of help is your teenage next-door neighbour. Cathleen couldn't imagine Betty going through something like that now. Betty was still so childlike at times, even though she had a boyfriend. Some hippy looking long haired kid named Andre. Cathleen didn't like him, she found him too tactile at the party; he followed her around like an injured dog waiting for his owner to pet him, eager for any chance of affection. Joe had told her to stay tight-lipped.

"Let's learn from the past now, Cathleen," he advised in a half-humorous tone. "Things are different now, it's okay to date someone and do more than walk around the park for months until the guy gets down on one knee."

"And is that what you and my sister did, do more?" Cathleen said irritably.

"Exactly that, and we were happy which is more than I can say about you and Rupert."

"Me and Rupert were happy once."

"Maybe, but your different with Frederic, and Betty will probably have lots of Ruperts until she finds her Frederic."

"Would Charlotte have found her Frederic?" Cathleen asked wishing she hadn't when she noticed his face drop a little.

"Charlotte already found him." He made his excuses to check on Madeline after that, making Cathleen feel awful for taunting him. The truth was he was right, and she hated it when he was right. She had to let Betty be Betty and make her own choices, and together they would all support her no matter what happened because that is what a family does, and she would never repeat history. Joe was also right about Rupert—she did feel different with Frederic. It was as though he had given her a brand-new outlook on life. He had been her rock throughout her worries with the pregnancy, but he had total faith that it was all possible; always talking to her bump, telling their unborn child all the things they were going to do together. Cathleen had wondered if Rupert had found the same kind of happiness. She also wondered whether he would have still left if she'd been able to give him a child of his own; would he be looking at her the same way Fredric does. With these thoughts, Cathleen felt thankful to have her husband, for Rupert was not the type of man she had thought him to be, since he had left no word was ever heard from him, not that she or Betty needed him, yet his name would forever be printed on her birth certificate reminding her that he left them without a backwards glance.

Another jolt of pain had her kick Frederic's leg, but he did not wake from his slumber. A flat-pack cot stood to attention in the corner of the room filled with soft blankets and cuddly toys. Drawers were filled with tiny clothing and terry nappies ready to keep the baby warm and fresh. Cathleen lay there in quiet discomfort for another hour until the pain grew harsher, and she knew laying in her bed was no longer an option.

"Frederic!" she called out, giving her husband a shake. "Frederic, wake up now. Its time. We have to get to the hospital."

Cathleen tried her hardest not to show Frederic how much pain she was in as he stayed by her side cheering her on.

"You can let the pain out, Mon Ange, you are acting like a nun who has got in trouble by a wild man," Frederic laughed.

"What if this ends badly, Frederic? You will stay strong for Betty if anything happens to me, won't you?"

"Cathleen, stop distressing yourself for no reason, nothing is going to happen to you."

"What about the baby? What if I am punished for all the things I have done wrong, to Charlotte, lying to Betty, not telling Joe the truth." Cathleen let out a high shriek no longer able to contain them.

"Mon Ange, I ask you to please calm down, would it help if I said a prayer?" he asked, cupping his wife's hands into his ready to ask God to bring safety to his wife and child.

Cathleen cried in fear, Frederic kissed her on the head and reminded her of all the times she had wished for the very moment she was in. He reassured her that it was her time, and that God was watching over ready to give her a child.

God quickly got to work and gifted Cathleen and Fredric with a baby boy, a healthy boy with ten fingers, ten toes, and good lungs.

"We have a boy! You did it my sweet, sweet wife!" Frederic exclaimed, kissing Cathleen repeatedly.

"A boy!" Cathleen gasped.

The midwife took the boy away and showed him to another midwife who was preparing the plastic crib. The nurse's faces were grave, sending shocks of panic through the new parents.

"What is it? What's wrong with my son?" Cathleen shouted across the bed.

"Dis-nous s'il te plait!" Frederic pleaded with the midwives to tell them what the matter was.

The two ladies gave each other a quick glance before approaching the bed where Cathleen lay impatiently waiting to hold the small bundle that was wrapped in a white cotton blanket. Handing him over, the couple took their first look at their child. His small almond-shaped eyes stared back at them; his tiny little ears peeked from the blanket around his head. His hair was dark, and there was plenty of it, and he had a little flat nose.

"Il a le syndrome de Down," a midwife said gently.

"Frederic," Cathleen whispered to her crying husband, "he is perfect."

Frederic placed a kiss on Cathleen's forehead followed by a one on the baby. "Theodore," he said. "We should call him Theodore; it means blessed by God."

Cathleen loved the name and felt as though her heart could burst from the love that she felt for Theodore. She already felt protective of him and knew he may face difficulties, but he would be cared for unconditionally by those around him. They did not hear the staff leave, it was not until Betty took a stance beside them that they noticed their whole family were present and alone for the first time, and they couldn't be happier.

1980s

Chapter Nineteen

May 1981

Music blasted from the art gallery in celebration of the engagement party of Betty and her partner Julian, a university student from the countryside studying in Paris. Red roses decorated the frames of the art pieces, as well as a grand table filled with enough food and drink to feed all of Paris. Theodore never left the makeshift dance floor, always on the lookout for his next dance partner, Joe and, the now, Madeline Hollister's twins, Isabelle and Louis, along with Peter's son, Charlie, darted around the tables and guests in a tiring looking game of chase. Madeline's older children were often seen taking short breaks, sweating in their chairs hoping Theodore would stop picking them to dance with him. Theodore's favourite dance partner of all however, was Aiden. He loved visiting their house to listen to Aiden and Cedella's records. Motown had become his absolute favourite.

During an earlier speech, having gone through it prior with Cathleen and Frederic, Betty asked Joe if he would do the honour of walking her down the aisle. He of course accepted; he couldn't hide the pleasure of being chosen to take the job that was so rightly his. Frederic nodded in understanding when Joe looked over at him as though asking for his permission. Even Cathleen shed a small tear at the pure emotion from Joe. Joe had always played the part of Uncle Joe but those who knew the truth knew he took the role of dad seriously, and he had done a great job, that much Cathleen had to admit. When Joe had the twins, Betty was thrilled to have two new cousins, not knowing that she had really gained a new brother and sister. Giving her a grand total of two brothers and three sisters. There were times Cathleen felt like she should have reached out and tried to find her sister. There were so many events in her life that could have been better with her there; when she lost her babies; when she and Rupert were having troubles; her life in France—Charlotte would have liked Frederic she imagined, as their Nana Florence would have as well. Cathleen reminisced on their holidays in London to spend time with their nan, they always had the best time. The only rule had been to have fun! Back at home, where things were different, Cathleen and Charlotte would stay up late chatting making the school mornings harder. Their mam would tell them to take their elbows off the table and wake up. Cathleen had stopped doing this as she got older and would give her sister a shove if she wouldn't zip it and go to sleep. She remembered all the times she tried to shield her sister from their dad's trauma, the times he screamed through the night from his nightmares, the nights he came home from the pub or a regimental reunion in a state that led him to stay awake all night playing Vera Lynn.

Cathleen stepped outside for air, her mind buzzing with too much wine and thoughts of her sister. Joe was also standing outside, leaning on the gallery wall, smoking a cigarette. His tie was loose, and he was looking up at the night sky. The stars seemed to be shining brighter than usual.

"Are you okay?" she asked, noticing his sombre expression.

Joe quickly wiped his cheek before declaring that he was fine.

"You thinking about her as well then?" Cathleen quizzed, leaning on the wall beside him.

"I hope she can see what an amazing woman she has turned out to be," he said with a sniffle. "I often imagine her up there with your nan and my mam. I picture them having their own celebrations alongside ours. Do you think of things like that?"

Cathleen nodded, feeling as guilty as Judas.

"I hope my mam will be proud of me now," he added.

"I believe she would be very proud of you Joe. You have become the man she and your dad always wished you to become," she said truthfully.

"Did your parents not attend because I was here?"

Cathleen laughed. "No, don't you take their absence personally. My dad has chosen never to fly again. Doesn't like France you see, brings back too many memories. And my mam, well she doesn't leave his side any longer than it takes to pop to the shops. It is no surprise that they will not be attending the wedding either. I'm just glad Peter and Aimee made it."

"I didn't recognise him; I was surprised he remembered me, him being so small the last I saw him. I hesitated that he might throw a punch or something, but he was pleasant."

"My brother will love anyone Charlotte loved. You are obviously no exception to that. After all this time he still idolises her."

"There you two are," Betty beamed as though she had just found treasure, stepping out and closing the door behind her leaving the noise indoors. She snuggled her way in-between Cathleen and Joe, taking a cigarette out of her bag.

"Do you both believe in angels and stuff?" she asked, looking up as Joe had minutes earlier at the starry night. "Or signs from a loved one?"

"Like white feathers?" Joe asked.

"Kind of, only I was thinking earlier, I met Julian in a bookshop of all places to meet your husband and then when he proposed after only four months, I thought he was crazy, but I had a magazine on the coffee table and one of the headlines on the cover said *dis oui."*

"Say yes," Cathleen repeated.

"Yes!" Betty exclaimed. "So, I said yes, and it felt right as I said the words out loud. Do you think it could have all been a sign from Auntie Charlotte?"

Cathleen felt the dreaded knot form in her stomach as she watched Betty and Joe's faces light up at the possibility Charlotte could somehow be guiding Betty towards the love of her life. Of course, she knew it could not be, as Charlotte was very much living and breathing in England.

"She did love books," Joe smiled.

Joe would have believed it was Charlotte if Betty had told him she met Julian at a fish market Cathleen believed. He would look for any indication that Charlotte was around them. It was painful to see how much love he still had for the teen he'd dated for less than a year. His heart was still in some way bound to his first love. All Cathleen could wish for is that Julian could love Betty the way Joe loved Charlotte.

Chapter Twenty

August 1981

Betty and Julian hadn't beat around the bush when it came to planning their wedding. The big day was planned to go ahead at Julian's parents' farmhouse in Noyers-Sur-Serein, two hours away from Paris.

"The backdrop will be beautiful for the photos," Betty had told them all. "They have their own vineyard so there will be unlimited wine!"

The wedding was to be a small and intimate event at the couple's discretion, nearest and dearest only. Being an only child, Julian had asked Theodore to be his best man. Ever since being asked to take on the important role, Theodore had been counting down the days and had his suit hung up on his wardrobe door for eight weeks. The upcoming nuptials had everyone excited. Cathleen didn't venture far out of Paris too often; they had all taken a camping trip to Burgundy once, before Theodore was born, where Cathleen had concluded that camping was not her cup of tea.

The last wedding they attended was Peter's—they all made a quick visit to England for the event. It was Frederic's first time in England, and he quite enjoyed the rowdy evening with Peter's military friends, getting extremely drunk, their mam had to step in and stop one squaddie from performing a striptease, much to Frederic and Betty's amusement. While Peter's wife-to-be, Aimee's family filled out her side of the church all six members of Peter's filled the front row of his side with Theodore on Cathleen's knee. The rest of Peter's pews were filled with friends.

"Thank goodness for the army," Cathleen had whispered to Frederic.

Again, Charlotte entered Cathleen's mind, perhaps Frederic had been right, maybe she was a little obsessed with her sister or was she just consumed with constant guilt. It got her thinking about who would have sat on the pews at Charlotte's wedding when she married her children's father, whoever he may be, if she ever had married. Did she have many friends? Had it been the best day of her life? It wouldn't have surprised her if their cousin William had been present with his parents. To have taken Charlotte's side would be no shock to her at all. Her Uncle Albert had detested the whole idea from the start. When Cathleen had married Rupert, the church was filled to the brim on both sides. The two young lovers had been at the centre of the community. Aside from locals and work colleagues, Cathleen's pews had been filled with her parents and Peter. Charlotte had stayed by her side at the altar as a bridesmaid. There was also her family from London: Nana Florence, Uncle Albert, Auntie Emily, and William. Joe and his brother Henry with their parents, Betty and Walter, her parents' best friends, and the lovely Mr Flint. The party had lasted well into the night at her parent's terrace house. It would turn out to be the last event where everyone there was together for it was not long after Cathleen's wedding that Betty Hollister had a heart attack sending a ripple of shock through those she had held close; only for there to be a second wave weeks later when Cathleen lost her nan. The loss of both women had changed everything, there were those who could carry on despite the pain and those who hit rock bottom. Charlotte's grief was the reason why the pews for Peter's family had been almost empty.

Some say God has a plan, and Cathleen used to believe that but had his plan worked? If Betty Hollister had not died would her sister have ever built a relationship with Henry, who beforehand did nothing but torment her? If her nan had not died and Charlotte had left for London, Cathleen wondered if she would have led a completely different life, would she have given a backward glance to the teenagers next door? It was the loss of the two woman that led her sister to the Hollister web, she was like a fly captured by two spiders, and she was unable to get away from their clutches. The only difference was that Charlotte, unlike the fly, did not wish to be set free. She did not wish to leave their clutches because she felt safe with them, the spiders cared for the fly, and with them she knew she never had to leave, she never had to venture too far into the painful, real world.

Betty would have a strong group of people attending her big day, people who loved her dearly. She had strength and support, love, and protection. Never would she wish to be a fly in a spider's web.

The night before the big day, the wedding party arrived at Julian's parents' farmhouse. The hosts were incredibly generous, and alongside the excited couple, they had transformed the place into the perfect setting—one that Betty had envisioned. The nuptials were to take place outside in the back garden, garlands of white roses were hung everywhere giving a simplistic and romantic vibe. Unlit candles made an aisle between rows of rustic chairs.

"It is beautiful, Betty!" Cathleen cried, hugging her daughter as tightly as she could. When she looked at her, she was still just a baby, despite the fact she would perhaps have children of her own in the coming years. Her bright blue eyes were the same ones that had looked up at her when she first held her, the arms wrapped around her, despite the length they had grown, were still the same ones that hugged her every day when she had picked her up from school or had clutched onto her fearfully after a nightmare.

"Maman do not cry yet, save the tears for tomorrow," Betty said.

"I have a whole box of tissues for your maman for tomorrow," Frederic smiled. "You're a lucky man Julian," he said, turning to the groom.

"I couldn't agree more," Julian beamed. "Why else do you think I had to snap her up quick. Didn't want my luck to run out."

"Come." Julian's mam gestured to the group to follow her. "Inside. Please. I have wine."

The evening was spent getting to know the in-laws, retelling stories to embarrass Betty and Julian (Frederic's favourite part) and singing the likes of Smokey Robinson & The Miracles – *You Really Got a Hold on Me* and The Jackson Five – *I Want you Back.*

To separate Betty and Julian for the night, Betty and Cathleen had a room in a converted outbuilding at the front of the property. Outside they sat under blankets and candlelight quietly away from the main house on Betty's last night as an unmarried woman. Other guests were checking in to the recommended local hotels. It gave Cathleen and Betty some much-needed private time.

"How do you feel?" Cathleen asked.

"I don't know, excited, I guess. I thought I would be more nervous, but I only feel joy," Betty smiled. "How did you feel when you married Rupert?"

"I too felt joyful, but I was extremely nervous. Unlike you and Julian, Rupert and I were not already living together. In my time you only lived with a man once you were married. We had been courting for many years though, so it felt like it was the right time."

"So, you hadn't already, you know…done it?" Betty laughed.

"No, we had not *done it,"* Cathleen laughed, blushing.

"Had you kissed him at least?"

"We had pecked. I know it sounds strange to you, but it was what it was like back then. You met someone you liked then you courted them for a while."

"Courted them, that does sound old fashioned."

"We are talking about thirty years ago here Betty. We lived at home until our wedding day and only then were we allowed to take things further."

"Were you not ever tempted to go that step further?"

"Not really, I knew what my role was, and I played it perfectly. I believed if we did anything more that our marriage would be sinned upon, that I would have sinned and upset God."

"I remember all the prayers you used to say and the songs you taught me, are you and the guy upstairs still friends?" Betty asked.

"We are more like pen pals these days," Cathleen said, wrapping the blanket a little tighter.

"Perhaps if you had been allowed to do what you wanted in those days you would have known that Rupert was a bad egg," Betty suggested.

"Perhaps."

"I am glad things didn't work out with him though otherwise we wouldn't have Frederic and I can't imagine a life without him. Did you wait with Fredric before you *did it?"* Betty asked, eager to know the details.

Cathleen blushed again, causing Betty to let out a roar of laughter.

"Maman, you dirty girl."

Cathleen shrugged her shoulders unapologetically. "I couldn't help myself."

The duo laughed once more.

"It is good to try before you buy, Maman."

"Betty! That sounds awful."

"But it is true, I should know, I have tried plenty!"

"Betty!"

"Sorry. Seriously though Maman, I couldn't imagine myself now about to marry Julian tomorrow knowing that all in one day I was going to be leaving my childhood home, living with a man for the first time, and letting him be the first to water my flower."

Cathleen pulled a face at the latter, making Betty chuckle.

"Nana Mavis and Grandad Frank sent me and Julian a card and a silver horseshoe."

"How very traditional."

"It still had the price tag on, £9.99 from Woolworths."

Cathleen tilted her head. "I suppose their pension doesn't stretch far these days. Be sure to give them my good wishes when you see them next week."

For their honeymoon, the newlyweds were planning a different kind of trip. While most prefer jetting off somewhere romantic like Italy or the Caribbean, the two were spending ten nights in the UK climbing mountains followed by seven nights skiing down them in Finland.

"You will always be my baby you know, that doesn't change just because you're going to be married," Cathleen said sentimentally.

"I know, Maman, and I will always need you. You are my first go-to for my future babysitter."

"I hope so," Cathleen said, now unable to hold back the tears.

"Oh, Maman, you are setting me off now."

The two women embraced, and Cathleen wrapped her blanket around Betty to bring her closer in.

"I love you Betty," she whispered.

"I love you too."

A distant roaring noise that quickly grew louder was heard in the distance. The girls let go to try and see where the noise was coming from. They were surprised to see a car speed up the driveway, the headlights making their eyes squint. It wasn't until the engine was turned off that it became apparent that the car was Joe's. His eyebrows were pointing to his nose, and he had a grim mouth, he slammed his door with such force that the car shook.

"Betty, can I have a word with your mam in private?" he said marching over to the small terrace.

"Is everything okay Uncle Joe?" Betty asked alarmed.

"Please could you just give us a minute," he said calmly kissing her forehead. Betty obediently walked back to the outbuilding with a little hesitation.

"What is it? What's going on?" Cathleen asked once Betty had gone inside.

"This!" Joe shouted, slamming two books onto the table. Picking one up for closer inspection, Cathleen realised she was holding a French copy of her sister's book.

Chapter Twenty-One

August 1981

Panic rose as Cathleen inspected the French cover version. Two books. Her sister was doing well, she thought, and not only was she successful in getting her books published in French, but she had also been successful elsewhere in her life. *Lottie Ridley* had been replaced with *Lottie Hollister.*

"You told me she was dead!" Joe shouted. "You told me she burnt in a fire! What is wrong with you Cathleen?"

Dropping the book Cathleen sat back in her chair. "I swear to you, Joe, that is what I was told, that is what we were all told. My uncle told my family and yours in person himself. It was the police who told him."

"You watched me grieve for years for a woman who was alive," Joe continued, ignoring Cathleen's words.

"I grieved too; I attended her memorial, remember. This is just as much a shock to me as it is to you."

"A memorial with no body, a body taken away for science before any witnesses. Her body was so badly burnt she was unrecognisable, yet her nana's ring turned up in one piece. Why were these questions not put forward?"

"My uncle tried, they just kept telling him the same thing."

"When did you really find out Cathleen? How long have you known the truth for?" Joe asked glaring into her searching for answers.

"I told you this is a shock to me too."

"STOP LYING! I saw your face when I put the books on the table. It wasn't the face one makes when they realise their little sister is alive after years of grief, it was the face one makes when they are scared. Now tell me Cathleen how long have you known? Was it before I turned up on your doorstep for the first time? Soon after? Before Madeline? When?"

"Joe, I didn't know," Cathleen lied, sinking further into her chair hoping it would morph itself around her completely and take her out of the situation. Joe stepped away from the table and laughed.

"You are fucking unbelievable; do you know that? I just nearly crashed my car with my entire family in it when Isabelle asked me if we were related to the author of her new book by Lottie Hollister." Marching back to the table, Joe picked up the nearest book flicking it to the back page where now above a description of the author was a photo of Charlotte. "She shoved this in my face! Have you read the back yet, do you know what it says? How about I translate it for you, it says she lives in Cornwall, Cathleen, fucking Cornwall. That's a little bit different to heaven in case you didn't know. It also says she has four children and lives with her husband—Henry."

Four children, married to Henry. To Cathleen those details were news to her, she had her suspicions that Henry may have known the truth, and he was the only face she could ever picture alongside Charlotte. She couldn't help but notice the small break in Joe's anger as he mentioned his brother. It must not have been an easy acceptance regardless of where they all were in their lives now.

"All this time, I have walked around with a ring I bought for your sister feeling guilty that I got to be a part of Betty's life—feeling guilty that I got to watch our daughter grow up."

"Joe, quiet!" Cathleen sat up in a flurry looking back over her shoulder to the outbuilding.

To her fury, he replied with an unfriendly smile. He knew how to get to her, which buttons to press, he always had when it came to Betty.

"You frightened she's going to hear me? Frightened that she will find out that you had me believe that all this time her mam was dead when she was alive and you knew all along, didn't you? DIDN'T YOU!" Joe pointed at her inches away from her face. "You shit yourself when I first turned up, you didn't want me anywhere near Betty, you told me Charlotte was dead so that I wouldn't go and find her, you wanted to keep Betty all to yourself from day one!"

"Please keep your voice down," Cathleen pleaded.

"I don't have to do anything you ask of me, not anymore. You lied to me, you're a fucking liar!" he said, punching the table, making Cathleen jump. "You knew the truth; I know you did. You watched me cry, you listened to me talk about her for years. You made sure there was no way she could be in Betty's life. She should be here now for Betty's big day; she is her MAM!"

Cathleen shot up off her seat, anger raging through her as she stood before Joe. "I want you to leave, I get your angry. This is a shock I get it, but it's done now. Go back to your family, Joe, go back to your wife and your kids—forget about Charlotte. She is happy with Henry. You were a mistake; she was grieving and once she came to her senses, she returned to the one she really loved."

Joe instantly retaliated—his face red—he pulled himself so close to her face she could feel his breath. "YOU'RE A HEARTLESS BITCH!" he yelled in her face.

"STOP!" Betty shouted in tears, running out to the terrace.

Joe was enraged even more so; Cathleen had made things worse by mentioning Henry she realised.

"Tell her the truth," he said. Cathleen tearfully shook her head. "TELL HER!"

"I ALREADY KNOW!" Betty screamed.

As Joe and Cathleen both stared dumbstruck at the young woman whose eyes appeared red, tears streamed down her cheeks and her hands were shaking.

"I heard it all," she confessed.

Cathleen gasped, holding the table tightly for support. Her daughter looked painfully at her. Joe stepped forward to comfort Betty, but she pushed him away.

"Betty," he said stunned.

"Go, please," she cried.

"Darling, we need to talk."

"I've heard enough, please go."

Joe nodded, respecting her request. His shoulders dropped and with his head low he returned to his car, giving Cathleen an awful glance before making his exit as painful as his entrance.

1980s

Betty

Chapter Twenty-Two

August 1981

Uncle Joe had left—if that was even the correct term to use, Betty felt guilty. She hadn't meant to push him away like that, but she couldn't have him around her right now. He was her best friend, the one she had trusted all her life with every secret, yet he had been keeping one from her the entire time. As for her maman, she sat in hysterics in her chair, rocking back and forth the words *I am sorry* replaying like a broken record player, like a child with her blanket wrapped around her. Betty couldn't bear to look at her, instead, she looked at the books that had been left behind flicking to the back page, there she was, her Auntie Charlotte, much older than the picture they had of her, but it was easy to recognise her. Only her Uncle Joe had made out that she was not her auntie but her maman. He made out he and Auntie Charlotte were her parents, and maman never rectified it, she only wanted to keep him quiet. She had been too curious to head inside when she saw how angry her uncle was, she had never seen him so angry before, so she stopped by the door and listened to it all. Her whole life had been a lie, she realised, her gaze transfixed on her auntie's picture. Rupert had never abandoned her as a small child—she was never really his to begin with. She had brothers and sisters in England—three of them, which meant her cousins, Isabelle and Louis, were also her siblings, and regrettably

Theo was in fact her cousin. Her maman was her auntie and her uncle was her dad. It was all too much to take in, closing the book she collapsed into a chair. It became hard to see as her eyes were drowning in water, she felt her maman's arms wrap around her. Crouching at her knees, Cathleen wiped the tears Betty shed. Betty let her, wanting to feel small again, wanting to feel her maman's love.

"I am so sorry that you had to find out this way, Sweetheart," she sobbed.

"I wish I never listened, I wish I never knew," she cried.

"I am still your maman, Betty, please know that. This does not change that; you will always be my daughter. I'm sorry I wasn't honest with you, but I was frightened of losing you."

"Why would you lose me?"

"I was scared you would love her more than me if you met her. I see how close you and Joe are and I imagined if she were here, or you knew her true identity, you would want her."

"When I go to Uncle Joe it doesn't mean I love you less, he just—he just gets me sometimes when you don't."

Cathleen nodded. "As would she, perhaps."

"How could you know that. I love Uncle Joe but you're my maman, you always come first."

Betty noticed that her maman could not bring herself to say Charlotte's name. Even in the present conversation, she struggled to speak of Betty's biological maman.

Despite Uncle Joe's happy marriage, and it was a happy marriage, everyone knew how much Auntie Charlotte had meant to him, her maman had lied to him just like she had to her, which was cruel. There was so much to process and the more Betty thought about it, the more she realised she needed to get away from it all.

"I have to go Maman," she said, grabbing the books off the table.

"Betty where are you going? We need to talk about this."

"I don't want to talk about it with you. I just need a little bit of space from all of this," she said waving her arms.

"From me you mean?" Cathleen asked sulkily.

"I will see you in the morning Maman." Betty didn't have it in her to confirm it was her she needed space from. Leaving her maman behind to spend an evening that was meant to be special for them, she headed to the farmhouse to find Julian.

"Betty!" Cathleen shouted. "We should really talk!"

Betty painfully ignored her, closing the heavy oak door behind her, making sure to lock the catch just in case she thought about following her and waking the whole house up with the big revelation. Grabbing a bottle of red wine that had been put out with many others for the big day, Betty crept quietly upstairs to her fiancé's room. Julian was still awake; she could hear music playing quietly. She let herself into the childhood bedroom of her husband to be, posters of scientists were stuck to the walls, books filled a large bookcase, and more were scattered across a messy desk. Julian was currently studying to become a physicist, and Betty had taken on shifts at the gallery unsure of what exactly her calling was. Laid across the bed, Julian sat up alarmed as Betty closed the door behind her and bounded for his arms. She broke down again once she felt safe.

"Betty, should I be concerned? What's wrong?" Julian pulled Betty off his chest just enough to see her face. "Are you having second thoughts?"

Betty shook her head. "No, not at all. I can't wait to marry you."

"What is it then?" Julian sat more upright pulling up his pillow to lean back, pulling Betty in close to his side.

"It's Maman, she's been lying to me. They all have. My life has been a lie, Julian. No one is who I thought they were, I am not who I thought I was." Betty wiped her eyes on the sleeve of her cardigan. "She isn't my real maman."

Julian's eyes widened. "She isn't? Did she just decide to tell you this now? The night before our wedding."

"I overheard her talking to Uncle Joe. He turned up and they started rowing over these." Betty showed Julian the books that had been tucked tight under her right arm. "My Auntie Charlotte wrote them."

"Your Auntie Charlotte who passed away?"

Betty nodded and showed him the photo of her on the last page. "She isn't dead after all; she has got to be in her thirties now. She lives with her family in England."

"I don't understand, Betty, why does everyone think she is dead. Your Uncle Joe, he loved her, didn't he?" Again, Betty nodded. "They were fighting over these you said."

"Yes, Uncle Joe just found out that she was alive. He was angry at Maman for not telling him the truth."

"She knew your auntie was alive?" he asked surprised.

"He believes so."

"But why would she make something like that up."

"To keep her away from me," Betty sobbed.

Julian stared at her for a few moments, processing the information before coming to a conclusion. "Your auntie is your real maman?"

Betty's head silently made another slow nod.

"And your Uncle Joe, is he?"

"My dad, he's my dad, Julian," Betty cried out, trying hard not to make too much noise because of the other's sleeping feet away down the hall.

"Wow! I see why you brought wine. Did you bring a corkscrew?"

"Oh, I forgot."

"I will go and grab one, do we need glasses or is this a drink straight out the bottle kind of night?"

Betty smiled through her tears. "We can drink out of glasses."

"I will be quick." Julian left, his feet could be heard hastily making their way down the stairs. Staring back at Charlotte's photo, Betty noticed that her eyes were dark like Cathleen's. She had always been told that her bright blue eyes came from a relative of Rupert's. Now she realised that, of course, her eyes were from Joe. Her uncle had often made comments over the years about how similar in looks Betty and her auntie were, the way her hair parted to the left or her dimples came out when she smiled.

"One corkscrew and two glasses for my lady," Julian said slightly out of breath.

"Do you think I look like her?" Betty asked, holding up the picture to her face.

"I am not sure," he said, not even looking properly.

Betty knew he was just trying to save her feelings. He poured them each a large glass and together they sat legs stretched side by side. "I was thinking Joe being your dad kind of makes sense. Who decides to live in a foreign country, pretty much bringing up their teenage girlfriend's niece when they, let's face it, don't get on with her maman. He obviously loves you."

"He was so angry at Maman; he was shouting at her. It scared me a little."

"You can't blame him, can you?"

Betty took a big gulp of wine. "I can see why he was upset but he lied too, he could have told me the truth many times."

"Do you believe he never wanted to? I like Joe a lot and I can see how much you mean to him. Look at the lengths Cathleen went to, to keep you away from Charlotte. I wonder what loops Joe had to jump through."

"If he loves me so much then why did he not keep me himself? Why did Charlotte not want me?"

Julian kissed Betty's anguished face. "Those are questions you are going to have to ask Joe."

As they guzzled their way through the red wine, the pair became historians with very few sources to try and piece together the many questions they kept asking themselves. Why had Charlotte and Joe separated? Why had they not kept Betty? Why had Charlotte married Henry—Joe's brother? Is that why Joe and Henry did not speak? Is that why Charlotte didn't keep her baby? How did Cathleen get her if Joe wanted her so much—if Charlotte would have wanted her? Who else knew? Why did her grandparents also believe Charlotte to be dead? None of it made any sense and the more they tried to figure it out the more exhausting it became, especially for Betty. The tradition may be to not see your fiancé the night before your wedding, but Betty didn't care about tradition at this point. Fuck tradition she thought as she fell asleep in Julian's arms.

Chapter Twenty-Three

August 1981

As the sun crept through a gap in the wooden shutters guarding the windows, a beam of light lay upon Betty making her dark hair appear golden. Julian shuffled closer to her, pulling her in close to him. She slowly came round to the new day smothered in delicate kisses across her back.

"Good morning, welcome to our day. The start of our forever," he whispered.

Betty's body caved at the feel of his lips on her bare skin, it left her aching more despite the heavy weight that sat in the pit of her stomach. Everything from the night before had made its memories known before she had even opened her eyes. She had no intention of it allowing her to be pulled down on her wedding day. The day was about them. Betty was not a Brown or a Lemieux, nor was she a Ridley or a Hollister. She was, as of today, a Babin. An identity of her own, a family line she would create with Julian, the right way. As she rolled over and took in Julian's olive skin, jet black curly hair, and green eyes she allowed herself to be consumed and together they began their wedding day how they imagined it should end.

You could cut the tension with a knife in the outbuilding. As Cathleen helped Betty into her wedding dress, they both stayed silent. Betty made it clear upon arrival that they were not to talk about the night before; she just wanted to enjoy her day. With the elephant taking up a lot of space in the room, they said nothing else. It was a relief to them both when Betty's bridesmaids arrived, followed by Frederic and a very excited Theodore.

"Oh Ma Chérie!" Frederic beamed, when Betty made her way into the main living area in her white gown. She had three layers of ruffled skirt as well as poufy short sleeves. The top of the dress was shaped in a love heart coming off her shoulders a little. A white laced headband sat on her head and attached to it was a long chiffon veil decorated in more lace and pearls. "You look as beautiful as Princess Diana did on her wedding day."

Betty blushed. "Thank you, Frederic."

"I am so proud," he cried, dabbing his eyes with an ivory handkerchief. "Look at my princess."

Everyone joined in, telling Betty how pretty she looked. Cathleen approached her daughter holding a small white box.

"For you, your something blue."

Upon opening the box, a pair of sapphire earrings dazzled; their diamond-encrusted edges sending a rainbow reflection of light on the walls from the sun.

"Thank you, Maman. They are beautiful."

Cathleen dived into her daughter's arms like a child being picked up from school. Betty squeezed her maman back, giving her the reassurance she needed. All heads turned towards the door as Joe opened it. He gave Betty a nervous smile before telling the party that people were taking their seats, that statement should have sent a wave of excitement through Betty. She was minutes away from getting married. Instead, she found she couldn't stop staring at Joe, she was looking at him as though she was seeing him for the first time. With small kisses on the cheek, Cathleen and Frederic left to take their places. Cathleen avoided Joe's gaze as she passed him, his head too was firmly down at all times Betty observed.

"Girls, do you mind taking Theo outside, I will be ready to leave in a moment."

As Theo and the three bridesmaids, all friends from school, headed out, Joe closed the door behind them. Leaving just the two of them.

"You look beautiful," he said. Betty found no words left in her mouth even though she had thanked him for the compliment in her mind. "I know last night was a shock for you, you were never meant to find out like that."

"I wasn't meant to find out at all apparently," she said sternly.

Joe sighed. "If I had my way Darling, you would have known from the start however I didn't call the shots. Despite being your dad, Cathleen was in charge. Legally you belong to her and if I wanted to be in your life, I had to follow her rules. So, I did." Joe took a few steps closer to Betty. "I'm sorry I lost my cool the way I did last night. It wasn't my best move, I know that. I just…I was in shock. That doesn't mean how I treated your mam was right, I am not saying that at all. I'm sorry Betty. I am ashamed of my behaviour, I deemed myself a better man than that, nowadays."

"Is that why Charlotte left you, because of your temper?" Betty dared to ask; it had made Joe's face flinch.

"No, she didn't leave me for my anger. I left her, I left you both." Betty's eyes glistened, hearing Joe admit he left her made the heavy weight in her stomach grow larger. "I didn't want to," he continued. "I did it to protect you both. I got into some trouble, big trouble, and I couldn't have any of you get hurt so I left, leaving you and Charlotte, with my family."

"Henry?"

"Yes, Henry," he almost whispered.

"Did she hate me because of you?" Betty asked, clearing her throat.

"What? No!" Joe was standing in front of her now, both of her hands placed in his. "She loved you just as I do, she loved you with every piece of her. You were everything to her, Darling, everything." Joe lifted Betty's veil to wipe away her escaped tears.

"Then why did she leave me?" she cried.

"She was sixteen when she had you. Your grandparents decided for her, they believed they were doing the right thing in allowing Cathleen, who was married and older, to have you instead. She had less power than I have ever had, and I have forever felt guilty for it. I know you probably have so many questions, some I can answer and some I cannot, but together me and your mam will tell you everything. I can't say I have been your mam's number one fan, especially now, but she has done a brilliant job bringing you up and she is your mam, that will not change. As for me whether I am your uncle or your dad I will take anything so long as I don't lose you."

"My head is fucked! It's my wedding day," she sobbed wiping her face.

"I'm so sorry Betty."

"You won't ever lose me though; I love you too much. I have to stop crying though. I have to put all of this aside for today."

"Of course, Darling."

Betty wrapped her arms around Joe, smelling his familiar cologne and feeling his stubbly face. He had always been her safety net; he was the one that made her feel like nothing bad could happen. As they pulled away, he fumbled in his blazer pocket.

"One last thing," he said, pulling out a shiny ring she recognised so well. "I was going to give you this before everything. I wanted you to wear it today, I want you to keep it."

Joe never had many things; he wasn't a materialistic guy, but the engagement ring that he kept safe in his vintage leather jacket was one thing for which he was known for. Many drunken tales ended with the ring being brought out, and many events where the candle was lit in memory of the young girl meant the ring was also taken out. Betty was touched that he wanted her to have it, knowing what it meant to him.

"I can't keep this, Uncle Joe. This is yours; it belongs with you."

"Wear it just for today then, please."

Betty could feel the ring sitting snugly on her finger as she walked down the aisle, with her head held high, towards a sobbing Julian. Her arm was clutched tightly around Joe's, and she hoped her maman would not see the vintage ring belonging to her auntie. Part of her felt guilty for wearing it and another part of her was left with flitting thoughts of Charlotte. Did she ever think of her? Did she miss her? Had she ever tried to get her back? Once she reached Julian, and parted from Joe, the thoughts stopped.

She was Betty Babin. The past had to be put on pause until she was ready.

Despite particular guests not speaking to others, the wedding played out beautifully and Betty became so engrossed she felt lighter and high on her love for Julian…and many glasses of wine. The setting was everything she had envisioned, and the cake baked by none other than Marcel went down a treat. Whose bloodline she did or didn't belong to was not an issue she thought as she danced with Theo for the hundredth time. They were family regardless. During the first dance, the pair danced to *La Maladie d'amour* by Michel Sardou. The song had played on repeat at a small restaurant they dined at on their first date and had become their special song. The party went on long into the night. Betty felt like she was on cloud nine when Julian carried her into the outbuilding which had been redecorated with roses and fresh bedsheets.

"Mrs Babin," Julian said coyly as he lay Betty on the bed pulling off one of her high heels.

"Mr Babin, I see you have taken to your new role well," she teased as he pulled the second off.

"Just you wait until the morning, I'll need a coffee and breakfast in bed."

"Ha! I don't think so. You have obviously married the wrong type of woman."

"I married a feisty one," he said, kissing her ankle. "A wild one," he said, kissing behind her knee. "A sexy one," he said, kissing the inside of her thigh. "The right one," he said, removing her white knickers.

Before leaving the farmhouse for the two-hour trip to Paris Airport. Betty left Charlotte's ring on top of Isabelle's books with a small note to Joe, he had volunteered to help Julian's family tidy up the place, so she knew they would be in safe hands.

Thank you for letting me wear this beautiful ring on my special day. Thank you for finding your way back into my life. Thank you for always being there for me. Betty xx

On second thoughts Betty grabbed the books and threw them into her handbag, scribbling quickly on the note.

P.S. I have taken Isabelle's books. Hope she doesn't mind.

Chapter Twenty-Four

August 1981

"Another funny part?" Julian asked groggily.

"Sorry, I didn't mean to wake you."

Betty had been unable to sleep in the small tent they'd pitched up in Wales, ready for their hike up Snowdonia. Julian had managed to fall asleep listening to his Walkman, whereas Betty had begun reading Charlotte's book, *Mischief in the Durham Lane,* aided by torch light. The book was based on three girls and two boys who lived on the same street in Durham. It was girls versus boys, and they did awful but amusing things to each other. Their mediator was an old couple, Rufus and Florence, who lived in a large house at the bottom of the lane and allowed the children to play in their enormous back garden. The truces never lasted long, much to the annoyance of the couple. Betty had ended up staying up much longer than anticipated and couldn't help but laugh out loud, waking her husband up a few times too many. He hadn't minded though, tucking his sleeping bag up to his chin he rolled over and fell back to sleep.

Much to Betty's amusement, Julian could not understand the Welsh very well, there wasn't much difference during their stay in Scotland either when trekking Ben Nevis. Abandoning the tent, they had a cosy room above a country pub overlooking farmland. They did not venture out much due to the rain so decided to dine by a log fire downstairs in the pub. The locals were friendly and after one too many drinks, accents didn't really matter too much as none of the conversations made sense anyway. It was a hotel stay in Windermere when they trekked up Scafell Pike at the Lake District. Their room overlooked the lake and had tea rooms adjacent to it that made the most delicious scones. They bought sandwiches and snacks from there to eat on their trek and sat with a small picnic in the evening on the rocks, dipping their sore feet in the lake.

"It's breath-taking," Betty commented.

"Is Durham this beautiful?" Julian asked, impressed with the land he had seen on his first trip to England.

"I don't remember too much of the place to be honest. My grandparents live in a small village away from the city. Time will tell, however. We best go and pack, we have an early train in the morning."

Mavis and Frank were not expecting the newlyweds until teatime for their short stay, so with their backpacks strapped on tight the couple explored the northern region, they toured Durham Castle and the Cathedral and ate lunch at a Tudor style pub.

"I can understand people here, they all sound like Joe and your Maman," Julian commented, tucking into a steak and ale pie.

"Yes, they do don't they. Are you almost done Darling?"

Julian looked down at his barely touched meal. "Not really, are we in a hurry?"

"I just wanted to check out that book shop over there," Betty said pointing it out.

Opposite the pub was a book shop, the front window was decorated in bunting with a large photo of Charlotte surrounded by five different books in the series Betty had finished reading.

Julian took one look at it and smiled. “Why don’t you go, and I will catch you up.”

“Are you sure?”

“Yes, go.”

Betty leaned across the table to kiss Julian on the cheek. “Thank you I won’t be long.”

“Are you eating this chicken?” he asked, grabbing Betty’s plate of Hunter’s chicken.

“No, you can have it,” she replied, rushing out.

She didn’t know what made her feel the need to go to the bookshop, all she found there was the decorated window and more books inside. Maybe it was the photo that drew her in. It was a slightly older picture of Charlotte; she was smiling from ear to ear against a pastel blue backdrop. Her large brown eyes stared back at her, when she looked into them it was like looking at her maman’s. They hadn’t spoken much at the wedding; Betty had spent the day avoiding conversation with her, nor did she really say bye when they left for the outhouse. Betty bought a copy of each of the three books she hadn’t read yet telling herself it was for Isabelle. Leaving the shop, she could see Julian sitting in the pub window still tucking into his meal. She stopped once more at the display, celebrating her new release.

“She’s brilliant, isn’t she?” a shortish woman with a blonde bob, wearing a beige mac asked beside Betty. “I used to be one of her best friends, always knew she’d be a great writer one day," she continued before Betty had a chance to answer. "Haven't seen her in years mind, not since—well since she left Durham."

"Where did she go?" Betty asked acting coolly.

"I have no idea, she ran away with her boyfriend then the next thing I heard she was sent off to London, she had family down there, but she didn't want to go, it was such a difficult time for her."

Betty could feel goosebumps rise on her arms, but she wanted more information from the lady. "I heard a story that people thought she died."

"Oh yes, I attended that awful memorial, me and our friend Molly. It was dreadful, there wasn't even a body. No one could believe that she was actually gone, a fire killed her they said. Her uncle was furious, and the family were not talking to each other. As for Henry, her partner, he was destroyed as you could imagine. We were only young but by God did he love her. Somehow along the line though they've managed to find each other again and that really does make me happy." The woman smiled wholeheartedly. "I never had a friend like Charlotte again, she was one of a kind. When I found out she was alive, my faith in God was restored."

"Was it Henry she ran away with then?" Betty asked, staring at the glossy-eyed face of Charlotte's old friend.

"Oh no, Charlotte got involved with his older brother. He was extremely good-looking mind, but trouble, he left her high and dry he did with a bun in the oven as well. Rumours are that she gave birth in a shed."

Betty clutched the carrier bag in her grip tightly. "A shed."

"An allotment shed, she and Henry used to hang out there with an old man. He plays a part in the book."

"Rufus?" Betty asked.

"Yes, Rufus Flint he was called. He wasn't married to Florence in real life though, they were just friends. Florence was Charlotte's nan. A lot of the characters are based on real people, the three girls…I see a resemblance to myself, Molly, and Charlotte as for the boys," the woman laughed. "They smell of Hollister's—Henry and his brother."

"Did you do the things she writes about?" Betty asked intrigued.

The woman laughed again. "Some things, not all, the war was really between Charlotte and Henry when we were children. He used to torment her at every given opportunity. He'd trip her up, pinch her sweets, throw bugs at her, you name it. As for that scene where he pulls her draws down in P.E at school—very true. She was absolutely mortified, rugby tackled him to the ground like an angry man she did. Gave him a black eye."

"Do you ever think of finding her?"

"Oh, I have thought of it many times but so much time has gone by and so much has happened that I fear I belong to her past. Sometimes people belong in different chapters of your life, and I don't believe I belong to this one."

"But Henry does?"

"Henry plays a part in all the chapters; he is one of the main characters of her life after all."

"And Joe?"

"Joe shouldn't have been written, the baby he left her with—a baby girl—I saw her a few times in church such a beautiful bairn—they ripped her from Charlotte's arms. It was her downfall. He was her downfall."

"But he loved her," Betty said quickly.

"Joe only ever loved himself, his own dad was ashamed of him, his brother hated him, he was a waste of space."

Betty felt heat rise within. "No, he…"

"You done; thought we could visit the Finchale Priory before heading to your grandparents?" Julian asked rubbing his swollen stomach.

"Oh, don't let me stop you," the woman said. "The Priory is lovely this time of year. It was lovely to meet you, sorry I've been chatting so much I didn't even catch your name Pet."

"Amelie, my name is Amelie."

"What a lovely name, I'm Carol."

Betty filled Julian in on what she found out, Carol was all for Henry and Charlotte, unlike Joe. She was rather confused with the timeline of Charlotte's relationships with the brothers.

"What if I am not even Uncle Joe's?" she asked in a panic.

"Joe seems pretty certain you are, as does everyone else. As far as he's concerned, from what I've heard, the two of them were very happy, living in their little flat."

"His story has flaws though. Oh, and apparently I was born in a shed!" Betty sulked.

"Maybe that is why you like gardening?"

Betty gave Julian a dig. "This is all frustrating, Julian! I don't even want to stay with my grandparents anymore. I barely know them, and they too are two eagled eyed liars!"

"Will you tell them you know?"

"I really don't know."

Mavis and Frank's small bungalow was pristine. The whole house was made up of three rooms, the kitchen living area, one bedroom and one bathroom. Frank barely moved from his recliner, positioned beside a large vintage gramophone. The table had been set upon their arrival with an *English spread,* and Mavis made a fuss of them. She wouldn't let them do anything themselves, if you wanted a drink, a snack, to bin something, move something, she was there ready at hand.

"We don't get many visitors," Frank said from his chair while Mavis showed Julian how to use the shower. "Your Uncle Peter sometimes pops over with Aimee and the bairn. They're only based at Catterick, but they don't come as much as we would like. Ya fella seems canny."

"Canny? Oh, I remember what that means—good. Yes, he is *good.*"

"How's your ma?" he asked.

Which one? Betty thought. "Fine, she's fine."

"Be nice if she could see her ma sometime, Mavis would like that. Ask her will ya?"

"I'll ask but I can't promise anything."

Mavis, having left Julian in the bathroom, joined them. "Oh, it's so nice having you here Betty. I have missed having family around."

"I was just saying our Cathleen should come over," Frank said removing a cigarette out of his green cardigan pocket.

"Oh, that would be lovely, ask her for us, will you? We will make room," Mavis beamed.

"I will ask," Betty informed her, knowing damn well she wouldn't come. She had always told Betty she was afraid of flying, but something told her perhaps that too was a lie. "The bungalow is in a nice area."

"Yes, it is quiet around here isn't it, Frank." Frank nodded taking a puff of his cigarette. "We get no bother round here, the street we used to live in began to get a bit rowdy, a few rough-looking families were moving in, and it just wasn't the same as it used to be, was it Frank?"

"I lived in that house all me life, as did me da. Thought one day I would leave it to Cathleen or Peter, but ne one wants to live round 'ere anymore. This place is alreet though. Tucked away from the riffraff."

"When Julian gets out of the shower, I'll dish out some chocolate eclairs. I bought them from Greggs today. French people like eclairs, don't they?" Mavis asked, almost hanging off her floral seat.

"Yes Nana, they do."

There were so many photos dotted around the bungalow, some faces Betty recognised others she didn't. There was so much family history that she knew nothing about. She knew about her great-nana Florence and her rich relatives that lived in London but only by name, not by personality or stories. She knew nothing about her great Uncle Albert or his wife Emily. She guessed who they might be in the photos, it had never bothered her much before. The family she had in France was all she knew and needed. She never cared for Rupert and the family who abandoned her, or so she thought. She never cared for Maman's family in England who they barely saw. Now, however, it suddenly mattered. She had seen the desperation in her Nana Mavis to please them, they were lonely—partly their own doing she concluded but nonetheless it wasn't easy to see. Asking her nan about the people in the photos had crossed her mind, she thought it may lead to a talking point, as they had all struggled to keep a conversation going longer than five minutes. Knowing they were the heads who produced the planning of her future and ultimately Charlotte's, she decided to stay quiet and endured their company for the rest of the evening.

As the house grew quiet, Julian fell asleep on his makeshift bed on the sofa. Mavis had pushed the man into a food coma with her eclairs and vanilla slices. Betty, who couldn't sleep, found herself crouched with her knees tucked in under her chin on Frank's chair staring out to the night sky. A large oak tree stood proud in the centre of a green, guarding the small houses surrounding it. Branches moved gently in the small breeze and Betty thought about the number of people, seasons, and years the tree had seen in its lifetime. Julian began to snore softly, warming her heart as she watched him with his feet and arms all dangling off the edges of the sofa. A camp cot had been pulled out beside him for Betty, which was beginning to seem more inviting considering it looked uncomfortable. Pulling herself away from the chair, Betty lay on the khaki meshed bed pulling a thin duvet over herself. Sleep found her quicker than she thought, and the morning greeted her with more fussing and a packed lunch for two prepared by Mavis for their journey to Newcastle Airport.

"I can see why Maman does not visit," Betty quietly said to Julian as they waved goodbye to Mavis and Frank.

"They mean well," Julian mentioned. "Frank is a little hard to read though."

"Maman said the war gave him an extra shell."

"War will do that, my grand-pere came back with one leg and one hell of an attitude. It destroyed his relationship with my grand-mere. She left him within the year."

"Well luckily for Nana Mavis, she is the only person Grandad Frank has ever truly cared for, or so Maman says. Enough talk of the past, we are still on our honeymoon. Let history stay where it belongs."

Chapter Twenty-Five

September 1981

They chose to sit outside at a small wooden table, the Eiffel tower could be seen in the distance, its twinkling lights exciting tourists below. Even though she had lived in Paris all her life she could still appreciate its beauty. Sat opposite her were Cathleen and Joe. They had chosen a quiet corner to have their chat and Betty had suggested alcohol should accompany them to take the edge off.

"Okay, tell me everything," Betty commanded.

Joe went first, he told Betty about losing his mam and giving himself a bad name with all the trouble he got into. He told her how he fell in love with Charlotte even though she was dating his brother and how she made him want to be a better person. He told her that no one approved so they dated in secret until they got found out and decided to run away. They were happy there above the bookshop and even more so when he found out Charlotte was expecting. They had it all planned, they were going to be a family. Joe filled Betty in on the night Charlotte got spiked by his ex and he feared he would lose them both. Anger had got the better of him, and the woman he threatened happened to be related to the worst thug going, and it put them all in danger. He left them both to protect them, not because he wanted to.

"It was the hardest decision I've ever had to make. Charlotte wanted to come with me on the run, but I couldn't do that to you both. I was on the run for years before I heard Bill was dead, by then I had found you again and thought Charlotte was dead." Joe took a drink before continuing, "I left thinking you both would be safe and loved surrounded by family. I almost turned round when I found Charlotte's engagement ring and note stashed in my pocket, but I knew I wouldn't be able to provide for you. It wasn't until I was on the streets in London months later that I bumped into Charlotte. She was a mess, distraught that you had been taken from her. She told me you were here with Cathleen, and I felt like a failure all over again. She blamed me, told me it was all my fault, and it was. All of this is my fault, if I learnt to keep my cool then we wouldn't be sitting around this table right now."

"Am I the reason you came to France?" Betty asked.

"It certainly drew me here, I never thought I would actually be lucky enough to find you but like magic there you were, and I knew then that I had to find a way to stay in your life."

It was Cathleen's turn next, she told Betty how Charlotte had everything going for her before her nana died and the impact her death had on her sister. She told her how lovely her relationship was with Henry; the family believed her grief was subsiding until they learnt she had been mixing with Joe. Frank had gone berserk, and the relationships Charlotte had with others began to deteriorate. Cathleen explained how worried they all were when she ran off with Joe. They had been gone for almost a year before Cathleen got the call from her mam that Charlotte was in the hospital with a haemorrhage.

"We had no idea she had been staying next door."

"Is it true she had me in a shed?" Betty asked.

"How do you know that?" Cathleen asked. "Yes, an allotment shed. Henry delivered you."

"Henry seems like a very forgiving person by the sounds of it," Betty commented avoiding Joe. "So, Nana and Grandad decided to send Charlotte away and I ended up with you, Maman."

"Yes, I adopted you," Cathleen said, then explained why they moved to France, being nothing but honest to Betty and how she had felt. She also came clean to Joe about when she found out the truth that Charlotte was alive and why she chose to stay quiet.

"Can we have another round please before we continue?" Joe asked, fidgeting in his chair.

Apart from letters about Charlotte's well-being from London and Joe running into her, no one knew too much about what happened while Charlotte was in London or what had really happened to her.

"Henry had to have something to do with it," Joe suggested.

"I don't think he did, not straight away anyway. He was devastated at the memorial. No one can act that well," Cathleen said.

"Why disappear?" Joe quizzed. "Why Cornwall?"

"Maybe she didn't want to be told what to do with her life anymore," said Betty. "Maybe she just needed to get away from everyone and start again."

"I can't imagine she wouldn't have tried to come for you though, Darling," Joe said.

"Perhaps she did," Cathleen proposed. "Who knows if she tried to write to my parents once she was settled. They moved away and no one but me and Peter knew where to. Everyone we know has moved on to pastures new. Charlotte has no other connections."

"Whether she tried to get in touch or not, it could be that I just didn't fit in her chapter."

"Her what?" Cathleen asked.

"It doesn't matter."

"What would you like to do now?" Joe asked seriously. "Do you want to find her? I will help you if you like, it can't be too difficult if we write to her publisher."

"Is that what you want Uncle Joe? To find Charlotte."

"Only for you. As much as I would love to sit at a table like we are now, face to face with her, able to chat to her. I don't think it is the right thing to do. Charlotte has found happiness…she is married to Henry; they have children, as do Maddie and I, the last thing she needs is me rocking up."

"What about making amends with Henry?" Betty asked.

"Or your dad?" Cathleen added.

Joe laughed anxiously. "Last time I saw Henry I was leaving with the girl he loved. He told me he would kill me if I hurt her, and I believed him. I was selfish when I pursued Charlotte and I was selfish when I abandoned him and my dad when Mam died. Some things are unforgivable. I put my dad through so much stress I think seeing me again would be the death of him. They are all better off without me. You on the other hand would be welcomed with open arms."

Betty noticed that Cathleen was sitting rigid in her seat, she stared back at her daughter with glossy eyes waiting for her answer. Betty had thought about this a lot, she imagined meeting the smiling author and her siblings and, in her head, it was all picnic and roses and then she'd remember the lengths her maman went to keep her for herself. Her maman had told lies and kept secrets that were cruel and hurt many people, but she knew deep down it had all been for love. It was love for her. She knew it would upset Cathleen if she got to know Charlotte and the thought of crushing her maman's heart always pulled the reunion party in her mind to a close.

"I don't want to find her," Betty informed them, Cathleen's shoulders dropped a little and Joe sat up straight.

"Are you sure that is what you want?"

"That is what she has decided Joe," Cathleen fiercely injected.

"I am only asking if she is sure."

"I am sure. Charlotte sounds intriguing, Uncle Joe, she really does. She was so young when she had me and both our lives went differently to what was planned but we've both turned out okay. I love the life I have; I love living in Paris, I've met Julian and I love the pair of you and Frederic so much. I feel lucky to have you all in my life. Somewhere in England Charlotte is, by the sounds of it, living her best life. She's an author…something she always dreamt of. She has other children and is married to a guy who loves her just as much as you did. I think she probably feels lucky too. I know you want us to meet each other but I ask you to please respect my decision. I want things to go back to how they were, I don't want anything to change."

"I respect your choice, of course, I do," Joe said unconvincingly, he was saddened by her decision, she knew this, but in time he would come to accept it. "Can I ask for one small change?"

"What small change?" Cathleen asked.

"Now, everything is out in the open and you know who I am. Do you think you would feel comfortable if you dropped the Uncle Joe. Maybe one day I could be Dad."

His heart was right there on the table for Betty to choose either to toss it aside or cradle it. Joe had always felt much more than an uncle and she couldn't remember Rupert at all. This small change meant a lot to him she could tell, but by calling him Dad wouldn't that be hypocritical towards Charlotte?

"Perhaps," she concluded. "In time."

Joe nodded with a smile. "I can live with that."

1970s

Grace

Chapter Twenty-Six

August 1970

"You're pregnant, Miss O'Connell."

The words the doctor said played on repeat in her mind, the world now looked less colourful than it had before her appointment. She thought her alcohol intake from celebrating her nineteenth birthday had been the cause of her missing her course along with the nausea, she had heard that could happen, or was she foolish and the old wives tale was now laughing at her. She was meant to be the mature one, that is what everyone said about Grace. She had believed it was due to growing up without a mammy, Linda O'Connell had run off with a Spanish man when she was only four leaving behind her small daughter and loving husband. Her daddy had become both parents overnight. He taught her everything she needed to know to grow up to be a confident young lady, even all the parts men are normally too afraid to speak of such as her courses and other changes her body would make as a teenager. Her daddy was her rock so telling him that she was in the family way felt disappointing despite his instant support.

"You're pregnant Miss O'Connell."

These very words had instantly changed everything. Despite her daddy suggesting hiring a nanny and offering her financial support, it was not enough. She had to say goodbye to her studies at Cambridge University and her dream of becoming an archaeologist, travelling across ancient worlds. If she were to become a mammy then she was going to do it properly, she was going to be present—something Linda had failed to do. She wanted to give her child a life as beautiful as the one her daddy had given her in their country estate in Ireland. The only question left to answer was whether she would be a sole parent or would the father be involved.

She had only slept with him five times, and each time left her desperate for more. He had been called to Ireland from England to oversee plans for the old barn houses to be converted into holiday apartments. He was the best guy for the job, Daddy had told her. She first clocked eyes on him when returning Chestnut, her horse, to the stables, standing outside the ruins deep in conversation with Mr O'Connell. He was devilishly handsome she thought, much older than herself—thirties perhaps. He was in a suit, which was not appropriate for the humid day, but he pulled it off well. Not a drop of sweat, he looked as cool as a cucumber. She hadn't thought much more about him until she spotted him the following evening in a local pub on his own. He looked exhausted sitting over a glass of whiskey, his tie lay on the table, three shirt buttons were undone, and he looked miserable. She hesitated to approach him at first; they had never been introduced and he looked as though he wasn't looking for company, but Grace couldn't stop looking at him, only half listening to the conversation of her friends. His sadness drew her in until she found herself sitting at his table.

"Hi!" she said almost too cheerfully. "I'm Grace O'Connell," she finished, holding out a hand, to which he ignored. “You’re working on my daddy’s estate,” she added.

“The barn conversion, yes. Pleased to meet you,” he said in an accent, sitting slumped over the table.

“You looked like you could do with cheering up.” Grace smiled; however, he did not notice as he sipped the burnt orange liquid.

“I’m fine.”

As he glanced at her she noticed his eyes were blue, he had large veins in his hands which wore no ring, broad shoulders, an unshaven face. He was irresistible and she had to have him. Grace had lost her virginity to her high school sweetheart whom she left when she got into university, so she was not frightened to make a move on the older gentleman sat opposite her, she was brave and daring and went in for a kiss. He did not return it, he had in fact pulled her away, but she had got his attention. Her heart plummeted as he gave her a confused glare. She tried to keep her cool staring him out with a smile, she wanted to appear sexy and confident. He broke the stare first, drinking the last of his whiskey and stuffed his tie into his pocket before standing up. She watched him leave the table, a wave of embarrassment washing over her. He probably saw her as just some kid she thought. The gentleman stopped and turned around leaning onto an empty table.

“Are you coming then?” he asked her, before continuing to walk out of the pub.

Without hesitation she leapt out her chair and hastily followed. The warm air of outside hit her first before he pushed her against the wall and kissed her ferociously. Grace’s body instantly craved for his attention to be all over her, including in her. She knew by the way he kissed her that his love making would not disappoint. They had gone to his B&B, that is always where they met up after and the evening always played out the same. They would have sex, great sex—he met all her sexual needs, he was attentive and passionate but as soon as it was over, he reverted back into himself. He was quiet, they would have drinks and Grace would do all the talking, all the questions. He was a mystery to her, a closed book. This made her want him even more. She didn't want a man who was predictable like Oskar—their Norwegian farmer who was madly in love with her. If she asked Oskar to jump, he would say how high; her English lover however, she couldn't make heads nor tails of him. Which is why as she left Ireland behind to go and tell the dark and handsome lover her news, she had not the slightest idea to what he would say. She told herself it would be okay if he didn't want to be involved, they didn't really know each other and part of her wasn't sure if he even liked her. He never smiled, he always wore a serious face, none the less she had fallen for it—hard—and hoped he would want to be involved. Grace wasn't stupid, she knew they weren't going to run into the distance together hand in hand, but with their baby growing inside her perhaps they somehow stood a chance.

Chapter Twenty-Seven

August 1970

Grace headed towards the double glass doors that led into a great big warehouse. The floor was made from renovated wood as was the reception desk by which she was greeted. A plump woman wearing bright green cats eye spectacles and a bright purple dress smiled from her chair that was draped with a pink knitted cardigan.

"Good morning, madam, how can I help you?" she asked in a strong southern accent. Bright pink lipstick stained her mouth, thickly applied making her lips look far larger than they were.

"Morning, I am here to see Henry Hollister, I am a friend of his."

She stood tall and held back her nerves. She was doing this for her unborn child she had told herself throughout her journey, and she was doing this for herself. Henry had played a part in making this child, he had a right to know and she had to see him again, be near him.

"Do you have an appointment with Mr Hollister?" the lady flicked through a diary. "I don't have anything written down."

"No sorry, I didn't have time for that, please I won't take up much of his time."

"One moment please, I will just give him a quick call." She felt herself start to overheat with a sickly feeling just like she did when hungover. Grace tried to hide it by slowly pacing the small room as the receptionist made the call. "Mr Hollister, it's Margret. You have a visitor here at reception…I know you do not have any meetings scheduled Sir…she said she is a friend. What is your name Honey, sorry I should have asked?"

"Grace—Grace O'Connell."

"She said her name is Grace O'Connell…she said she didn't have time…I can check the diary now…you're free Friday at nine-thirty."

"Tell him it is important," Grace anxiously interrupted. "Tell him it cannot wait, and I won't leave until he sees me."

"Did you hear that Sir? She said she won't keep you long…okay." Margret put down the receiver and smiled once more. "He is on his way down."

She did not have to wait long before the doors leading to the main warehouse were dramatically swung open, with Henry attached to the door handle his face was flushed and his tie swung from side to side.

"Grace." His lips moved a little into a half smile. "I will take it from here Margret."

Henry led her through the doors to his empire, Walter and Sons. The warehouse looked so much bigger on the inside, sawdust lay on every surface, the noise was deafening, and his workforce were busy on all kinds of large machines, wearing goggles and headphones. Henry led Grace up a short flight of narrow metal stairs to an office overlooking the production room. The noise immediately decreased as he closed the door behind them. The office was quite large and incredibly tidy. One wall was filled floor to ceiling with identical black files all dated and labelled. The wall opposite was mostly made of glass with white blinds stopping prying eyes from below. A large lamp filled the corner, Grace could envision Henry sat up late in the office by the glowing light. By the door, a row of blueprints lay carefully rolled up in pigeonholes.

"Please sit down." He offered Grace a green leather chair as he took a seat opposite her behind a large rustic desk. Like the room the desk was also minimalistic, a stationary pot filled with identical black pens sat behind two black trays filled with paper labelled *Done* and *To Do.* In front of Henry lay a closed heavy diary, a ribbon marking a page. He sat back, his hands clenched together. "So, what is so urgent?"

Grace gripped the leather seat, her nails dug into the bottom. She swallowed the bile that was rising back down. She had to tell him she thought, she wished now he were a little more predictable as his posture made her feel a little hopeless.

"I'm pregnant," she blurted out, her heart falling out her mouth as she saw his face drop. He looked at her as one might when they mishear someone but feel too rude to ask them to repeat what they said.

"You're sure?"

Grace nodded.

"And it's mine?"

Grace gasped. "I know we don't know each other that well, Henry, but I can assure you that I don't go round opening my legs for anybody who wants a turn."

"I'm sorry, I just… Fuck!" Henry stood up and walked over to the window, peeping through the blinds. He was biting his clenched fist; his face was growing red. Grace's nails dug deeper into the leather fabric. "This is huge! I don't even know you, you're so fucking young. We were careful, fuck." It was probably the most words Henry had ever said in one go and Grace wasn't sure she liked it. He returned to his seat pulling himself up to the desk, fists still clenched in front of him. "Sorry, how do you feel about this?"

Grace tucked herself in closer to the table, closer to Henry. "I am keeping the baby if that is what you're really asking. I am going to drop out of uni to bring my baby up. Where I do this depends entirely on you. Daddy said he would support us if you chose to not be a part of our child's life and we will live in Ireland, however if you decide you do want to play a part in their lives then I will stay here in Epsom, for you."

Henry sighed; his head buried in his hands, his elbows hanging off the edge of his desk. He pulled open a draw under the table and produced a bottle of whiskey and a glass tumbler. Silently he filled the tumbler and downed the whiskey in one go. He looked troubled; his silence was unnerving. Yet as Grace looked at him, he still looked good enough to have, she would have him now if he asked, right there on top of the table or mount him on his chair, she wasn't too fussed.

"We will sort something out; I will have to let you go, Grace. I have a lot of work to be getting on with."

"Henry," Grace said, her thoughts of their naked bodies interrupted. "I need more than that, what does that even mean—we will sort something out—I have come all this way I deserve more? If you don't want to be a part of our lives just say it now, rip the plaster off. I will leave and you will never have to see us again. Daddy will get someone else to work on the barns."

"I'm sorry it isn't what you want me to say Grace, this is a shock, I'm not going to lie, and I just need to get my head around it all."

"How do you think I feel? My whole life changes no matter what you decide."

"Please, Grace, just give me some time. I'm sorry."

Henry didn't move from behind his desk, the clear tumbler was once more glowing amber. He couldn't even look at her, she observed. Her chair legs scratched the wooden floor as she pulled it back, her blood rising at his cowardice. Legs shaking in frustration she stormed out the office, slamming the door behind her. The noise was blaring once more as she carefully took the stairs desperate to get out.

She ignored Margret as she joyfully waved her off. "See you later, Love."

She breathed in the outside air like the first breath out of water. As Grace walked away from Walter and Sons, she realised that although she told herself that it would be okay if Henry didn't want to be involved, his reaction made her think otherwise. Without him she would be a single parent living in her childhood home for the foreseeable future. The local women will hide away their good sons from the whore who had a baby out of wedlock. She had been crazy to even have the slightest hope that he might have wanted to give it a go for the sake of the baby, it was clear that he wanted nothing to do with them even though he never said it.

"Grace!" She turned around as she heard Henry running after her down the street. He looked a fool running in his suit she thought but couldn't help but be pleased to see him. "Maybe, I could come to Ireland for a little while. We could get to know each other," he said breathlessly.

Chapter Twenty-Eight

August 1970

The first thing Mr O'Connell and Henry did was speak privately in the office of Grace's family home. She had tried to listen to what they were discussing but the door was too thick. They must have been chatting for almost an hour before Henry emerged eyeing her up suspiciously. Neither of them told her what was said, which she found infuriating considering it was her life and her child they were talking about. All her daddy said was Henry was a good egg.

To try and break the ice, Grace invited Henry on a horse ride. The only activity they had engaged in previously was in the bedroom. They did not need to get to know each other more in that department, so a horse ride she felt could ease them into conversation in a relaxed activity. Henry met Grace at the stables where she was getting the horses prepared.

"Have you ridden before?" she asked him, as he approached in a pair of linen trousers and a polo top. She had only ever seen him in a suit, he looked younger and more vulnerable out of his work clothing. The horseshoe in his triceps were in display making Grace's stomach flutter.

"Never," he replied, she could hear a hint of nervousness.

"You can ride Oakley; he is Daddy's horse. He is the oldest and is a little slower. He will look after you. I'll take Chestnut, he is mine and is a little wilder," Grace said kissing the side of Chestnuts face.

"Should you be riding a horse in your condition? Is it safe? What if you come off?"

Grace smiled at Henry's concern. The man of stone did have some care in him after all. "We will take a leisurely ride. I have ridden Chestnut all my life. Don't worry, we will be fine."

Seeing Henry ride beside her, his knuckles white from his grip on the reigns pleased Grace. She was seeing parts of him that were not all straight and serious. They headed to a fishing lake that she had visited many times growing up. Some days she and her daddy would stay till the dark hours, waiting patiently while chomping on sandwiches and crisps. Their lines laying still for hours while the thought of dining on salmon or trout filled their minds. Grace loved fishing with her daddy, it was always just the two of them, sometimes they would talk about anything and everything and other times they sat in a peaceful silence which was just as perfect.

"I will teach our child to ride a horse and bring them out here, just as me and Daddy did," Grace told Henry, whose grip was a little more relaxed.

"That sounds nice," he said, not taking his eyes off the footpath ahead.

"It was just me and Daddy growing up, we used to trek along this footpath all the time. I was four when he bought me Chestnut, not long after Linda left us." Grace gave the badious horse a loving pat. "Did you have a big family growing up?"

"My mam died when I was a fifteen, then it was just me and Dad from then on."

"I'm sorry to hear that, was she a good mammy?"

"She had the patience of a saint," he said. "She was the best," he added glancing her way.

"If you are an only child then why is your business called Walter and Sons, if there is only one son?"

Henry looked ahead once more, his grip tighter on the reign as the footpath narrowed and large roots stretched across. "I had a brother, he…he died not long after Mam."

Grace watched his body stiffen; it was no wonder he was so closed off; he had experienced so much heartache in his teens. A family of four to a family of two must have devastated both Henry and Walter. At least Linda left when Grace was young with few memories of her to ache her heart like it had to her daddy. She could barely remember Linda ever being present.

"That must have been awful. How did he die?"

"A motorcycle accident, he was drunk."

Grace wanted to hold Henry in her arms, despite him being much older than her she didn't feel a difference in their ages.

"What will you teach our little one?" Grace asked, changing the subject. Henry shrugged his shoulders. "Well, what do you like to do? What skills do you wish to pass on?"

"I could teach them a trade, joinery, electrician, business perhaps."

"Okay, a trade is a clever thing to have, what else? What do you like to do when you're not at work?"

"Drink whiskey, although I don't believe I should teach them to do that."

Grace agreed, pressing him for more. There had to be more to him than work and drowning his sorrows for that she learnt was all he was doing.

"Gardening," he suggested.

"Gardening!" She couldn't help but laugh, she noticed a crack of a smile in his face. "Sorry, I just never imagined you to be a one for green fingers. Well, that settles it doesn't it. Our child will know how to ride horses, catch fish, learn a trade and garden."

"What a lucky duck."

They tied their horses to a tree branch by the grassy bank of the slow flowing lake. The grass was long and tickled the back of Grace's legs. Wildflowers grew around the trunks of the trees and the sky was clear above them, as they lay inches from each other side by side.

"It's beautiful here," Henry commented.

"Yes, it is."

It felt unbearable for Grace to be so close to him without feeling his touch. He was like an itch that was in desperate need of scratching. She shuffled a little closer to him, his trousers brushed against her legs. His eyes were closed, his body still only his chest was moving with each breath. She had to make things work with Henry, she thought. She had feelings she couldn't understand, all she knew was she wanted him. She leaned closer and gently placed a kiss on his cheek. He didn't move, nor open his eyes.

"I know you don't love me, and I know this baby was not planned but together I believe we can give them a wonderful life and maybe you could learn to love me in time, if you don't dislike me too much."

Henry's eyes slowly opened, and he turned his head towards her, the bright sky reflected in his blue eyes like in water. "I don't dislike you Grace, I think you're incredibly brave and attractive. Having a child was not the plan, no, but it's happening anyways, and I want the best for them just as you do. I don't love you, you're right, but in time perhaps I might."

Time, she just had to give it time. It was early days after all, but she would do everything she could to make Henry fall in love with her. When they made love, you would think he was madly in love with her already, but the moment it ended so did his affection. Grace nuzzled her face into Henry's chest, and he wrapped his arms around her. Time. She just needed time.

They were in separate bedrooms, but Grace waited until the house fell silent before creeping along the dark corridors in her black silk night gown. A small orange glow caught her attention when she passed a window. Oskar was still awake in his cottage across the grounds on their home farm. He hadn't spoken to her since her return with Henry. For a split second she thought she should go and call on him, but the temptation to slip into the door across the hall was too much.

He was asleep when she crept into his bed, her presence stirred him awake. She pushed herself against his half naked body before he could resist. She traced his body with her finger starting with his chest slowly down to the bulge in his underwear. He stopped her, grabbing her hand before she could venture any further. He pulled her arm up above her head and lay over her, using his other hand to arouse her instead before releasing her from her torment of longing.

Grace woke up searching the sheets for Henry to find that he'd already left. She lay on her back, the sheets wrapped around her naked body, thinking of the night before. She was glad she had been bold and went for what she wanted, for it had been a pleasurable night and not much sleep was had. She had never stayed the night with him before, it was a first to fall asleep beside each other. She hoped it would be the start of many more firsts. She later found Henry and her daddy huddled over plans for the barns outside, she was going to join them when she spotted Oskar heading towards the house carrying fresh eggs.

"Oskar, do you need any help?" she asked, sprinting towards him.

"No thank you," he said, trying to avoid Grace's arm as she linked it through his.

"You're avoiding me," she said bluntly.

"I am doing no such thing."

"Yes, you are, Oskar, please don't lie to me. Is it because of Henry?"

Oskar stopped, pulling himself free of her grip. "Do you love him?"

He looked as though his own question was too painful to say and Grace felt pity for the man. He was good looking, that went without saying but he was more like a cute puppy rather than the great stallion that Henry was. "Yes," she admitted.

"Does he love you?"

Grace looked over at Henry deep in his work, he had quietly sneaked out without a word that morning leaving her alone in his bed. "Yes, he does," she said as confidently as possible.

"And you are happy?" Oskar asked.

"Very much so."

"If you are happy, then I am happy too."

Oskar hurried away before Grace could say more, she watched him walk the steps to the main house with care before picking up the pace once more. Turning back to Henry she decided to leave him and her daddy to it and headed to town to post a letter to Cambridge University to inform them that she would not be returning in September.

Chapter Twenty-Nine

December 1970

It was Christmas Eve and Henry's dad, Walter, and his wife, Gloria, were arriving in Ireland to spend their first Christmas with them as one family. They were her baby's family, and she couldn't wait to meet them, although she was a little nervous too. Her small bump was showing now, much to her delight. Henry would be arriving with them; he had been spending two weeks of every month with her and two in Epsom attending to work. He had been amazing; attending midwife appointments and his knowledge and understanding of her pregnancy was impressive. He had really done his homework. He knew what was happening to the baby at each stage of development along with what she should expect. Grace had learnt more through Henry than anywhere else. He made sure she wasn't doing anything strenuous and held her hair back when she was sick. She had found that he was a very caring person, and she was falling more in love with him each day. She could feel their relationship changing the more time they spent together, he spoke to her more, and she even managed to make him laugh a few times. The wall he had built up was slowly coming down. He wasn't chasing her into bed or trying to sneak her away for her attention, but they did share a bed. After they made love, he would cradle her in his arms giving her butterflies as she thought of his growing love. He met her closest friends who all found him to be a true gentleman, he had placed his hand on her leg all evening and they walked home hand in hand.

In preparation for meeting the family, Grace had wanted to know more about Henry and his childhood. She had learnt that he grew up in a small minor's village in Durham. It was a quiet village, and nothing much ever happened nor was there much to do, he had taken up boxing as a sport and an old gentleman who lived down the road taught him how to garden. Henry had been taught how to be a carpenter by his dad when he left school, joining Walter and Sons. After the tragedy of losing their loved ones, they put their heart and souls into the business and expanded it from a small village shop building furniture to a large warehouse outside London delivering every part of a renovation from start to finish with hopes to expand even further by opening more warehouses across the country.

Grace and Mr O'Connell greeted their guests as they arrived in the entrance hall. All nerves disappeared the moment Walter gave her a hug, he was cold from the winter air, but his embrace felt warm.

"Lovely to meet you Pet," he beamed.

Gloria was close behind him. "Henry never mentioned how beautiful his girl was," she exclaimed, bringing her in for a hug. *His girl.* Grace grinned. "Honestly, this is a real pleasure, I have never met a girlfriend of his before."

Girlfriend. Grace looked over to Henry who was quietly pointing over to the barns, both their dads hanging off his every word.

"Oi!" Gloria called. "We didn't come all this way to start talking about work. Walter, love, can you get the gifts out the car."

"Oh, you didn't have to bring gifts." Grace liked Gloria instantly, she was bold. Her grey hair was long, tied in a tartan head scarf. Long beaded earrings hung off her ears and she wore cowboy boots with a red woollen jumper dress.

"We have a new baby to celebrate, a new family. I have gifts for everyone!"

"Well, I hope everyone is hungry," Mr O'Connell said. "As I may have gone a little overboard with the food."

"Whatever we don't eat now we will eat in the morning," Gloria stated, as she stepped into the dining hall with Mr O'Connell.

Henry who was still wrapped in a black heavy coat, gave Grace a peck on the cheek. "Hi."

"Hi," she replied. "Oh, you best help your dad."

Walter was trying to juggle carrying a heap of presents up the icy steps. They really had gone all out, Grace thought. Everyone had. The Hollisters with their visit and gifts, her daddy with his hosting and slaving away in the kitchen all day. Her baby already had a mountain of love waiting.

Over dinner Walter couldn't seem to contain his excitement over the new baby. The more wine he drank the more he almost teared up at the thought of becoming a grandad and he and Gloria had lots of plans of places to take, in their words, the *bairn*.

"We will babysit anytime you want," Gloria offered. "And you Mr O'Connell are welcome to stay with us at any time as well."

"Oh, Gloria we can take the bairn to that park we drive past with the outdoor pool, the one near that new housing estate."

"We will, and we'll go to Chessington Zoo."

"And the beach."

"And the cinema."

Grace caught her daddy chuckling as he took a mouthful of quiche Lorraine.

"So, when is the wedding?" Gloria asked casually.

Beside her Grace heard Henry, who had been silent up till then, almost choke.

"There are no plans to marry, Gloria," he said, taking a large gulp of wine.

Gloria and Walter looked annoyed, whereas Grace didn't quite know where to put herself. The atmosphere had turned from charming to awkward rather quickly.

"Lad, it's the right thing to do," Walter quietly said.

"It's the seventies Dad, there is no need to make such rash decisions anymore," Henry sternly said.

"So the young folk might think, but to the majority, traditional family values are still just as important as ever. The bairn needs security, the lass needs security as well."

"And they will have my security, they have this huge house, loving grandparents, I will support Grace financially and visit as often as I can."

"I thought Grace and the little one were moving to Epsom with you." Gloria pointed her fork at Henry as she spoke.

"There is no need to change a good set up that is already in place. This works well, doesn't it?"

Henry directed his question to Grace, who felt a little wounded. She had thought once the baby arrived that he would stop travelling back and forth between County Tyrone and Epsom. She had thought perhaps he would ask her to move in with him where they could bring up the baby together properly. Grace nodded in agreement, avoiding eye contact.

"You're thinking about yourself Lad, if you don't marry Grace, she'll be frowned upon and your own bairn will be looked on as a bastard," Walter chimed in.

"It's true," Mr O'Connell interjected. "I see it all the time, still in this generation. Grace's reputation and treatment does worry me. She's come face to face with it already at the surgery that's why I have a private midwife come to the house instead. Grace came home in tears; they treated her so rudely."

"See, I think you should get married as soon as possible," Gloria said.

"I agree," Walter declared. "You're gonna be a family—why not make it official, to protect them."

"I have a friend in London that I met in university, who went on to become a priest. I could see if I can pull some strings," Mr O'Connell suggested.

Grace said nothing as their parents discussed their marriage plans, they had both been cut out of the conversation as they talked of quick licences and local venues. She dared not look at Henry. She couldn't help but like the idea of marriage, she got butterflies just imagining walking down an aisle all in white towards Henry. She would be his wife, she would belong to him, they would be a true family unit, she would share his name, and united he would fall in love with her. She would have dinner ready for him on the table when he returned from a long day at work, they would have date nights where she would show him how sexy she could be again without a bump, she would keep their house clean, and together they would watch their baby grow, tasting their first foods, hearing their first word, applauding their first steps as two proud parents, and each night she would get to lay beside her husband and have her sweet way with him.

"This is bullshit!" Henry shouted, slamming his glass on the table, and jumping out of his chair. "There is not going to be a wedding."

Henry left the dining room, leaving everyone stunned. Popping Grace's bubble along with it.

"I'll go and see him; you lot carry on," Walter sternly said as he gave a sympathetic smile towards Grace. "Don't worry Pet."

Gloria and her daddy carried on talking about the weather and the journey to Ireland. Grace felt hot under the collar, Henry and Walter had been gone for some time. Henry was furious she told herself. As close as they had seemed to be getting the last four months, he still did not feel the same as she did. He didn't want to live together let alone marry her. She had thought their time together had been pleasurable for them both, obviously not enough for him. Gloria had mentioned that she had never met a girl of Henry's before, perhaps he was a commitment-phobe. Maybe what he needed was right in front of him and he just couldn't see it. Grace excused herself from the table, letting out a large breath once alone in the hallway. The future frightened her. Without Henry's sole commitment was everyone right that she and her baby were doomed. She noticed the drawing room door was ajar and quietly tip toed across the hall for closer inspection. She was aware that eaves dropping was wrong but when it came to Henry, she couldn't help it. She could hear footsteps pacing the wooden floorboards and could just see the back of Walter sat on a plush pink chair.

"Please Son, you know it's the right thing to do," Walter snuffled.

"Dad, man, do you know what you're asking me to do?"

"I know, I just want us to all make sure we can be there, play a part in the bairn's life. You have to understand that."

"I'm thirty-one, Grace is nineteen. We're not kids, no one is going to take the bairn away, you don't have to worry about that."

"It will be good for you too; I worry about you. Since what happened last year when you saw…"

"Don't Dad," Henry said sternly.

"You need to move on, this is the best thing that could happen to you. Grace is a lovely lass; she is young and needs ya, man. You're gonna be a da, for heaven's sake. Give ya bairn the upbringing they deserve. If ya were willing to do it…"

"DAD!" Henry shouted, making Grace jump. "This conversation is over."

"Son, please listen to yourself. I know ya a good man, I'm proud of everything you've done. You've had a shit time since we lost ya mam, but you've always stayed on the straight and narrow. There have been times I thought I might lose you, but in the end, you always did the right thing."

Grace could see Henry now as he stood by the window, looking out. "Look where that got me."

"You have a successful business; you've got your own place…"

"I should have left Durham sooner; I shouldn't have listened to you," Henry interrupted Walter once more.

"I can't turn back the clock Son, I know you blame me for what happened but believe me Henry if you marry Grace, you won't regret it especially when ya meet ya bairn, your flesh and blood. This is your chance of happiness."

"Oh, stop it man! Cut the pretence, this has nothing to do with me and my happiness, this is about you and protecting you from what you lost out on. You were not the victim Dad, she lost so much more."

"I know, but it doesn't mean it hurt any less."

"As I said, you're going to get what you want regardless. You and Gloria will still get to play happy grandparents whether I am married or not."

"You're not thinking straight, Henry. If you don't marry that lass and bring her to Epsom you're going to miss so much. What about if Grace meets someone else, do you want another man bringing up your bairn."

"If he can do a better job than me then why not?" Henry said, shrugging his shoulders. He had turned to face Walter now; Grace could see the side of his face.

Walter shook his head. "I know what you're thinking."

"You have no idea."

"I have a good idea actually and you need to quit it, you need to start again. Wake up, Son. There is someone who wants you in that other room. Make an honourable woman of her."

Grace watched Henry breath in deeply, his veins were visible in his temple. "I'm done with this conversation."

Before Grace had time to move away, Henry opened the drawing room door. She felt ashamed when she met his gaze.

"You know Grace, one day you're going to hear something you wish you didn't."

Henry pushed past her and left the house through the double doors; she could hear the car start-up as he drove away into the night. Walter didn't move from the chair; his shoulders dropped and he stared into space. Grace had overhead so much, yet she couldn't make sense of any of it. Who had they been talking about? What demons did Henry carry? There was so much of Henry's life that she knew nothing about. She may never get to know about it either—she may have just blown it completely.

Grace called it a night, sulking to her bedroom, the conversation she heard played repeatedly. Why was Walter so afraid that he wouldn't get to be a part of her baby's life? What had he lost out on? Why was Henry so unhappy? What had Walter wanted to say when he said Henry had been willing to do something? What happened last year?

Henry's entrance to her bedroom woke her up as he fell into the wardrobe. She sat up and watched him silently as he removed his clothes and folded them into a neat pile. Not without using her dressing table for support. The clock on her bedside stated that it was quarter past three in morning. Henry got into the space beside her, pulling the sheets over his stark-naked body. He smelled like whiskey and cigarettes.

"What do you want from me Grace?" he asked.

Grace looked at his sombre expression. "I don't know."

"Do you want to move to Epsom? Do you want to get married? Would it make you feel better?"

Grace gulped. "All I have is your word that you will be there."

He nodded. "Ask your dad about that priest fella, see what he can do."

Grace watched Henry turn over to his side, sleep ready to capture him. It took a while to take in what he said as her mind went into overdrive, but he had agreed to it. They were going to get married. It wasn't a romantic proposal, far from it but it meant the same. She was going to marry him. She was going to be Mrs Hollister. She put off apologising about listening to Henry's conversation with Walter until the following morning.

"It's fine," Henry grunted, reaching out for the glass of water Grace placed on his bedside table.

"You both sounded pretty upset," Grace added.

"Forget about it."

"You can tell me if you ever want to talk about it," she continued, wrapping a silk robe over her.

"It's nothing honestly."

"Henry, if I'm going to be your wife then shouldn't we begin by being open with each other."

Henry placed his empty glass down, his glare unnerving. "My brother had a daughter. She got taken away by the mother's family and my dad hasn't seen her since."

"I see, that must be upsetting for Walter, and for you. You have a niece somewhere."

"France, she's in France."

"Wow, France, and her mother is she with her too?"

Henry shook his head. "She went to live with other relatives. No one has seen her since." Henry lit a cigarette, there was something about him that Grace found incredibly sexy when he took a drag.

"That's awful. I would never stop your dad from ever seeing our baby."

"I know. Anyways, come on, its Christmas we should be making our way downstairs."

Grace had almost forgotten about the festivities. Her mind was crowded with other thoughts circling around, weaving in and out, bobbing up and down.

"Your dad mentioned something happened to you last year where he thought he was going to lose you."

Henry gave her that glance again, it made her feel like she was intruding.

"Sorry."

"I just fell off the wagon a little, that's all. Too much whiskey. Come on they will all be waiting." Henry briskly got out of bed.

"Wait till we tell them our exciting news." Grace beamed wrapping her arms around his toned torso. She could feel his body stiffen at her touch.

Chapter Thirty

January 1971

Everything after Christmas happened so fast. Mr O'Connell reached out to his friend in London and an Epsom church wedding was booked and paid for before the new year was out. Grace could not contain her excitement although she tried her best to contain it around Henry. The Hollisters stopped in Ireland to see in the new year and everyday seemed to be an excuse to celebrate the upcoming nuptials and the new baby. Grace took Chestnut out as much as she could, although the weather was bitter, she was going to miss her old friend as she left Ireland behind to start her new life with Henry in England. It was more emotional than she first thought, leaving her daddy behind with the car filled with as many possessions as possible to last her until the rest of her things were shipped over.

"I will see you in a few weeks, on your big day," her daddy beamed, his eyes glistening.

She wrapped her arms around his large soft belly. It had the same squidgy feel it always had for as long as she could remember. As they drove out of the estate to head to the ferry dock, the car fell silent. Looking back on when she first met Henry, she knew something deep within her felt a plunge towards him right away, never did she think she would be so lucky as to be his wife-to- be and have his child. It was early days; they were still getting to know each other but they had so much time, especially now they were moving in together. Time together on their own would be what it took for Henry to fall in love with her. He cared about her she knew this for certain otherwise he wouldn't have listened to her and agreed to the marriage, nor would he have visited her every fortnight since he found out she was expecting. She smiled to herself. The future was bright with Henry by her side.

"Grace." Henry shook her gently. "Grace we are here."

Grace slowly opened her eyes, the last thing she remembered was arriving in England. She took in her surroundings, the car was parked outside a cottage, surrounded by plant pots that she imagined would bloom beautifully in the springtime—green fingers she recalled. The drive was large, overlooked by trees at the entrance, beside the property were frosty fields for miles reminding her a little of home. Walter and Gloria were already gone.

"You were out for the count," Henry said opening the driver door, the cold instantly hitting her. "Well, this is home—to you too now—sorry it is nowhere near as big as what you're used to."

"I spent days in the dorms of Cambridge, I am sure this will be grand." She stepped out and breathed in the country air. "This driveway is big enough for a small stable," Grace observed.

"Let's move you in first eh, before we start thinking about horses," he said. Grace was sure she saw a hint of a smile, it made her stomach flutter.

Upon entering the home, the first thing Grace noted was how tidy and minimalistic it was, much like his office at

Walter and Sons. The second thought was how wooden and dark it was, small spots of colour were brought out in the mustard yellow dining chairs and sofa along with the white kitchen tops. It was modern, very much unlike the French antiques that ran through her home in Ireland.

"You hate it?" Henry said scanning her face.

"No! Not at all. It's cosy, its lovely. Can we take a look upstairs?"

"Course."

Upstairs was much brighter; the windows were bare looking straight out to the open fields. Every wall was bright white. Even the bed sheets were plain bright white.

"This is the main bedroom."

The room contained a double bed, two bedside tables, a chest of draws, a single wardrobe and a bookshelf all made from the same dark oak.

"I will make room in one of the bedside tables, I prefer to sleep on the right if it is okay with you to take the left."

"That's fine," Grace said laying her beige leather case on her side of the bed. It was perfect she thought. It was where their bodies would lay next to each other every night.

"I will move my home office into a shed in the back garden so that the bairn can have a nursery, there is a small third bedroom. It is already empty I was thinking perhaps I could build some storage in there for you and a small table, a little walk-in wardrobe."

Grace smiled gratefully, full of glee. "That sounds wonderful Henry, thank you."

"I'll make a start on it as soon as possible; I will give you some time to freshen up and settle in. I will just pop out for some food; I will grab us a Wimpy. What do you fancy?"

"Cheeseburger and fries please with a Lemon Fanta."

"Noted, help yourself to a shower," he called as he proceeded down the stairs, leaving Grace in her new home.

The bathroom was pristine white with black accessories. She looked at her bump in the mirror. "We're home baby. It is me, you, and your daddy now."

Grace envisioned the life they would have in their new home, the birthday parties, the Christmas festivities, Easter dinners, and long summer fun in the garden. They were going to be so happy. Inspecting Henry's bathroom cabinet, she laughed as she saw how everything stood neatly in rows with about a centimetre gap between every bottle or item. She grabbed his aftershave and took a sniff of the small silver lid, *Eau Sauvage by Christian Dior.* The man had taste and he always smelt so good. She took a sniff of another bottle, *Aramis*—it smelt manly but with a hint of nature, it was what Henry had worn the first night they spent together.

Grace had a shower and got into a long emerald silk nylon night dress trimmed with white lace around the top and the edges along the high cut up to her thigh on the one side. She found a hair dryer to dry her long copper hair. She finished off by squirting a little bit of her perfume on her neck before rushing downstairs when she heard Henry return armed with steaming brown paper bags that smelt divine. She welcomed him with a kiss to the lips.

"What was that for?" he said walking past her, placing the takeaway on the table, she followed him and wrapped her arms around his hard body, her green eyes met with his sea blue orbs.

"For standing by me, for everything."

"You're the mother of my child, how could I not?" he said.

"And soon to be your wife," Grace added.

"And soon to be my wife," he repeated in a whisper.

She pulled at Henry's polo top to bring him closer to her, kissing him once more. "I'll make you happy Henry. I promise I will be a good wife."

To her surprise he tenderly, stroked the side of her lightly freckled face. "Do you love me, Grace?" he quietly asked.

"I do, I love you so very much. Since the day I met you, I knew you were the one."

She was too fearful to ask him the question back, too afraid that the response would not be what her heart wanted to hear, however her heart bolted as he placed his soft lips on hers. His hands pulled her closer to him, before becoming tangled in her hair, their lips never parted as he slowly edged her towards the couch.

They fell into a routine with each other for the next two weeks. Henry would go out to work each day, leaving Grace to settle in. She took walks around the local treks, noting the best ones for when she could walk with her little one or when she could bring Chestnut. She had hinted many times to Henry about building a stable for her horse to which he always replied with, "one day". Sometimes she met up with Gloria and her daughter, Polly, and they would go shopping or for coffee. Baby shopping had become a little bit of an obsession amongst the women. Henry joked that they would have to change the baby's outfit three times a day to allow them to get a single use out of them. He began work on the nursery; the first thing he had given himself to do in his list of jobs to prepare for the baby's arrival, every evening and weekend he was up there painting or building furniture. They had gone for beige walls and white furniture; Grace bought some orange floral curtains to brighten the room. Bare windows were not going to work for a baby. Henry thought they were vile, but she was pleased with her purchase and bought a matching rug the following day. Before Henry set to work with the house renovations, he always cooked a home cooked meal. Grace had offered to take over on many occasions, but he insisted and said he found it rather therapeutic. He just wanted her to rest up and relax. Grace felt like their romance was slowly blossoming, they had made love most nights since their first night on the couch. Their Wimpy had got cold by the time they got to eating it, but they were so famished not a crumb was left. He was always gentle with her during their love making, and he always fussed about the baby. Grace was always reassuring him that it was perfectly safe. Every kiss sent electricity through her body; every hug made her feel safe. Every day she felt his heart beat a little more for her. She felt like over Christmas they had a small blimp when the talk of marriage began, but now they were back on track and Grace couldn't have been happier, especially when Henry gave her one of his special foot massages.

The day before the big day, a large van pulled up with Grace's belongings from Ireland.

"Jesus," Henry exclaimed nervously. "What is all this, I thought it was just clothes being delivered?"

"I think it is just my clothes," Grace replied with a huge grin on her face, she loved how worried he looked. "I have a selection for each season."

As Henry and the delivery guy carried the last two boxes into the living room, even Grace began to worry that there would not be enough room to store everything.

"This is ridiculous, there are fifteen boxes!"

"What can I say, I love clothes. I will go through them on Monday, put the things I wish to keep up in the box room and the rest can go to charity or I will ask Pol if she wants to take a look at them, plan?"

"Okay," Henry said, looking around the piled boxes in disbelief.

"Now though, we must get a move on. It is my hen night after all."

Grace was going to be spending the night at Walter and Gloria's for a girls night before the big day. Her daddy was due to arrive there today, he had hoped to have a drink with Henry and Walter, but Henry had chosen to spend the night before their nuptials alone.

"Did you know Gloria has given birth five times naturally, not even with gas, at home. She has been giving me breathing tips," Grace mentioned as they drove over to his dad's house. "She said I should pant, like this." Grace demonstrated, making Henry laugh. "I was thinking, do you want to be there? At the birth. I would like you to be if you feel alright with it. You don't have to look down there or anything. That will most likely be traumatising for you."

"I'll be there," he said not removing his eye from the road.

She placed her hand on his leg. "Thank you, I don't think I can do it without you otherwise."

"Oh, believe me when baby wants to come, they will come whether you're ready or not."

"We don't really have that much to go now, do we?" she said stroking her erupting bump. "I can't wait to meet them; I was thinking for a boy we could call him Damon or Danny."

"Not Danny, that is horrific!" Henry almost yelled.

"Alright, my goodness. What did that name ever do to you. Damon then?"

"Maybe."

"For a girl I like Meredith or even Sarah. My favourite doll was called Sarah." Henry did not state his opinion so Grace carried on talking. "Can you believe tomorrow we are getting married?"

Unlike any wedding she had ever known, they were getting married on a Sunday. It was the only date available at such short notice and before the baby was due. Henry said her daddy must have paid the church extremely well to get them to agree to such arrangements. They were going to have a small reception at Walter's after the ceremony. Gloria had given her full power to decorate her home however she liked. The last time she checked it had looked more like a florist than a home. Polly was going to do her hair and makeup, and her dress was already hanging up on Polly's wardrobe for safe keeping away from Henry.

"Are you sure this is what you want?" he asked as they pulled up outside the house. "To marry me, it isn't too late if you're not sure."

"I couldn't be surer. I want to marry you, Henry. Not just for security but because I want to be your wife."

Henry nodded. "I just hope I'm good enough for you."

Grace held onto Henry's hand and gripped it tight. "Just keep doing what you're doing. What are you going to do tonight then? Daddy and Walter are probably drinking beer as we speak on your behalf, you still not tempted to join them?"

"I'm going to head to the office, just want to finalise a few things and then probably have an early night."

"You're a workaholic Henry. You are going to be there all night, I know it. Make sure you get some sleep."

Gloria and Polly appeared at Grace's window bearing a bottle of champagne. "Come on, leave him alone now!" Gloria shouted.

"I think that is my cue to leave." Grace laughed, sharing a quick parting kiss.

The kitchen was a woman only zone, Walter and her daddy were banished elsewhere. Polly had pulled out a white veil from when she had her first holy communion, the child's garment was sat quite snug on Grace's head.

Gloria's neighbour Ruth had popped round, she looked sweet in her floral apron and hair net, but when she opened her mouth the sweetness evaporated."You're a lucky girl, that Henry is a gorgeous fucker! If I were younger, I would sit on that no questions asked! God he must look good naked."

Ruth went on to tell tales of the days back in the war when for a girl in her forties with two marriages already under her belt who looked good for her age, had a pick of men at her feet. "Those were the days."

"Weren't we at war?" Polly asked, pouring herself another glass of champagne.

"I don't mean the war was the good days, just the feeling of freedom for us woman, to go out and let our hair down without judgement. Everyone wanted to have a good time while they could, while they were alive. They fell in love hard, partied like it was for the last time, made love like it could save us, and we worked jobs we had never been allowed to do before, and you know what we were fucking good."

Gloria rolled her eyes and Grace jumped a little in her chair, resulting in all eyes on her.

Grace beamed. "I felt a kick."

"The first one?" Gloria asked.

"I've felt loads before but never that strong—" Grace gasped again. "Quick."

Grace grabbed Gloria's hand and placed it on her stomach and together they waited for the next kick. The room fell silent, all the women were leant over the table waiting for the unborn baby to make their next move. They didn't have them waiting too long as the next movement caused an eruption of excitement.

"I'm sorry but I have to break the rules—WALTER! WALTER GET IN HERE!" Gloria screamed.

"WHAT?" Walter shouted from the living room.

"GET IN HERE BOTH OF YOU!"

The two men came into the kitchen each carrying a bottle of Tennant. Their faces were flushed, and they hobbled over to the group of women.

"What is it? Thought we were banned," Walter said, leaning on the back of Gloria's chairs.

"We've decided that you're the stripper for tonight," Ruth teased.

"Yuck!" Polly said sticking two fingers into her mouth.

"It's the baby, we can feel kicking," Gloria said.

"Here, give me your hand." Grace placed Walter's hand on her stomach and watched his face change as he felt his grandchild.

"That's lovely Pet," he said, rubbing his eyes.

"You're a soft git," Mr O'Connell said, thumping Walter on the back.

"I canna help it."

As Grace watched her soon to be father-in-law cry, she felt sorry for him. Walter had lost his first grandchild; the feeling was obviously still raw. He put his arm around Gloria who kissed his hand before clutching it.

"You're going to be a great grandad, Walter. You both are," Grace said looking at her own dad. "This baby is going to be incredibly lucky."

"I second that," said Gloria.

"Are you sure about this Darling?" Grace's daddy asked, as the car pulled up outside the church.

"Yes, I do wish everyone would stop asking me that. I love Henry, we are starting a family together," Grace sulked, her hands were wrapped around a bouquet of red roses and white gardenias. She had gone for a straight white bohemian dress with a chiffon floor length skirt and off the shoulder straps. It felt tighter than the last time she tried it on. Her hair lay straight topped with a ring of white gardenias for decoration.

"I just want you to be sure that is all."

"I am, I promise."

"Let's get you in there then," he said, placing a gentle kiss onto her forehead.

With her daddy tightly by her side Grace made her way down the aisle to Henry. It was a small stone church, with only a few family members. Polly and her siblings joined Gloria; they couldn't take their eyes away from the young bride. Walter, who was Henry's best man, gave Grace a look that made her anxious, he could not look her in the eye as she got closer to her destination beside Henry. To her great sadness he had yet to look at his bride. She had walked towards the back of him the entire time. His very posture made her concerned. His head was bowed down, shoulders slumped, hands chained together, and legs slightly apart. As she reached her fiancé, she kissed her daddy on the cheek as she passed him her bouquet. Mr O'Connell grabbed her now shaking hands and stared at his daughter, his face matching her own.

"It's not too late to change your mind," he whispered.

Grace gulped; she didn't have to marry Henry, but without him she'd be alone—a single mother. But also, she really did love him and was desperate for him to love her back. She had started to believe, before today, that he was falling for her; perhaps it was just nerves. Marriage is a big commitment. Whatever it was that was running through Henry's mind, she could not read him. He had yet to look at her even when she did make the decision to leave her daddy and stand by his side. The priest began to say words she could not hear, for her mind was buzzing with questions and loud thoughts, she stared at Henry. He looked almost angry, whatever for she tried to think. Grace tried to reach out for his hand, to be able to signal to him that she was there, and everything would be alright, but his clench was too hard and with no give she had no chance of claiming it. Tears brimmed her eyes, not tears of a bride's joy but tears of despair. Henry could not bear to even look at her, all the effort Polly had put in doing her makeup and hair had all been in vain, as was the dress she found so difficult to find because of the growing baby bump. It was their wedding, and he could not even have the decency to glance at her. Panic rose higher when they had to face each other to repeat vows that were meant to be of great importance, the words that were what was binding them together in a lifelong union. His gaze fell past her face to a place beyond, his eyes were red rimmed and blotchy. She needed a sign, a smile, a touch any kind of reassurance to let her know that things were going to be alright, and that possibly Henry had a reasonable explanation for his behaviour, but none came. They said their vows as though they were forced at gun point. Henry's tone was sorrowful, her own must have reflected the pain her heart felt. As the silver metal ring ran along her finger, the small brush of Henry's fingers tore through her body. He made her weak, he made her long for him even when she received nothing back, even when he was destroying what was meant to be the best day of her life, she still desperately wanted his love.

"You may now kiss the bride," the priest said.

Henry swiftly kissed her cheek, missing her mouth completely. The church clapped in chorus, Grace didn't dare look at her guests, she felt mortified. They must have all seen that the groom couldn't bear her. Had she mistaken their growing bond? Had she imagined it? Had it all just been in her head.

She was now Mrs Hollister.

Yet she felt nothing like it.

Chapter Thirty-One

March 1978

Grace crept into the house as quietly as she could hoping to not make too much noise, but she bumped into everything. It was as though it was all jumping out at her just to fuck her off. She had really over done it this time, even she could admit that. The sick that was stuck to her hair was evidence alone, but she would do it again, she always did. Grace spotted Sarah's school bag propped up ready for school at the end of the sofa and was filled with guilt. Her small black shoes sat by the door and her navy ruffle coat hung up on a peg halfway up the wall so she could reach it. Henry would no doubt have her packed lunch neatly ready in the fridge alongside a carton of apple juice. Turning away from the small items, Grace crawled on her hands and knees up the stairs. Sarah's bedroom door was firmly shut tight, it always was at night, a red light glowing beneath. She imagined her daughter, peacefully sleeping, her arms tight around a soft brown bunny whose ears really were the floppiest, dressed in a pink floral dress. A gift from her Irish grand pops when he first met her. Sarah Rufina Hollister had been born on the 27th of April, weighing seven pounds and nine ounces. She instantly stole both her parent's hearts. At seven years old she looked like a mini-Grace with her shoulder length red hair and freckles. She worried that was all her daughter had inherited from her as the blue eyes, her tidiness, and her quietness she definitely inherited from her dad. As much as she craved to see her sweet girl, she swayed against the idea. Sarah didn't need to see her mum like that. That is what she called her—Mum. It used to Mama, then when she began school it was Mummy, just like the local children, before she shortened it to Mum. Grace recalled the first day she heard it, they were on an Easter egg hunt on Easter Sunday, Sarah was almost four when she handed her wicker basket over to her and said, "Can you hold these, Mum?" Mum. It sounded so grown up, she called her own dad, Daddy still at the age of twenty-six. It had hurt her, for she would never be Mummy again, nor hear the words come from her daughter so sincerely.

Grace entered her own bedroom. Under the white plain sheets, her husband lay sleeping on his side, his back towards her. She didn't have the energy to get the sick out of her hair or change her clothes, instead Grace collapsed on top of her neat bedsheets, the hospital corners still tucked in. As her head hit the pillow, the bedroom began to spin until sleep caught her and kept her until Sarah stood by her bed in the early hours of the morning.

"I'm going to school now Mum," she said.

Grace forced a heavy eyelid to open a little. Sarah was fully dressed in her uniform. Her hair was in a perfect ponytail finished off with a blue bow matching the same royal blue of her cardigan.

"Sarah, we have to go!" Henry called up the stairs.

Sarah stepped closer to Grace and kissed her cheek. "I have to go."

Grace thought she saw her daughter's nose wrinkle. She tried to reach out to grab Sarah, but she had already stepped away from her. Grace watched her leave before closing her eyes again unable to deal with the new day just yet.

By teatime Grace had herself looking presentable for her family's return. She had soaked in a long hot bath and washed her hair until it was silky and shiny once more. With the sick long washed away, Grace tied half of it up in a little ponytail with the rest of it flowing down her back. She was dressed in a forest green V-neck wrap dress. She felt too sick to cook, just brushing her teeth had made her gag, so instead she made up an assortment of sandwiches and filled small snack bowls with crisps and fruit.

"You're back," Grace said in a sunny tone.

Sarah and Henry removed their shoes at the door eyeing up the table almost suspiciously.

"I would have cooked," Henry said, hanging up his coat.

"It's fine," Grace said, waiting for her loved ones to join her at the dining table. Sarah came over first, Grace opened her arms for an embrace, aching to feel her arms fill. "Have you had a good day?"

Sarah nodded taking a seat.

"Will you sit with us tonight?" Grace asked Henry.

"Sorry, I'll grab something later."

It was rare for Henry to sit with them to eat, most evenings he took himself to his shed, where he told them he had work to do, but Grace knew all he was doing was drinking whiskey and listening to depressing music such as *Ebb Tide* by The Righteous Brothers or *I Can't Stop Loving You* by Ray Charles. Grace watched Henry leave through the back door before turning her attention to Sarah.

"So, what did you do today?" she asked, pouring a glass of orange juice, and a large glass of wine for herself along with two paracetamol. As they tucked into the food, Sarah told Grace how she got full marks in her spelling test and won a Headteacher Award during school assembly.

"That is fantastic! Seeing as your dad is busy tonight with work, why don't we snuggle up on the couch, see if there is anything good on TV."

"I'm going to Grandad Walter's tonight, remember?" Sarah said, wiping orange juice from her lips with kitchen roll.

"Oh yeah, I forgot." Grace gave a little laugh hiding the sadness that her plans with her daughter were ruined.

"That is okay, Dad dropped off my things this morning before school. I'm staying all weekend; Auntie Polly is going to be there tomorrow with the new baby. I can't wait to see baby Evie; Freddie is so upset that he has a baby sister, he wanted a brother." Grace smiled as her daughter spoke. "What will you do this weekend?"

"Oh, I don't know. I will just wait for my darling to come home."

"Mum why don't you and Dad see what is on TV. That would be nice."

"Hmm, that would be nice."

Saying bye to her daughter, Grace made herself scarce upstairs when Walter arrived to pick her up. They were not on great terms. A few months previously, when collecting Sarah from his house, she was incredibly tired and crashed the car into a streetlamp. Sarah was in the car with her and was crying from the shock; she was not hurt but nonetheless it didn't stop Walter from erupting in her face full of hot rage. He told her that she had to grow up and be more responsible. Grace was mortified as people emerged from their homes to see what all the commotion was. She would have never intentionally put her daughter in harm's way. That didn't matter to anyone else though. Gloria took Sarah into the house, leaving Grace to wait for Henry to arrive. Unlike Walter, Henry waited until they were alone before he told her how he felt.

"How could you be so reckless?" Sarah was tucked away in bed and after what had felt like hours of silence, her husband finally spoke.

"It was an accident, Henry. I didn't see it."

"It was a fucking lamp post not a pigeon, Grace. You had Sarah with you. You should have let me pick her up if you knew you couldn't concentrate."

"I could concentrate." She hadn't told him that she was aching for sleep.

"Don't lie to me, you probably haven't yet recovered from that three-day bender! You're a mother for Christ's sake be more responsible for once in your God damn life."

"Responsible! Like you, you mean drowning your sorrows every night in your fucking wooden shed!"

Henry had laughed, making her more frustrated. "I may allow myself a drink privately at the end of the day, but I will never allow myself to not be able to function and therefore be unable to take care of my daughter's needs. That is the difference between me and you, Grace, I'm not selfish like you."

"I'm irresponsible and selfish now, well at least I have feelings and emotions. I'm not some hard empty shell that walks around emotionless and serious every day of their life. In the same routine, putting everything back in the exact same place, living life in black and white."

"You can leave your car keys on the table; I'm going to bed."

Henry was clearing away tea when Grace returned downstairs.

"I would have done that."

"It's fine," he said, throwing her empty bottle of wine in the bin with a clash.

She lay down on the couch and observed her husband as he pottered around the kitchen. His braces sat snug on his shoulders; his shirt rolled up at the elbows. He was a good-looking man in his late thirties, grey whispers of hair now outnumbered the brown locks, wrinkles danced across his forehead and around his eyes. His hands got to work on the dishes, the very hands she craved to touch her bare skin like they once did. After they had Sarah, she felt like they had made a breakthrough from their silent awkward start to married life, they were bursting with joy and Henry thanked her every day for their daughter. They appeared smitten, he was loving and kind and when he touched her, she could have exploded, but the bubble didn't take flight for too long before it popped, and he had never been so loving again. Grace could count on her fingers the amount of times Henry had made love to her during their seven years of marriage and on most of those occasions it was purely down to alcohol.

"Should we do something tonight, with Sarah gone for the weekend?" Grace asked.

"Can't I'm afraid, got a ton of work to attack. Sorry maybe another time." Henry dried his hands and took off back to his hideout. Grace mindlessly sat in front of the TV, with a bottle of gin to herself. The lonely night disappearing before her eyes with each sip.

Chapter Thirty-Two

April 1978

Grace was sat in the corner of the pub when Henry arrived, his bed hair stood on end and the small hand of their daughter clutched his left hand, her body stood as close as possible to her protector in the grubby loud room she found herself in, in the middle of the night. Tim, the bar owner, gave Henry a sympathetic look as he spotted him, shrugging his shoulders behind the bar.

"Didn't know what else to do fella."

"It's fine, Tim."

"Sorry little one," he said to Sarah. "Do me a favour and make sure your mum goes to bed when she gets in."

Sarah nodded, her eyes widening as she spotted Grace.

"Don't look at me like that Darling, it doesn't hurt as much as it looks."

Grace hadn't looked at her face herself but was aware that her lips were bleeding as was her head where the crazy bitch had clawed her with her talons. Henry walked out with Sarah without a word, Grace followed obediently giving Tim the middle finger on her way out. The journey home was excruciatingly painful, the silence cut deeper than her wounds.

"Henry, I'm sorry."

Henry held his hand up to shut her up, his fists were white as he clutched the steering wheel. She had done it again, she thought to herself looking mindlessly out the window, rain began to attack the windows, she could see Sarah sat in the back of the car through the mirror. She looked exhausted. She had been dragged out of her warm bed because of her.

Henry's first thought was to get Sarah back to bed when they returned home. Grace sat herself at the dining table, listening to the muffled voices of her husband and Sarah above her head. He was probably comforting her—comforting her for the mistakes that Grace herself had made.

"Good night Darling," she heard Henry say on the landing, followed by heavy footsteps down the staircase. He hesitated when he reached the ground floor clocking her at the table.

"You can't keep doing this Grace."

"I know, I'm so sorry."

"It's not me you should be apologising to. It's not the first time I've had to get her up because you're too drunk to even stand or you've got yourself into some hideous fight."

Ashamed, Grace said nothing. Henry fetched the first aid box out of the kitchen. Her tears stung as they drenched her wounds.

Quietly he tended to her cuts, gently washing them away with antiseptic.

He frowned as he concentrated. "She got you good."

"I didn't do what she accused me of Henry, I wasn't trying it on with her boyfriend. I borrowed his lighter and we just got talking. Nothing more I swear." Grace placed her hand on Henry's knee. "I only ever want you. I know I disappoint you. Both of you. I am no better than Linda. At least she had the decency to leave, I never could walk away from Sarah though. I love her so much." Grace was an ugly crier but couldn't fight the tears from flowing. "I get lost sometimes Henry, I feel so alone and then I make awful choices. I don't mean to hurt any of you. I just—I have no control anymore."

"Come here." Henry pulled Grace closer to him allowing her to rest her head on his shoulder whilst he stroked her hair.

Grace could feel the warmth of his body, the skin of his neck close enough for her to give him a kiss. She could see a hint of chest hair peeking from his shirt, carefully undoing another button she exposed more to her delight. She could feel his breath intake deepen.

"Could you love me tonight?" she whispered in his ear.

Henry pulled away from her giving her no choice but to sit back up. He took her hand and together they stood up on their feet, with a gentle nudge Grace was pushed up against the dining table. Henry's hands searched for the loop to unfasten her trousers.

"Is this what you want?" he murmured.

Grace nodded and Henry's kiss delicately covered her neck. Aroused she could not wait for more.

Grace gathered their clothes as Henry poured two glasses of water for bed. Despite the hour he still stopped to sort the clothes into piles of darks and lights before jumping into bed, giving Grace a peck on the cheek before rolling over to his side. Staring at his back, Grace felt a mixture of emotions, she would have liked to have had his arms wrapped around her through the night, like lovers did until they got hot and sweaty, but she was aware that she'd already received more than enough from Henry Hollister for one night and to ask for more would be pushing it. She had to get better she told herself, for Sarah and Henry's love. Perhaps it wasn't too late to gain his heart.

The following day Henry returned home in a large white van rather than his black convertible. Sarah looked excited in the front seat. Grace greeted them outside, luckily, she had managed to get herself dressed. The smoke of the pub still sat in her hair.

"What's all this?" she asked.

"It's for you, Mum," Sarah said, as Grace helped her out of the high vehicle.

"For me?"

Henry came out the van with a smirk on his face. "I had an idea today. Come here."

Grace and Sarah followed Henry to the back of the van where he opened the doors to reveal piles of wood stacked from floor to ceiling.

"Wood?"

"I knew a girl once, who wished for nothing more than a stable for her horse. Thought maybe it was time to grant that wish."

"Are you serious? You're going to build a stable?" Grace exclaimed, with the fleeting thought that she had wished for far more than just a stable, she had wished to be his. Yet the excitement was real. "We could bring Chestnut!"

"And Dad said we can get me a pony," Sarah squealed, jumping up and down. She was already a fairly confident horse rider from their trips to Ireland, a trait of hers she had managed to pass on.

"I thought it would be good for the two of you to go out together, have some girl time." Henry smiled. "Sarah, why don't you go in and put your school things away. Me and Mum will only be a few minutes."

Sarah almost skipped into the house. "I'm going to draw a picture of me and Mum's new stable!" she called back, making Grace's heart melt.

"You're a good mum, Grace," Henry said once Sarah was out of ear shot. "You need to control this drinking though; you can't keep doing what you are because you might lose her, and I won't be able to fix that. You need to get yourself into a routine, if you feel the urge to get a drink, get on the horse."

Grace nodded, the smile never leaving her face. "Thank you, Henry. I promise I am going to sort myself out." She wrapped her arms around his neck and was delighted to feel his arms wrap around her waist.

"I will also try to be more present," he declared.

The household was in a horse bubble all evening. The dining table was covered in paper, showing the horse drawings the three of them had done. Henry's horse had the girls laughing it was so terrible.

"It looks like a big cat with a wig on," Sarah giggled.

"So, I may not be Van Gogh but at least mine is the right colour, look at Mum's."

"Mine is a unicorn, I will have you know. So, the bright pink is a reasonable colour."

Grace took on the duty of tucking Sarah into bed, she had requested the story *Black Beauty*. It had always been one of Grace's favourites growing up, so much so that her daddy could recite it. As they both snuggled under the pink gingham bed sheets Grace began to read, her mind was going into overdrive with the excitement of bringing Chestnut to Epsom. She would be able to ride him on the treks she used to walk Sarah when she was a baby, her pram jumping up and down on the uneven ground.

"We are going to go on so many adventures," Grace merrily said, putting the book down. "We can pack a picnic and stay out in the sun."

"We can pack apples and carrots for the horses."

"Yes!"

"Can you carry on with the story now Mum."

"Of course."

They would need to buy a picnic blanket, Grace thought as she read on. Maybe they could find a river to dip their feet in and make jewellery out of flowers.

"You will need to decide which colour horse you want and pick a special name. Grand Pops will know where to get you the best pony. We should call him tomorrow."

Sarah nodded.

"Then we will have to go into town and get all the equipment for the stables and for us. We could get matching helmets!"

Sarah let out a long yawn. "Can we read the rest tomorrow, I'm sleepy."

"Of course, good night my Darling. Sweet dreams."

Placing a kiss on Sarah's cheek, Grace tucked the blankets in and closed the door firmly behind her.

Something Henry had insisted on—to keep the noise out he had said but Grace knew really it was to protect Sarah from her.

"She settle okay?" Henry asked from the leather chair, a hardback book laid out on his knee.

"Yes, she was very tired after all the excitement of the horses. It really is going to be so wonderful," Grace sighed in joy collapsing on the couch, her legs dangled at the bottom. Henry returned to his book; head bowed in concentration wearing his new reading glasses. They made him look older she observed. They were getting older, each day. Yet they still had so many years ahead of them that could only get better in time. "What are you reading?"

"*The Mayor of Casterbridge*."

"Ah, Thomas Hardy. I prefer *Far from the Madding Crowd.*"

"Perhaps you should take up reading again then."

"You know what, I might. Right now, though, I am too hyped. We should celebrate!"

"Celebrate?"

"Yes!" Grace exclaimed, heading over to the drinks trolley. It had been filled so exotically when she first moved in. Nowadays Henry kept his own stash in the shed, leaving the trolley almost bare as whatever she filled it with never lasted, there was a bottle of red wine left however today to her glee. "We should celebrate the stables, the horses, the memories that will come from it, the changes to our family."

"Grace," Henry said sternly. "That is not a good idea. Why don't you fill yourself a nice bath and I will make us a hot chocolate."

"Come on Henry, one glass won't do any harm. We can both have one. It will be my last one, then no more I promise."

"It won't be the last one, if you open that bottle, it will become your last bottle instead, just leave it."

"I'm just so happy Henry."

"Which I am glad to hear. You don't need the wine though, Grace."

"Oh, come on, don't be a bore!" she said, irritated.

"Think of what's more important, Sarah or that wine."

"That's not fair!"

"Is it not, what about the promise you made to me only today? Pick Grace."

"It's just one glass, your being irrational. You drink whiskey all the time."

"This isn't about me."

"Course it isn't. It's about me, it is always about me."

"It's all about change. I'm here now aren't I, with no more than a glass of water by my side."

"I just want one glass of God damn wine, why are you making me feel so bad about it?"

"Because you don't know how to have one glass of wine!" Henry yelled.

"Let me show you then!"

"No!"

"Agghh," angrily Grace threw the bottle across the room narrowly missing Henry's head, his quick reflex managed to duck before it came down smashing onto the floor instead. Blood like liquid spilled out across the clean wooden floorboards, seeping through the gaps. Green shards of glass found its self-scatter across the room. Grace collapsed onto the rug; her joy turned to sorrow.

"You need help," Henry said coldly, his face pale.

"This is all your fault, you made me like this," she said tearfully.

"We both knew we were no fairy tale; I'm going to fill you a bath."

The bath felt soothing. The hot water infused with lavender salts calmed her rapid beating pulse. She had just wanted one glass, but she knew in her heart that Henry was right, one glass was never enough. Now she had nothing left, unless she went to the pub. The longer she stopped in the bath tub the later the evening got, and Tim would lock up for the night. She was pulled from what she wanted to what she needed, forcing herself to stay under the water until it grew cold, and the palm of her hands and the soles of her feet were like prunes. She could hear Henry clearing away glass as she tiptoed to her walk-in wardrobe. He had stuck to his word and did a beautiful job of turning the small space into a girlie haven. She had a place for everything, dresses, coats, and shirts were hung up, bags, shoes and trousers were neatly placed on shelves and in front of a pink velvet stool stood a small table with all her beauty products on. Grace sat down and stared at herself in the small bronze vanity mirror that once stood on her dressing table back in Ireland. She was in her twenties yet could pass for a woman in her thirties, the bags under her eyes told the tale of numerous late nights, lines of age through her unhealthy lifestyle, and wounds from uncontrollable moments. She tied her long locks into a damp plait and covered her body in moisturiser; a desperate attempt to reclaim her youth. A pastel blue satin camisole shorts set was carefully chosen. Grace did not own anything in cotton or baggy for nightwear, her collection included satin, silk and nylon night dresses and short sets, trimmed with lace and no longer than her knee. Her aim was to always look sexy, never to fall into the everyday housewife look, she wanted there to never be a time that her husband might look at her and see her as someone unattractive. Not by her clothes anyway. She had messed up once more, Henry had only been trying to help, she knew this. It was up to her to make it up to him.

Downstairs Henry was ringing out a cloth, red residue trickled into the white basin. Her rage had been cleaned away leaving only a patch of a red stain on the white wall above the skirting board. Two mugs of steaming hot chocolate sat on the table. Grace hugged Henry from behind, trapping him at the sink. "You're right, I knew we were no fairy tale when we got together. I did think over time you may have grown closer to me. Even learnt to love me."

Henry pulled her arms away with his wet hands. "I care about you; you are Sarah's mum, and she needs you," he said turning to face her.

"And you? Do you need me?"

His lips formed a straight line, his blue eyes stared deeply at her, yet no words were shared. It stung but she could understand why. No one needed someone like her. She was nothing but a burden. She fell into his arms.

"I'm sorry," he whispered.

Chapter Thirty-Three

April 1978

"That was Daddy on the phone, he has just checked in to his hotel. Asked if we could meet him for dinner."

"Sounds good to me," Henry said, taking a swig of water.

It was warm for April, and Henry had been out all morning working on the stables, sweat proceeded to drip from his forehead, which he dried off with a flannel.

"I thought perhaps we could make a night of it; we could get some theatre tickets. They are playing *Annie;* Sarah would enjoy that. I read some good reviews about it in the paper."

"Great, why don't you give them a call see how many tickets are available and ask if we can reserve some. I don't mind paying."

"Thank you, Darling, make sure you take a shower. We are meeting Daddy at five-thirty at The American Eagle Hotel."

"Fuck!" Henry stood up too quickly, knocking his head on a beam he had built to form the frame of the door. "We're not going there!" he called rubbing his head.

"Why not?" Grace asked confused.

"Well, because—well it is expensive."

"Oh Henry, we have been to far pricier places."

"I'm not going there, ring your dad, ask him to book somewhere else."

"Henry, it is a Saturday; it's London. He has already booked it and I've told him we will be there so stop being childish about it. I'm sure Daddy will pay anyway," she said, leaving him to get on.

"Stop fidgeting with your tie, you look fine," Grace told Henry as they walked up the marble steps of the London Hotel. "This does look fancy."

Grace's heels tapped loudly on the black marble floor of the hotel lobby of The American Eagle. The 1920s vibes were felt instantly upon arriving, the gold and black screamed Gatsby. A huge chandelier hung in the centre of the round shaped room, a large mahogany desk stood proudly to the left, two double glass doors were on either side of a vintage elevator on the back wall. Black velvet chairs were positioned facing each other with small mahogany coffee tables with large white flowers in gold vases between them. A huge gold mirror almost the whole length and width of the wall was hung to the right.

They approached the reception desk where a kind looking man greeted them.

"Good evening, welcome to The American Eagle Hotel," he smiled politely.

"Oh my God, Florence," Henry said quietly but loud enough for all to hear.

"Florence?"

"Ah, yes," the gentleman turned to face a large painting hung on the wall behind the desk. "Florence Anderson, the original owner of the hotel."

The painting was of a young woman, in a pale blue long gown, she had a brown curled bob and hazel brown eyes.

"She's pretty," Sarah commented, which Grace had to agree with.

"When Florence's grandson sold the hotel, it was sold on the condition that the portrait stays. So here she stays, continuing to welcome our guests."

"He sold the hotel, whatever for?" Henry asked, a look of concern on his face.

"His family all emigrated to Australia. They grew tired of the London life."

"Australia!" Henry gasped.

The man nodded. "May I take your name please?"

Henry stood gazing dumbstruck at the vintage painting on the wall.

"Hollister," Grace said, taking lead. "Although we have dinner reservations booked by a Mr O'Connell."

The gentleman shot a glare at Henry, before looking at her and back to Henry which she found rather uncomfortable. He cleared his throat as he looked away, scanning a large book. "I detect an accent."

"Yes, I am from the North of England. Durham," Henry said.

"Durham," he smiled.

"Northern Ireland," Grace replied.

"Surrey!" Sarah shouted, to which the man laughed. "Where are you from?" she asked on her tip toes peeking over the top of the reception desk.

"I'm a born and bred Londoner."

He was tall and slim with long fingers—piano fingers Grace noted.

"Mr O'Connell has yet to arrive so please feel free to take a seat in The Albert restaurant through these doors here to the left where you can order a drink, I highly recommend the *Lottie's Lychee Martini,"* he said with a twinkle of the eye, staring at Henry.

"*Lottie's Lychee Martini,*" Henry repeated with a broad smile.

"It was named after Florence's favourite grandchild. If you need anything Mr Hollister, anything at all, please, I am happy to help. My name is Laurence," he said tapping on the small badge that read, *"L. PORTER."* Henry thanked him, taking the hand he had offered for him to shake.

How pretty Florence's granddaughter must have been, Grace thought fleetingly before grabbing Sarah's hand.

"Come on then, let's get seated," she said tugging on Henry's arm.

Henry moved an inch before stopping once more.

"Florence's granddaughter. Did she emigrate to Australia also?"

"No, she moved to Cornwall."

"Cornwall," Henry whispered.

Grace found his newfound fascination with the history and family of the hotel quite amusing.

"She and her children live there happily, not far from the sea."

Henry nodded. "Thank you, Laurence," he replied, and allowed them to finally leave the lobby.

Grace found the martinis to be rather sweet. Henry however consumed many and had chosen to switch his whiskey for the clear drink much to Mr O'Connell's amusement who called it a girl's drink.

"I found the receptionist rather rude," Grace said sipping her sparkling water.

"Manager," her daddy corrected.

"Whatever he is, it doesn't change the fact that he was completely ignorant. He just wanted to talk to Henry. It was as though I wasn't even stood there."

"I thought he was fine," Henry said, tucking into his steak.

"How did you know that painting was of this Florence woman anyways?" she asked, cutting a baby potato.

"Everyone knows about her."

"I've never heard of her before."

"You must be too young," he said.

Grace shot her husband an irritated look. "Have you heard of her before Daddy?"

Mr O'Connell nodded, wiping his lips with an Egyptian cotton napkin. "Years ago, I came here on a business meeting. I never got to meet Florence herself, but I did meet her son, Albert. I first noticed him one evening carrying a young girl in his arms, down the staircase, he was rushing down, and I held the door open for him to the lobby. She was out cold, blood pouring out her head. An ambulance had pulled up just in time outside and off they went."

"Oh my, was she alright?"

"Rumour was she was a member of staff who got intoxicated in one of the rooms with some vodka she stole from the bar. Trashed the room while she was at it, only a young girl as well couldn't have been much older than sixteen or so."

"I imagine she was fired after that ordeal."

Mr O'Connell shook his head. "Albert didn't have it in him, I found him down here at the bar drowning his sorrows. She was his niece; he didn't say too much but you could tell he was in turmoil."

"Poor man, what a way to treat your family."

"You're one to talk," Henry piped up. "Hardly Mother Theresa yourself."

Grace felt her face flush, it was a low blow in front of Sarah she thought. Her daughter was mindlessly not aware of the grown-up conversation as she tucked into her dinner on the promise of a fancy pudding, but it still stung regardless.

"Now, now," Mr O'Connell said.

Henry continued to eat silently; he looked as though he was agitated. They spoke no more around the table about the Anderson family. They could overhear other tables cheerful conversations, the sound of everyone's clattered cutlery amplified. Their table was situated at the back, their backdrop a large oval window overlooking a garden. Grace could see a pretty bandstand on the grounds surrounded by outdoor seating and a pond. The inside of the room was like it was set up for a wedding reception, nothing like what she had, but something she would imagine she could have had, had they not rushed to marry. Great big pampas pieces sat in tall vases as centre pieces on crisp white tablecloths. They sat in gold vintage chairs under a ceiling of a painted night sky lit up by magnificent sparkling chandeliers.

"I can't do this!" Henry dropped his cutlery on the table with a clash, just as he had that Christmas Eve back in

Ireland when talk of marriage first occurred. "I will meet you at the theatre," he said.

"Henry!" Grace called after him as the table watched him charge out of the restaurant ignoring his wife, whose face grew a deep shade of pink.

"Why don't you go and look at those fancy puddings in those glass cases over there, Sarah. Pick something good," Grace's daddy gently said to steer the child away. "What was that about?"

"He hates London, that's all," Grace said, taking another drink of her water wishing it were something far stronger.

"Are you two getting along?"

"Yes, we are fine Daddy, in fact the past few weeks have been really great. He is building us a stable, he is helping me stay on the straight and narrow. I haven't had a drop of alcohol in almost three weeks now, he cares about me Daddy."

"Is that enough?"

"For now. You never know, if I stay good, things might deepen. They almost have before, haven't they? We have Sarah, we are family. Like I said, he just hates London."

"So, what will you do when Sarah grows up and starts her own life. What will hold the two of you together then? I only ask because I care about you Grace. If ever you want to come home the door is always open for you and Sarah."

"We will be fine Daddy, promise."

As the small red-haired child sang on stage wearing rags and danced around barefoot, Sarah was transfixed. As was Henry who was sat on the end of their box seats. He never took his eyes off the stage. Grace had no idea what had happened to put him in such a foul mood, was it really the comment she made about the drunk niece back at the hotel? Did she miss something? Or did he really detest London that much?

Chapter Thirty-Four

August 1978

The long summer days were met with horse riding through the countryside with enough food to keep them fuelled for the day. Grace had been advised to leave her faithful Chestnut in Ireland, he was an old horse now and had never lived anywhere but the manor since he was a pony, nor had he lived without Oakley by his side. The move would depress him, Mr O'Connell advised, so instead two new horses were bought. A small black pony for Sarah and a dark chocolate horse for Grace. Sarah had the grand task of naming them—Sooty and Sweep —after her favourite TV characters. Grace could feel her daughter warm to her with each ride. She was thankful for the open space they lived in and the sweet animals they had adopted. Every day Sarah helped muck out and brush their long manes. It was hard work; Grace had not appreciated the help Oskar had given her with her own horse. The stables not only had become a new home or a place to spend time with Sarah, but it had also become a place Grace could call her own. Henry showed no interest in the wooden house, once Sarah was in bed it was hers, and hers alone. A place of sanctuary at the end of the day. She began to understand why Henry enjoyed escaping to his shed so much. Under a stack of hay Grace kept a stash of wine, which she enjoyed on the warm quiet evenings.

The noise of an engine could be heard as Henry's car rolled into the drive; Grace wasn't afraid of him catching her having a drink as she knew he would head straight inside. She was more in control of her drinking now. She knew when to stop, she knew how one too many would anger Henry as soon as he noticed.

"Grace!" Henry called, Grace almost spilt the white wine over her top as she jumped in fright, hastily putting the bottle in its hiding place and grabbing a yard brush.

"Hi," she said, as naturally as possible.

"I have to go to Edinburgh first thing tomorrow for a few days." Henry had opened up a Walter and Sons in both Edinburgh and Liverpool, much to his delight. It really was starting to expand beyond London. "Will you be okay?"

"Course, me and Sarah will be fine."

"Why don't you go to Ireland for a little bit, see your dad."

"I can't leave the horses Henry, honestly, I will be fine. We will take the horses out and I will plan some trips."

Henry looked deep in thought. "Hmm, okay. You had a good day?"

"Yeah."

"Good, well I'm going to go and pack." Henry hesitated at the front door.

"You sure you're going to be alright."

"I've got this Henry, trust me."

Polly called by the house early in the morning inviting them on a trip to the seaside with her brood. She was married with three children, to a banker whom they all called Mr Banks. He was a chubby fellow but with a heart of gold.

Grace buried her feet in the sand watching Sarah jump over the waves with her cousins, Freddie and Maisie. A plastic fence and a large umbrella kept the mums shielded from the blare of the sun; it was a must with the baby sleeping in her pram.

"How are things?" Polly asked, lounging back in her deck chair, large sunglasses covering her tired eyes. "Feel like I haven't seen you in a while."

"I'm good, yeah," Sarah replied, gazing out to the sea. "How is being a mother of three?"

"Exhausting! Henry mentioned you have also become a mother again, to two strapping horses," she laughed.

"Well, one is Sarah's so that must mean I am now also a granny."

"Oh dear, at such a young age," Polly teased.

"You should come over and bring the children some time. Sooty is only small. They'll love it. I could teach them if you like, Sarah has come on leaps and bounds this summer."

"Maisie would love that she's the brave one out of the older two. Freddie may need some persuading. Have you ever thought of doing something with horses as a profession?"

"Me?"

"Yes, you. You're a natural Grace, I saw you galloping everywhere that spring we went to visit your dad. I felt nervous just watching you. Maybe you could open your own school, teach the kiddies to ride. *Grace's Equestrian!"* Polly called out, lifting her arm up as though imagining the place was before them.

Grace laughed, brushing it off but as she sat on the sofa with her glass of evening wine, she couldn't stop thinking about it.

"Grace, Grace, Grace man! Get up its eleven o'clock."

Grace felt distorted as she hazily lifted her head from the couch cushion. Her feet kicked three empty bottles of wine as she pulled herself upright. Walter was stood at the door looking unimpressed whilst Sarah was sat at the dining table with a sandwich, she'd made herself, accompanied by a glass of milk and a story book. Grace put her head in her hands, the thumping headache was real as the sun blared into the house.

"I was just driving by, thought I would pop in. Good job I did it seems."

"I was just taking a nap," Grace lied.

"Ah ha, Sarah Pet how does a sleepover at Granda Walter and Nana Gloria's sound."

"We have plans, we're going to go to Cambridge or to visit The National History Museum," Grace informed him. "Sarah is looking forward to it." Looking over to her daughter, her eyes were downcast avoiding her mother's gaze. Grace felt betrayed by the young girl.

"Ya look like ya could do with a rest; I'll take Sarah tonight; allow you to have some time to yourself," Walter insisted.

"I'm fine, look I am up now. The horses need taking care of and I bought ingredients to bake a cake, Sarah has picked out all the toppings."

"I'll bring her back tomorrow; you can still bake ya cake then."

"But-"

"I won't be long Mum, you look tired," Sarah said from the table. "I can call you to say good night if you like. It is only one night."

Grace's heart sank, with the pressure against her she agreed. She could still feel the sand between her toes from their lovely time at the beach, Sarah had laughed all day, they built sandcastles and turned Polly into a mermaid by burying her in the sand, decorating her tail together with only the prettiest shells. She was her own worst enemy; she cried as she sat alone in her front room. Sarah had chosen to leave; she had tried so hard yet had failed at the first hurdle. With nothing else to lose, Grace changed into a navy-blue jumpsuit with spaghetti straps accompanied with large earrings and high stilettos. She painted her face then headed to the only place she knew could heal her current heartbreak—Tim's. She knew where she stood there, she knew all the locals, she knew the people she could get free drinks from, the smokers who would give her a cigarette, and the men who wanted her.

Chapter Thirty-Five

August 1978

With no memory of the night before, Grace dragged herself from Sarah's bed where she had crashed out. Sick destroyed the pink rug by her bed. She felt like she'd been hit by a bus. Dragging herself to the phone, she dialled Walter's house phone. After three rings he answered.

"Hi Walter, it's Grace, can I speak to Sarah please?"

"She has just popped out with Gloria."

"What time will you be dropping her back home?" she asked forcing back the tears, the curly cord wrapped between her fingers.

"We will have her back before bedtime, I best let you go, got someone at the door."

"Okay, see you later," she said, as the line cut dead.

Too rough to be productive, Grace pottered around the house not knowing what to do with herself. She felt a pang of guilt every time she caught a glimpse of the stables, she had managed to give them a change of water and some food but the mucking out she couldn't bear, the smell alone sent her puking on her driveway. She took up residence in the back garden, laid out on the grass. They had a beautiful garden, Henry did well to keep it tidy and blooming year after year, he even grew his own vegetables in a small green house beside the huge shed that always remained locked. It had no windows and Grace had only seen inside once or twice when she first moved in. Finding herself thirsty Grace moved to the living room, she poured herself a vodka and lemonade and put a Bee Gees record on helping herself to one of Henry's cigarettes. Laying back on the mustard yellow couch that she had grown to despise.

"Holy fuck!" Henry shouted, running over to the kitchen, waking a startled Grace who must have drifted off.

The rug was enflamed, and the fire was quickly getting bigger. Grace jumped off the couch pushing it away from the flames to stop it from spreading further. Henry threw a pan of water over the rug dying out the embers and leaving behind a black smoky hole.

"Henry," Grace gasped.

"Where is Sarah?" he bellowed.

"Your dad's," she said shamefully, she must have nodded off with the cigarette in her hand she realised foolishly.

Henry placed his fist in his mouth, biting his knuckles. "What the fuck, Grace! What if I hadn't got back in time? You could have burnt the fucking house down—with you in it!"

"I was bored."

"Bored? Then ride your God damn horse for God's sake, read a book, go for a walk! What if Sarah had been here?"

"Well, she wasn't, and this wouldn't have happened if she had been. We were doing fine until your dad came snooping round here sticking his nose where it wasn't wanted!" Grace shouted back.

"He came round because I asked him to check on you, I wanted to trust you Grace, I did, but this terrible inkling told me I couldn't, so I asked him to come round and take Sarah if he thought he ought to, and I was right to do so."

"We were fine! Ask Polly, she invited us out to the seaside, and we had such a great day and I had so much more planned, but he then took her away from me and then I had nothing to do in this fucking house on my own staring at the miserable bare walls!"

"I asked Polly to take you out."

Grace felt the tears hot on her cheeks. "That was you too?"

"I was worried you would spiral, I wanted to keep you occupied, I wanted to prevent this," he angrily said, pointing to the floor.

She had been in control; she had been doing well. Grace cried; she loved them both dearly, yet she was letting them down.

"You need professional help, Grace."

"I just need you and Sarah."

"You have us! Sarah is your amazing daughter who is desperate for you to be normal. I am your husband—I married you; we lay in the same bed every night. I provide for you every day."

"Well, that is not enough! You didn't marry me for love, you married me because I was pregnant. You lay cold next to me every night; you provide for me because you have to. I gave up my career for this family, my whole future, all you did was make room for us in your house!"

"I GAVE UP EVERYTHING FOR THIS!" he bellowed, thumping his chest. "Do you think this was the future I envisioned, my life could be so different right now. So, stop feeling sorry for yourself and grow up! We got married for Sarah, so get a grip and focus on that girl's life."

Grace cried—she cried for her mistakes, she cried for Henry's lack of love, she cried that she was a no better parent to her daughter than Linda had been to her, she cried that she wasn't strong enough to fight her demons and be a better person, she cried because she was frightened that one day she would be completely alone.

"I'm going to pack more things for Sarah and head over to my dad's. He can keep her again tonight; she can't come home to this. Get yourself washed Grace and try not to burn the house down while I'm gone."

Looking at her body in the mirror Grace noticed bruises and grazes on her knee that she had no memory of. Too out of her face, of course. She had dark bags under her red rimmed eyes, her skin was pale despite being in the sun often, and her hair felt like straw. She really was a mess.

Chapter Thirty-Six

January 1979

As Grace carefully applied her red lipstick followed by a thick layer of mascara, she felt the presence of her daughter squeeze onto her stool. Grace was on her way out; she was meeting a guy named Hugo who she had been seeing for a few months. It was casual, Hugo wasn't looking for a serious relationship just sex. He was aware that she was married and didn't seem to care, normally Grace knocked back seducers, but Hugo was different. The ex-serviceman had her hook, line, and sinker the minute they got chatting at Tim's. He was new to the area and like herself, he was in need of some company. She loved his straight talk, knowing where she stood all the time with him. She loved how her body fitted perfectly into his, he was rugged, and the sex was unreal. He made her feel beautiful and he brought her back down to earth.

"Do you have to go out tonight, Mum?" Sarah asked, picking up her lipstick and clumsily putting some on her thin lips. "Me and Dad are having a movie night, we've bought snacks."

"You know I have to work Darling; I will see you tomorrow and you can tell me all about movie night."

"We're watching Charro! You've seen it before," Sarah said, rubbing the makeup off and leaving Grace alone.

When Henry found out about Hugo, they both agreed that he was someone that had to be unknown to Sarah. So, they both told her that she had a job that meant doing night shifts when she had planned to meet up with Hugo. Henry wasn't bothered that she had a lover, he was almost relieved that she had someone. It had been the new underwear and love bites that had given it away. His one rule was that if she got too drunk, she had to stay the night with him. Hugo had his own flat about thirty minutes away from the cottage, he took her out for dinner, bought her flowers, and was always complimenting her, he was a dream. Grace always looked forward to seeing her lover, however, as she headed out, saying goodbye to Henry and Sarah she felt a knot in her stomach. The fire was blazing, they were wrapped together under a blanket, hands deep in popcorn, already waiting for the Saturday night movie to begin on BBC One. A part of her wanted to kick off her heels and join them but her taxi was waiting for her, and she knew if she stayed, she wouldn't be warm and cosy under the knitted blanket, but would instead be on the leather chair, hugging herself. Hugo on the other hand was waiting for her—he wanted her so that was enough to encourage her to leave her family.

Hugo was a lot more lenient with his flat than Henry was, Christmas decorations were still up even though February was a week away. Laundry was often scattered on the bedroom or bathroom floor—sometimes both—and dishes filled the sink. She'd found a woman's earring once but chose to say nothing, putting it in the bin. Hugo was single, he could do what he wanted she would be a hypocrite to complain. Their relationship was what it was, no complications needed. Unfortunately, Hugo was feeling under the weather when she got there. She found him lying on the sofa with a beer and a box of Kleenex.

"I would have asked Tim to give you a call to cancel but I couldn't be bothered to walk down the road, this daft cold has had my bones rattling. It's good to see you though babe, you look sexy as fuck." Grace was wearing all white, from her tailored flares to her low-cut top. "You're a mother, you know how to look after the ill," he added.

Grace couldn't remember the last time Sarah was poorly. Henry would remember. Feeling out of her depth, Grace decided to make Hugo some tomato soup she found in the half empty kitchen, for which he was most grateful.

"I would return the favour Babe, but I don't think I have the strength."

"Oh, it's fine. You're unwell, I understand. Why don't you lay back and let me relax you." Grace placed the empty bowl of soup onto the floor and then proceeded to pull down Hugo's jeans and underpants. "You're excited?"

"Always with you Babe," he said huskily.

Grace licked her lips and got to work pleasuring her sick patient.

Hugo didn't take long to fall asleep after the deed was done. As she lay in the rough and heavy arms that made her feel safe from the world, she couldn't help but think of her family back home. Sarah's arms were small and delicate yet getting bigger by the day, Henry's were warm and gentle. She cried quietly wishing she could be what they needed. Her own self-pity had led to her self-destruction; when if only she had tried harder, she may have got the life she wanted. Perhaps, Henry would have fallen in love with the mother of his child if she had been more nurturing, and available to see to Sarah's needs. Perhaps Sarah would want her more if she wasn't always hungover or too busy hurting herself and those she loved. She let them down over and over and the damage was done, she knew it. Although Sarah asked her to stay, she knew she wouldn't have sat close to her like she did with Henry, she would even go as far as to say it sometimes felt awkward trying to be the mother figure that she should be. Sarah was so used to how she was, that's why when she couldn't attend movie night, she wasn't exactly hurt by it. With Hugo out for the count and the hour still early, Grace tip toed out of the apartment and headed straight to Tim's—her enemy but also her greatest friend.

With her high heels in hand, and the bottom of her trousers brown, speckled in mud, her top not looking much better either with spots of tomato soup splattered on it, Grace made her way home.

Tim's had been quiet for a Saturday night, which meant she could sit at her favourite table perfectly situated a few feet away from the bar, a perfect view of the entrance to see who is heading out for a smoke and not too far to stumble to the toilet. Grace knew just about everyone who went to Tim's. They called her their Irish Beauty, Tim called her his Irish Baby instead, and was always trying to talk to her about her feelings and telt her when he believed she should call it a night. It was annoying yet sweet to know someone cared about her enough to not want her money.

As Grace fought to the open door with her key after what felt like ten attempts, she had come to realise that it was in fact unlocked already, with Henry's keys slotted into the keyhole on the inside. The logs in the fire were still burning hot with a scarlet red glow, but the flames had died out. The room was dark, no lights were on, the TV was off, no music played on the stereo; it was all but silent apart from the odd shuffling sound from the fire.

"Why are you back?" Henry asked from the dark corner of the room.

"Jesus, Mary, and Joseph! Why are you sitting in the dark?" Grace exclaimed, clutching her chest. "You made me jump out my skin."

"Are you okay? Is everything alright with Hugo?" he questioned, ignoring her surprise.

"He's sick," Grace said, stumbling over to where Henry was sat on the leather seat. She fell down to the floor, on top of the new rug at his feet. "If I was the perfect wife and mum, would you love me then?"

Grace could feel his trousers, his indoor slippers were on his feet, but she couldn't make out his face in the dim light.

"You still managed to get drunk though, so you should have stopped there. That is the deal Grace," he replied.

"Henry please, answer my question."

"No."

"No, you won't answer it, or no, you wouldn't love me?"

"The latter," he said softly.

"Why?" she asked, rubbing her face against his knees. "All the men at the bar want me, Hugo can't keep his hands off me. Why am I never good enough for you?" She got to her knees and pushed her way in-between Henry's legs, his face now in view. "Remember when we first met, you couldn't take your hands off me once we were in that B&B, especially in bed. Can you not remember the rush you felt when you wanted me?" Grace grabbed Henry's hands and forced them upon her torso. "You wanted to touch me everywhere."

"Grace," Henry pleaded.

"Touch me like that again, Henry."

"Stop this," Henry said, trying to free his hands from her tight grip.

"Please Henry."

"You're drunk."

"Touch me Henry, like you used to in the beginning."

Henry managed to pull free from her grip and stood up, forcing Grace to sit away from him. "Stop this nonsense!" he shouted.

"Why can't you just love me!" she screamed.

"BECAUSE YOU'RE NOT HER!"

Grace's body felt numb, she suddenly felt stuck to the floor in shock. Her heart began to beat rapidly, her breathing becoming heavy, and her palms grew sweaty, yet her skin had goose bumps. Henry let out one of his annoyed sighs and poured himself a large whisky knocking it back in one.

"Who are you referring to?" Grace gasped in a croaky voice she did not recognise.

Pouring another large whiskey, which again was knocked back in one Henry put down his glass a little too harshly on the glass trolley bar.

"Forget I said anything. It was a long time ago. I'm going to bed," he said, turning away from her and heading towards the staircase.

"Henry, you can't just say that then leave," Grace said, no longer feeling so drunk.

"I suggest you have some water."

"Henry!"

He ignored her, running off upstairs. Grace recalled once believing Henry was a coward, always running from his problems; he made her leave when he found out she was expecting; he left the dinner table several times when he didn't like the topic instead of just saying why he was unhappy; now he didn't want to talk about *her*. Who was she? Who had her husband's heart?

Chapter Thirty-Seven

January 1979

Once the house was empty, with Henry and Sarah out to some unknown place, Grace let out a howl. She cried knowing the man she loved with all her heart would never love her, no matter what she did. It was impossible because he was in love with someone else. Eight years they had been married, and in that time she thought they'd shared moments that felt like real love, but it had probably just been her imagination running wild with her own wishful thinking. Sitting on the edge of her bed, Grace scanned the bedroom that she called theirs, but really it wasn't theirs—it was his. Every part of the room, minus her side of the bed and the small table that came with it, all belonged to Henry. Nothing had an ounce of her touch to it, there were no pictures of them together or pretty bedsheets, it was all Henry. All her belongings had a place in the tiny walk-in wardrobe, that is where she belonged pushed aside to a room no one needed so that she couldn't clutter up the rest of the house. The whole house belonged to Henry, he had not moved her into his home, he had made her nothing more than a tenant because he felt obligated to do so. The more Grace contemplated her position in Henry's life, the more the anger brewed, and she begun taking her anger out on the pristine room. Grace knocked down the books on his shelf, she used all her strength to knock down the chest of draws, neatly folded clothes and colour matching socks sprawled across the floor, she ripped apart feather pillows and smashed his bedside lamp against the wall making a black mark on his boring white walls. She pulled clothes off their rails and the contents of his bedside table onto the floor. Sitting on a heap of clothes, surrounded by the beautiful mess Grace slowly caught her breath and calmed down. Tears still fell upon her cheeks, and she felt hopeless and scared. She had always hoped one day Henry would come to her. She always wished one day, time would make him see that she was the one for him. Amongst the chaos, she spotted a set of keys. Taking them for closer inspection, she realised she recognised some of them as spare keys to the house and the cars but some she did not. Both curiosity and excitement ran through her as she raced down to the lower floor, still dressed in the clothes from the night before. She ran across the frosty grass of her garden and stopped outside the shed. There were four spare keys on the hook and one tiny one. She guessed some belonged to the HQ warehouse; she hoped, however, that one would fit into the lock of Henry's secret hideout that no one, not even Sarah, was allowed to access. Part of her was relieved when the keys she was trying didn't fit. She knew she was trespassing, and Henry would go berserk, but when she found the key that worked, she knew she wanted to go in.

To no surprise it was just as neat and tidy as any other place owned by Henry. It was much larger than it looked on the outside. To the left rows of black files dominated the shelves.

"So, he does actually work in here," she said out loud.

To the back wall was a pine homemade desk with a black leather chair pushed under it. A British map was pinned to the wall above with small red pins marked in various places, *Epsom, Edinburgh, Liverpool, York,* and *Birmingham.* They were all the places that had a Walter and Sons. Other cities were marked in blue pins *Aberdeen, Belfast, Newcastle, Leeds, Cardiff, Kent,* and *Manchester.* His aims perhaps, and a yellow pin—the only one on the board—was on *Cornwall.* Taking her attention away from the map, Grace found Henry's drinks collection beneath a large radio where he played his depressing records. Playing *I Can't Stop Loving You* and helping herself to a bottle of Glenmorangie, Grace sat back in the chair and gazed around the wooden shack with distaste. For years he had hidden away within the timber walls to stay away from her, she admitted to herself taking a big swig straight out the bottle. He would rather be alone at the bottom of the garden than with her, he didn't realise that she was who she was mainly because of him. She had fallen hard for the older man and believed deep down he could see what many before and after had seen, but he never did. She was never enough. She gave him a daughter, she left her home to come to England, she left all her friends behind, and with none of Henry's to meet it was lonely in Epsom, but she did it in the hope that one day he could at least give her a small part of his heart. Instead, she got a box room and was told to be grateful for it.

Grace noticed a red tin box in one of the draws she had been snooping in. It was locked. On her quest to anger her husband further, Grace began to slam the tin box against the desk, which resulted in nothing. She urgently looked through more draws looking for some kind of tool to prize it open with. Under a pile of unfiled papers, very unlike Henry, she came across a picture frame. The black and white photo was taken outside in someone's garden. She could see the glimpse of a picnic hamper in front of two people sat on small chairs—an elderly gentleman who looked rather scruffy with dirty fingers clasped around a mug and beside him sat a young girl. She could tell from the photo that her hair was dark, her eyes were wide, and she was wearing a gingham dress. They were both smiling from ear to ear. Grace had no idea who either of them were or why Henry had put it away in a draw. Looking straight at the young girl whose picture Henry had kept when he hadn't seemed like the sentimental type made Grace think was she looking at *her?* Finding herself more desperate to see what was hidden in the locked box, it dawned on her that the set of keys had one small key attached. Finding herself exhilarated once more she was ecstatic when it fit like a glove.

Inside, a carefully tied pile of envelopes were found. After further investigation she learnt that they were all written to Henry at an address in Durham. Prying open the first letter so harshly the paper ripped; Grace began to read.

Dear Henry,

It is me, Lottie, as you know I am here in London. My parents have all but abandoned me and stolen Betty as well. How could they do this? I'm their daughter, my dad talks of pain and loss, yet they torture me with a life sentence of grief. I don't even have a picture of her.

If you ever see her, please describe her to me, how she looks as she grows, describe her cries you hear through the night, the songs she falls asleep to. I need to know every detail. I can only imagine her angel face and the feel of her soft skin. I'm a mother without a child, Henry.

I'm sorry I couldn't say goodbye, my uncle outright refused, he along with the rest of my family want to keep me away from you. I miss you already. I can't not have you in my life that is why we need to be careful. My cousin William is going to post my letters for me, you must reply to the address that will appear on the front of the envelope. This is the address of his school, address it to Master W Anderson. I will be able to receive them each weekend. Please write to me Henry. I already feel like I'm losing my mind.

Love you always,

Your Lottie xxx

"Lottie!" Grace gasped.

Grace looked through more letters, words jumping out to her.

"I'm sorry you have fallen out with your dad, putting money away for us is a good idea. I wish I could do the same but pay at The American Eagle is shit! Hold on, our time will come."

The American Eagle, Grace thought. Her mind began to go into overdrive, as she read more.

"I would never pry you away from Walter and Sons, our home will be wherever you are."

"I love it when you talk of our future, I can't wait for the day you get me Henry."

"William believes I should start writing again, what do you think? Is this a dead-end dream?"

"Happy Birthday Henry! I so wish I were with you on your special day. I would buy you a cake and we could go and sit in the allotment with Mr Flint. Instead, I had to endure a celebration for Danny's birthday that filled me with guilt the whole time. I only went because I felt like I had to, and I really wish I hadn't."

"I miss you too, so much, it hurts me just as much."

"You have always wanted to keep me safe; you have always been my knight in shining armour."

"It's not fair that I should be trapped here while my sister enjoys my baby for the rest of her life."

"I saw him—I saw Joe."

"Your dad might want to know that he is at least alive. I feel like I cannot breathe. Lottie x P.S. love you always."

"I feel like I'm losing it, Henry. I am losing the will to live."

"I still can't believe that we got to speak on the phone! Hearing your voice was music to my ears. I just need to see you in person now."

Her sister had taken her baby. She had saw someone called Joe that she believed Walter would be happy to know was alive—was this Henry's brother? How crazy was it that she didn't even know her own husband's brother's name. After their small talk on Christmas Eve, he never mentioned him again. It was a subject that both Henry and Walter refused to speak of. Her sister had her baby, Grace thought back—she had mentioned she had been sent away. Baby Betty. One thing she did know was Henry's mum was named

Betty. All the pieces then slowly came together. Henry said his brother got a young girl pregnant, but her family took the baby away and sent her to live with family. This is the girl…Lottie. Who was sent to London and worked at The American Eagle and whose cousin was called William Anderson. Anderson was the surname of that woman whose picture was in the lobby and that fucking drink that Henry loved so much was called a *Lottie's Lychee Martini.* Not only that, but she recalled the annoying receptionist telling Henry that the granddaughter of that famous hotel lady now lived in none other than Cornwall, where the only yellow pin on the map was. Henry was in love with his dead brother's ex, and she must be the same girl from the picture frame.

Grace felt embarrassed as she thought back to how both Henry and the guy from the hotel behaved. They were discussing her in front of her and she had not an inkling. She thought of when she questioned Henry about what happened to his brother's girlfriend, and he told her that no one had seen her since. Had Henry seen her since? Grace searched every nook and cranny for more letters but there were none. Looking at the map she wondered if Henry really did have all those warehouses dotted around the country, taking trips away for meetings. Was he really going there or was he going to Cornwall to see her, where she was living with her children—were they his children? Did he have another family? Grace smashed the photo frame of the pretty girl against the wall, then tore the map off the wall. She cried in outrage and couldn't manage to calm herself down. She was fuelled with anger and all she wanted to do was hurt Henry like he had hurt her. Gathering all the letters she took them to the garden and threw them onto the floor before lighting them on fire with Henry's lighter. As she watched the flames erupt, they died quicker than anticipated on the wet grass, so Grace placed them on top of a few of Henry's files and watched them as they burnt to a crisp. It didn't make her feel as satisfied, as she had hoped although she knew it would devastate *her husband,* but she didn't feel guilty either—he deserved to know what it felt like to be wounded. He had married her with his heart already full of love for another knowing they never really stood a chance.

Whereas she had loved him so much and had been in denial, that she had married a man whose heart had already reached full capacity, leaving no room for her. He deserved it she told herself again. All she had to do now was wait for the coming storm.

Chapter Thirty-Eight

January 1979

Grace impressed herself by managing to pull herself together and cook a roast dinner for her family's arrival home. She looked every bit the perfect housewife. She had put on a floral frock. A gift from Gloria one year for Christmas, that she had never worn before, along with some pearl jewellery and pale pink high heels. She laid the table to sit two and had placed Henry's away separately on a plate covered in foil. She played the radio softly in the background and was ready just in time before they tumbled in.

"Mmm, smells nice," Sarah said, looking cautiously at Henry as they hung up their coats and took off their shoes. Grace had intentionally worn shoes indoors knowing it rattled Henry.

"Come and sit down Darling." Grace smiled pulling out a chair, making sure her heels could be heard on the shiny wooden floorboards.

"Will you sit with us Dad?" Sarah asked.

"I have some work to do first, I'll make something later."

"No need, I thought you might say that, so I wrapped some up for you to take to your shed," Grace said.

Henry took the plate as though it may explode in his hands. "Thanks, you shouldn't have."

"It's the least I can do, and for pudding we have chocolate muffins," Grace said cheerily, as he headed out.

Sarah tucked in hungrily and as she sat opposite her daughter, she felt a pang of guilt knowing her meal was about to be interrupted the moment Henry realised what she had done. Grace's hands began to shake as she cut into her chicken.

"GRACE!" Henry shouted from the garden.

Sarah looked at her mum with wide eyes, and a mouth full of instant mash.

"It's okay," Grace reassured her.

"GRACE!" he bellowed, throwing open the back door. "WHAT THE FUCK HAVE YOU DONE?" His face was scarlet; his veins almost popping out his head.

Grace stayed completely composed pouring a little more gravy on her plate. "Darling, you mustn't use that type of language in front of Sarah."

"Sarah, go upstairs," Henry demanded. Sarah looked hurt at his instruction and immediately jumped off her chair.

"Here, take the cupcakes." Grace passed her the plate with three chocolate muffins with chocolate icing on top to her daughter. "Eat as many as you like," she said with a wink.

With a last glance at Henry, who was breathing heavily and had thrown himself into her seat opposite Grace, Sarah went upstairs. As they waited to hear her door close, Grace carried on eating her meal. Henry's eyes bore into her.

"I have to say for me, this is actually quite good."

"What the fuck have you done?" he repeated once Sarah was out of ear shot.

"I was just having a clear out, I thought you would be pleased. I know you like things tip top around here."

"Don't play games with me Grace, you had no right to go through my possessions."

"Your secrets you mean."

"You have no idea what you have just done, I can never forgive you for this."

Grace sat back on her chair and grinned. "That is absolutely fine with me because Henry I do not seek your forgiveness, I seek nothing but a divorce."

"A divorce?" he repeated, sitting back on his own chair.

"Yes, I've called Daddy already. I am flying back to Ireland first thing in the morning, bags are already packed upstairs, and I am taking Sarah with me."

Henry laughed sarcastically. "Like fuck are you taking Sarah."

"Henry she is my daughter."

"You're a drunk!"

It was Grace's turn to laugh in Henry's face. "Darling, you are as much as a drunk as I am, you can just hide it better."

"It's not happening Grace; you want a divorce I will give you one. You want to leave in the morning, I will drop you off at the airport, but Sarah, she stays here with me," he said tapping the table.

Grace had felt brave deciding to leave Henry, after the letters burnt out, she had packed her and Sarah's bags feeling exhilarated, feeling like for the first time her heart had truly been lifted. She pictured herself and Sarah in Ireland going fishing in the river, catching up with old friends and their children, feeding the animals on the farm with Oskar, playing hide and seek in the great big house. It would be a fresh start, but it only felt right to have Sarah with her, she had issues she knew this, but she was not Linda. She could not abandon her child and walk away without her. Sarah was closer to Henry, she was aware of that, and leaving him would distress her, but she would get used to it. Hearing Henry put his foot down frightened her to the core, her strength disappeared, and the fear took over.

"Please Henry, let me take Sarah. It is the least you can do. You work all the time; I can be there for her. I will get help—real help—and I will have Daddy there to support us. I promise I will be a better mammy, but I can't do that here. I want to start again, to turn things around. We will be happy in Ireland. I promise you can have her every school holiday and any other time you want her, and you can stay with us whenever you like—in separate rooms of course. I really mean it Henry I want to better myself and being away from you, I really think I can."

Henry's face softened, though his glare was still intense, but his face was returning to its natural colour. "I am sorry that I have not been the man you wanted, the truth is I should never have agreed to marry you. You could be with someone better now, someone who you deserve. Despite our differences you have a good heart Grace and like you I too believe Ireland will be better for you. I want you to be happy and someone is out there who you will make you incredibly happy."

"Just not you."

Henry shook his head.

"Please, Henry, tell me, I have to know, have you seen Lottie since you found out she lived in Cornwall behind my back."

"No, not ever," he said, grabbing her hands from across the table. "I have not seen her for years."

Grace nodded. "Why haven't you? If she has meant so much to you all these years."

"When you have said goodbye to someone as many times as we have it starts to tear you up inside. I couldn't do that again."

"Would I like her?"

Henry shrugged his shoulders. "Do women like their husband's ex?"

Grace smiled. "I don't know, depends how they parted I suppose, how did you two end?"

Henry looked down. "The situation wasn't nice, but we weren't on bad terms with each other if that makes sense."

"Can you tell me about her?" Grace asked, wanting to know more about the woman Henry held a torch for.

"I don't think that's a good idea, it wouldn't be fair and to be honest I find it too difficult to talk about."

Grace nodded again, feeling strange to hear Henry filled with emotion. What she would have given to have had that, things could have been a lot different.

"Grace, I want you to know that I tried to love you. I really did, and like you I thought in time I would grow to. I'm sorry I couldn't and all I have ended up doing is hurting you instead. From the moment you met me, you met an emotionless man, and it was wrong of me to pursue you, wrong of me to bring you here to Epsom and marry you. I thought it was for the best and I don't regret having Sarah with you. She is the best thing to ever happen to me. Thank you for telling me when you didn't have to. You could have carried on studying and let your dad look after you both. I was a chance you took, and I am glad you did."

"If it weren't for you, I like to think I would be in a better position but being a young single mum out of wedlock is never easy. People look down on you and treat you different and you saved us from that—but now I feel stronger, and a failed marriage is not uncommon. So please Henry, can I take Sarah with me?"

Henry sighed, "Why don't we trial it. You take Sarah with you tomorrow, but you must get professional help as soon as possible."

"I promise I will!"

"And she has to come and spend the full Easter break with me."

"Of course."

"I will be ringing Sarah and asking how she is, how she feels, and I want to hear good things Grace, otherwise I will have to bring her back. It's going to break my heart having her leave, but me and Sarah have a great relationship and I want you both to have one too, but I will be keeping tabs, you have one shot at this Grace."

"I get it, thank you, I promise Henry this time it's going to be different."

"The road is going to be tough."

"I know, but I will do everything it takes."

"Okay, well we best get Sarah down here and tell her what's going to happen. Don't take it to heart if she needs a little persuasion."

Grace nodded, smiling from ear to ear. She meant her promise to Henry, and she would promise Sarah and her Daddy as well. She would get better. She had to. She was going to change her life for the better. Tomorrow morning, she was going to leave the tidy box she lived in, and the man who had her heart, but it was all going to be for the best. She had to start living in reality and say goodbye to broken dreams. She was going to save herself from the nightmares of being no better than Linda; and be Grace, mum to Sarah who was her number one.

1970s

Sarah

Chapter Thirty-Nine

April 1979

The noise from Sarah's shoes hitting the floor amplified as she ran into the arms of her dad at the airport. She had been longing for Easter to arrive ever since she moved to Ireland to live with her grandpops and her mum. She spent the first few weeks crying for her dad and everything she was used to, her bedroom, her school, her friends, Granda Walter and Nana Gloria, Auntie Polly and all her cousins. Sarah loved her grandpops and of course she loved her mum too, but she didn't like her new bedroom it was far too big and filled with toys she would never play with that once belonged to her mum. The teachers were mean at her new school and the children picked on her for her strange accent. Grandpops suggested home schooling one evening over tea, but her mum said she had to give it time, she believed she had to become a member of the community and the children would soon get used to how she spoke. Sarah wasn't upset when her parents decided to split up, she had friends who had separated parents who were devastated, whereas she never saw her parents as a normal couple, not like her Auntie Polly and Uncle Banks, or her grandparents. They held hands and pecked each other on the cheeks. Her's argued and threw things, and they never did anything as a family. What devastated Sarah was having to live with her mum when she really wanted to be with her dad. He was her everything, he knew how she liked her crusts cut off, or how to French plait her hair for school, he knew she didn't like her juice too strong, and that she was embarrassed that she couldn't grasp skipping. He was her best friend, yet everyone said her mum needed her. They told her she was poorly and was trying her best to get better just for her. So, Sarah felt like she had no choice but to be with her mum. She didn't want to tell her that she didn't like their new life and wanted to live with Dad because it was better there. She thought that might hurt her mum, so she said nothing, however school was over for two weeks and she was finally able to return home and be with her dad.

He picked her up and spun her round as he caught her after she'd lunged into his arms. Her grandpops had brought her over and was slowly making his way over, not able to keep up with his granddaughter.

"I missed you, Dad!" she squealed.

"I missed you too, Darling," Henry said pulling her closer to him. "How is Mum?" he asked.

"She is okay, she rides Chestnut most days and is going to special meetings."

"That's good," Henry said, putting Sarah down.

"Yesterday she had to go to her room, Grandpops said we had to lock her in."

"She relapsed," Mr O'Connell said, having caught up. "I've left her with Oskar, so will be heading straight back over. She was doing well though, Henry. She was getting upset about the holidays that's all. We will have her back in no time."

Henry nodded. "Ring me when you get back to Ireland, we will chat about it then. Well then, we best be off, got lots of fun to be had."

In the car, Henry told Sarah that they had to pop over to the office before heading over to see her grandad. She couldn't wait to see everyone, she had so much excitement building up inside her. Normally she would find sitting in her dad's office boring, but she actually found herself looking forward to it.

"Sarah!" Margret exclaimed from behind the reception desk. Her bright face looked pleased to see her, Sarah thought, taking in the bright orange lipstick and multi coloured top which reminded her of Elmer the elephant. When Sarah used to join her dad at work after school, she would spend the hours sitting at reception with Margret completing her homework while sharing her stash of sweets she kept in her top draw. She was like an auntie to her, she had known her, her whole life, saw her almost every day and every Christmas she was always given the wackiest pyjamas that were always her favourite pair. Today, however, Sarah wanted to sit with her dad in his office. She didn't want to miss one minute with him.

As her dad got on with his always very important work, Sarah sat opposite him in a leather chair diving into the book she'd been reading on the short plane ride. Her grandpops had bought her it before the flight, and so far, it had been a very good read, it had lots of funny parts that she couldn't help but laugh at. As Sarah let out a large belly laugh, Henry looked up from his work with a smile.

"What you reading there?" he asked.

"*Mischief in the Durham Lanes*, it's new, Grandpops said I don't have to read picture books anymore because I'm a big girl now and I'm a good reader."

"I lived in Durham when I was younger," he commented, before retreating back to his paperwork.

Sarah got stuck back into her book, she had never read anything like it before; every page had something she found either shocking or hilarious. Sarah reached a part of the story that made her both shocked and laugh so much at the same time that she found that she was gasping in between breaths.

"It can't be that funny," Henry said, laughing at his daughter. "Read some of it out, I want to hear it."

"Okay," Sarah said, wiping her eyes from joyful tears.

"*Colette believed Harry was the worst person in the whole entire world. During a P.E session at school she was happily skipping around the great hall in her underwear, trying to miss the bits of potato and mince still stuck to the floor that the dinner ladies had missed, when Harry crept up behind her and with one big tug pulled down her knickers. Colette was mortified and her face grew as red as a tomato. Her whole class erupted into laughter pointing at her with her knickers round her ankles. Harry's laugh was the loudest. As soon as she managed to pull her knickers back up, she launched herself at the horrible boy and began to slap him all over. She could feel his feeble hands trying to knock hers away, but she managed to keep slapping him as he screamed. Their teacher, Mr Evans, then pulled her off him.*"

Looking up at her dad she realised he was no longer smiling but looked deadly serious. "Do you not think it is funny, Dad?"

"What name is on the front of that book?" he asked.

"Erm…Lottie Rid-ley, Ridley."

"Do you mind if I take a look, please?"

Sarah passed her book across the desk to her dad who beamed upon inspection. He stroked the cover like you might stroke a cat before fanning through the pages. He then turned it over reading the blurb and opened the back page and gave a little gasp. Sarah thought he might even cry, his eyes went all watery. Sitting on her knees, leaning across the table she saw that the last page had a photo of a woman.

"Is that Lottie Ridley?" she asked.

"Yeah, that's her."

"Can I have my book back now please, Dad?"

"You have book three Darling; do you have any other ones?"

Sarah shook her head.

"Then we should go and check out the book shop. Get ya stuff, we should make it before closing time if we leave now."

Sarah laughed at her dad as he ran around his office turning everything off quickly as she put on her backpack. With her book still in his hand they jumped into the car, Sarah had only just managed to put her seatbelt on before her dad sped off. He had the roof down, and the wind was blowing her ponytail everywhere. Her dad was the best.

"How fast can you read?" Henry asked in the book shop.

"I don't know," she admitted.

"Okay, well we will buy two of each, and an extra copy of book three."

They didn't return to Walter and Sons once they had bought the books, nor did they visit Granda Walter like they'd planned. Instead, they headed straight home and spent the evening, legs stretched out, on the couch reading and laughing at the '*Mischief in the Durham Lanes*' series.

"Colette is my favourite," Sarah said, as they stopped to eat a Chinese.

"I agree," Henry said, shovelling chow mein in his mouth.

He didn't eat very grown-up Sarah noticed. "I don't like Harry and Jack very much; they are funny but mean."

"Agreed."

They read well into the night, Sarah hadn't realised how much fun reading with her dad could be, bath time didn't happen and nor did bedtime, for the last thing she remembered was her eyes growing heavy on the couch.

Chapter Forty

April 1979

As Sarah slowly woke up, slightly achy from falling asleep on the sofa, she could hear her dad pottering about in the kitchen. Sitting up she could see him wrapping up sandwiches in foil.

"Morning sleepy head," he said, as she yawned. The books they had been reading were sat on the coffee table with the pages folded like a dog ear to hold their last place. Sarah couldn't remember there ever being a time she had slept downstairs all night, normally her dad carried her to bed if she dropped off. "We're off on an adventure as soon as you're ready, so I need you to quickly go and brush your teeth and get into some fresh clothes."

"Where are we going?" Sarah asked rubbing her eyes.

"Cornwall. We are going to meet Lottie," he said, his smile almost reached his eyes, his wrinkles becoming more present.

"How do we know where she is?" she asked, picking up her book and looking at the authors face. She looked kind and pretty, Sarah thought.

"I called up an old friend of hers this morning, a man she used to work with at a hotel. He gave me her address." Henry placed the sandwiches into a grey backpack. "We should have done this years ago," he said so quietly she barely heard him. "She doesn't know we're coming so it will be a surprise."

"Are we really going to meet a real author, Dad?" Sarah asked, excitedly jumping up from the sofa.

"Yes, we are so hurry! Get dressed, it's a long drive."

The address of Lottie's house was scribbled on the back of an unopened postal envelope and was stapled to Henry's map. Her dad told her when they set off that he once knew the author, they had grown up together in Durham where they were neighbours. Sarah thought it was so fascinating that her dad knew the author already, that they were friends. The journey was long, but they were both so thrilled and eager to get to Cornwall. It was a warm day, so her dad pulled down the roof again and Sarah kept eating her hair when she was trying to tuck into her pack up. Henry was in such a happy mood; he played good songs that didn't make you sad, the kind of songs that meant they could dance in their seats and sing along to. He was tapping away on his steering wheel looking relaxed out of his work suit. He was wearing a white polo top and a pair of blue jeans, and he had shaved she noticed.

"You smell nice today, Dad."

"Thank you, Darling, tried out a new aftershave."

"I like it, have you been to Cornwall before?"

"Years ago, me and Granda Walter did some work there for a few years before going to Epsom. You will like it; the beaches are beautiful."

As they got closer to Cornwall, Henry turned the radio off and didn't talk anymore, concentrating on his map. Sarah looked out at the crystal blue sea on the horizon. She had only been to Brighton and Southend-on-Sea before. The streets were busy with people buying ice cream and different coloured rock, gift shops lined up for miles, and as the beach came into view, Sarah could see people scattered across the golden sand, opened umbrellas and plastic buckets and spades lit up in a rainbow of colour. White buildings sat against the backdrop of tall green banks. As they drove away from the busy coast they drove through quiet streets with cobbled roads, white cottages standing on either side.

"Look for number 27," her dad said peering out the window, driving extra slowly.

The cottages were small, with little panelled windows and tiny front gardens. Each one replicating the other in neat rows. They eventually stopped outside a house with a red door and bright flowers bloomed from every inch of the garden with ivy spiralling over one half of the house. Henry turned off the engine and everything was quiet, but the seagulls flying above.

"Is it the red one?" Sarah asked, pointing to the house on her left. Henry nodded, his face had gone pale, and he carefully folded up his map and put it away in his bag keeping a close eye on the house. "Come on then!" Sarah shouted, wanting to meet the author of her books.

"Let me go first, okay. Lottie will be very surprised that we have come all this way she might get a big shock," he said.

Sarah was bummed that she had to wait in the car but watched on as her dad knocked on Lottie's brass knocker and stood with his hands in his pockets. Her heart began to drum in her rib cage as she stared at the red door waiting for it to open. She had never met a friend of her dad's before she realised. Only Margret but she didn't really count because he was her boss. Henry knocked again; he began to rock on one foot.

"They are not in," a sweet looking lady called from across the road with two small pugs on spotty leads. "I saw them go out about twenty minutes ago." The pugs were pulling the lady, impatient for their walk.

"Thank you," Henry replied, heading back to the car.

"We will wait," he told Sarah, as they watched the lady being dragged up the street, for two small dogs they were strong.

They waited for what felt like hours, her dad said nothing as he stared out into space. Sarah tried to read her book, but her stomach kept rumbling. The pack up they had eaten was long gone.

"Can we get something to eat, Dad, I'm starving?"

Glancing around the street, he agreed, driving them back towards the seafront where they grabbed some chips. Smothered in salt and vinegar they were the best chips Sarah had ever tasted. They were sat on a small brick wall overlooking the beach, their feet dangling off the edge. Children were screaming as the waves washed over them, siblings were competing for the best sandcastles, parents were deep in conversations, grandparents were taking a nap and one baby Sarah observed was eating the sand in large mouthfuls, no one realising.

"There is something I want to tell you Sarah," her dad said. "Long before I met your mum, Lottie and I had become a little more than friends. I actually wanted to marry her."

Innocently feeding her hungry belly Sarah listened to her dad's news of his relationship with Lottie. "Did you love her?"

"I did, very much."

"Did you argue?"

Henry scoffed. "Yes, we did, everyone argues but we always made up in the end. It was kind of our thing."

"Did you kiss her?" Sarah asked giggling.

"I'm not answering that," he laughed.

"That means you did! You kissed Lottie." Sarah proceeded to pucker up her lips and pretend to kiss the air imitating her dad. Henry threw one of his chips at her to make her stop. Cackling away to her own joke, Sarah spotted a woman with shoulder length brown hair that had huge curls in walk across the sand. She was in a long cream dress covered in pink and red flowers on walking barefoot with a pair of brown sandals in one hand. Sarah watched on thinking she recognised the woman from somewhere. Her dad hadn't noticed her, he was too busy eating, dropping a chip as he tried to put too many in his mouth in one go. Then it suddenly dawned on her like a lightening flash.

"Lottie! Dad! There's Lottie, over there!" she squealed pointing to her in the distance. Her dad scanned the beach his eyes searching for her. "There in the flower dress!"

"Oh my God it is," he gasped. "S-Sarah, just wait here a moment okay, don't go anywhere, j-just hold on," he said, giving her his cone of chips.

Her dad bolted across the sand towards the author, Sarah held both cones tightly trying to nod her head to bring her shades down from her head to her eyes for a better look. Her dad was shouting her name catching the attention of some beach visitors, but she hadn't heard him. When Henry caught up with her, he touched her arm to gain her attention and as she turned towards him, she looked startled at first, before breaking into a grin. They were both smiling but Sarah noticed they were also crying at the same time. Henry stroked Lottie's cheek; her hair was blowing in her face, but she didn't seem to mind. Lottie couldn't stop looking at her dad, listening to whatever he was saying. She then rested her head against his. Her dad was still talking to her, but they were too far away for Sarah to lip read. Lottie was next to talk before closing her eyes and pulling her dad close for a hug. Apart from Sarah, she had never witnessed Henry embrace anyone before, he was a serious man and could be quite stand offish.

Turning their attention to Sarah, her dad waved her over to join them. Still clutching both chip cones, Sarah scuttled over to them nervously. She was even prettier in real life Sarah thought; her lips were coloured in a natural colour, and she had no other make up on but a pinch of pink on her cheeks.

"Hi Sarah," Lottie beamed, her accent just like her dads. "It is so good to meet you Sweetie."

Sarah was honoured that the author was pleased to meet her, she was just Sarah, a school kid whose mum was ill and whose dad worked all the time. There was nothing special about her, she was just Sarah Hollister. Sarah felt shy now that she was face to face with Lottie.

"Hi," she said.

"Sarah has been reading all your books, well we both have really," Henry said, his cheeks going pink.

"They are funny," Sarah added.

"Well, I am so glad to hear that you are enjoying them, that's what I love to hear."

"Harry is mean to Colette."

"Harry is mean to Colette, he is definitely the naughtiest character," Lottie said, looking at Henry with a smirk on her face.

"I wouldn't say he was the naughtiest," he said.

"He is Dad, he's always playing tricks and he put a spider in her hair."

"That is naughty," her dad agreed, for some reason he and Lottie giggled but Sarah didn't understand why.

Three teenagers approached them armed with ice creams with chocolate flakes.

"This is my little gang," Lottie said. "This is Florence," she said, pointing to the tallest girl who was wearing a short lilac dress with white peter pan collars and large white buttons down the front. Her hair was long with a ribbon tied on the top. "This is Nancy," Lottie continued, pointing to the second girl who wore her hair in a ponytail and was wearing blue trousers and a floral shirt. "And this is Arthur," she said pointing to the boy, he smiled at Sarah shyly in his green tartan pants and white long sleeved polo top. "Gang, this is Sarah, and this here is my oldest friend, Henry Hollister."

With the greetings over, Lottie invited them all to have tea at her house and told Sarah she could have a sneak peek at the new book she was writing.

"Should I give Sarah your ice cream Mum, I can go back and get you and Henry one?" one of the girls asked.

"Yes of course," Lottie replied. "I don't think I can eat just yet any way."

"I'm good too, but thank you," said Henry.

"Thank you," Sarah said, taking the ice cream from the girl who she thinks is called Florence. Lottie kindly took the chip cones from her.

"Should we head over then, there is so much I want to show you?" Lottie gleefully said to Sarah's dad.

"Course," he replied.

Sarah thought he was going to hold Lottie's hand, his fingers brushed against hers before pulling them away into his pocket.

As they headed to the cottage with the red door and the beautiful flowers, Sarah and her dad left the car in the car park without a care in the world. The grown-ups took the lead, deep in conversation, their heads close together, and they kept touching each other's arms as they spoke. Florence and Arthur stood behind them, it sounded like they were bickering about something. The other girl walked beside Sarah, Nancy she believed, or was it Darcy?

"I love your hair," she declared. "It is a beautiful colour."

Sarah smiled, licking her ice cream.

She thought she might be experiencing the best day of her life.

2020

The Last Chapter

2020

"So, it's true then? She's dead and buried," Grace said over the phone.

"Yes Mum, please don't be too sad about it," Sarah said sarcastically.

"She wasn't anything to me."

"No, but Noah lost a nana."

Grace laughed. "I am his nanny—she wasn't blood related to Noah."

"Just like his Grandad Oskar isn't either, eh?"

For a moment Sarah thought her mum had gone from the phone. "Okay, you got me, I just didn't like her alright. She took my girl from me."

"She never took me away from you, Mum," Sarah said rolling her eyes. "I chose to move to Cornwall. It was my choice."

Once they met Lottie everything changed for Sarah and her dad. Henry never wanted to leave Lottie, so he moved his whole life there to be with her and once Sarah returned to Ireland, she knew she had to be brave and tell someone how unhappy she was. She was longing for the beaches and bike rides with the gang who included her in everything. Lottie's hugs were warm, and she smelt like lavender, and her dad learnt how to laugh and live a little. At the time her grandpops was talking about her mum having to go away for a while to get better, so he believed it was the right thing for Sarah to go and live with her dad. Looking back, Sarah knew it devastated her mum and for a while she felt guilty about how great she felt her life was and that she grew close to Lottie that bit more every day. She thought she had let her mum down, but everyone told her that she had a voice that deserved to be heard too. Grace's path was bumpy for years, but there was light at the end of her tunnel; she opened her own riding school, married Oskar, and had two more children. Grace was a great mum, and Sarah was happy that she got it right in the end for all of them. The time spent with her mum in Ireland had become something special to look forward to. She loved her dearly and as she grew up Sarah began to understand her more. Grace's bitterness however had never subsided, and she forever blamed Lottie.

"Right, I have to go Mum I have an extremely busy day ahead."

"Well, call me when you're free. I miss you."

Thankfully, she had missed the downpour before heading to the cemetery. The sun was now peeping out of the clearing, the dark clouds subsiding and making room for the beautiful clear blue sky. Sarah took the familiar path to the gravestone she was visiting with a huge bouquet of white chrysanthemums and purple lisianthus with a few yellow roses from one of Lottie's neighbours. Ahead she spotted an elderly gentleman leaning on a cane stood by the grave with an elegant olive-skinned woman beside him. They both looked at her almost anxiously as she approached awkwardly, she had no idea who they were, but Lottie was a popular woman and she had learnt that some people like to just stop at the resting places of new residents of the cemetery to see who they were, how old they were when they died, and who they were leaving behind.

"Good morning," she said, carefully placing the bouquet down. "Sorry to disturb you both."

"Not at all," the gentleman said, his voice croaky. "She's been spoilt." He gestured towards her many flowers.

"Yes, she has." The pain of losing Lottie was still too raw, yet not surprisingly ever since they lost her dad two years ago, Lottie never recovered. Although it was his heart that had failed him, it was her heart that felt the constant pain. Losing Henry had sent a shock wave through the family, he was fit as a fiddle helping Arthur decorate his son's new flat when he collapsed from the ladder and was gone just like that. Heart attack they were told, it was hereditary Lottie had said. From then on Lottie's health went downhill. "Were you friends of Lottie?"

"We go back a long time," the gentleman said, he looked familiar she noted, his eyes were shining brightly despite his age, and his hair flopped to one side thinly.

"We will leave you to it," said the woman, her English hinting a foreign tone to it. She placed a card into a new bouquet of flowers and linking the man they set off, not before the gentleman gave her a subtle nod.

Eager to know who they were, she bent down to read the message and gasped, skipping a full heartbeat or two as she read *Joe and Betty*.

"Stop!" she shouted. They abruptly stopped at her yell still only about two metres away. "You're Joe, my Uncle Joe. You're Betty—I'm Sarah, I am your stepsister." She couldn't help but laugh from pure joy. "I can't believe you're here. You came to see her."

Joe looked at Sarah with pure joy. "My niece, oh my." The cane began to shake a little under his grip. "Stepsister you said, not half?"

"I am Henry's daughter, but Lottie was as good a mum as ever, I certainly felt like her real daughter."

"And the others?" he asked curiously.

"They are all biologically Lottie's but like me, they all loved my dad as their own."

"Hmm, I always assumed they had you all together."

"I bet there is loads you both want to know, and I have to say seeing you both here, together, has baffled me. I know this may sound a little too much, but I am heading to Lottie's house now to meet with the others. I know they will all really want to meet you both and there are some things there that I believe you might be interested in. So, what do you say, will you come?"

Betty looked frightened by Sarah's proposal, Joe looked at her with a reassuring smile and held her hand.

"What do you say, kiddo? I think it's a lovely idea. You will get to meet your siblings."

"They are really good people, Betty. I would never throw you into an awkward position if I thought it would make you uncomfortable. I know it's a lot and all at once, but I just know what it would mean to them."

Betty nodded. "Alright, I suppose there's no time like the present."

"That's my girl," Joe said, kissing his daughter's hand.

Sarah felt like Father Christmas letting herself quietly into the beach house. She found the gang in the open plan kitchen area going through boxes of Lottie and Henry's belongings. The magnificent glass wall overlooking the sea brought in the sun as Sarah arrived with her newfound family.

"Wow!" Joe exclaimed taking in the view.

His voice caught the attention of the others who looked curiously at each other before Sarah introduced them all. It was a beautiful moment when they realised who they were in the presence of, Sarah was choked as she watched Florence, Nancy, and Arthur embrace Betty. She watched the Parisian woman's guard fall a little as her eyes glistened more with each arm that wrapped around her. Sarah passed Joe a tissue for his tears.

Florence began fussing in the kitchen getting the cups of tea brewing, while the rest sat down on the large couches overlooking the sea.

"This is impressive," Joe said, as he lowered himself slowly down.

"Mum and Dad bought it after they got married and sold both their properties. It was cheaper back then than what it is worth now and they did a lot of work to it," Arthur said.

While Betty sat fiddling with a diamond ring dangling on a chain around her neck, Joe asked question after question about what happened to Lottie, from being in London after Betty's birth to marrying Henry. There was a lot to talk about, but they filled Joe in the best that they could.

"This must be quite overwhelming Betty," Nancy said. "Is there anything you would like to ask us?"

"I don't know," she said shrugging her shoulders. "I suppose the only question I have is did she ever try looking for me?"

"Lottie wrote to her parents many times, asking for an address to contact Cathleen but she never got a reply, so she and William, her cousin, went back to Durham to ask them in person but were sad to find they no longer lived there," Florence told her.

"She was adamant they would never move out of their terraced house, that it had been in the family for years. She found that everything had changed, and everyone had moved on or didn't talk to her parents anymore," Arthur added.

"That was brave of her to go back there," Betty noted.

"Lottie kept you both a secret until Dad died. We thought Uncle Joe had died in a motorcycle accident, Dad never spoke about you but when Lottie began to get poorly, she told us the truth about both of you. She said it had been too painful to mention before," Sarah said.

"She even asked us to go back there again—to the village she grew up in, only about six months ago," Nancy told them.

"She said she wanted to see it one more time, so we all piled into my mini and took her where she wanted to go," said Arthur, chuckling at the memory. "The girls were squashed in the back, took us hours to get there."

"I still say the train would have been better," Florence piped up.

They all went on to tell Joe and Betty how when they arrived, Lottie had mentioned feeling like her life there had belonged to someone else. She hated that the fields and hills had become modern houses and office buildings. She even struggled at times to navigate where she was until she reached the terraced houses, which were like a time warp, they all stood to attention like rows of men on a battlefield, the small shops were all the same as she remembered minus the change of names.

"My goodness it looks all but the same," Lottie gasped as they stood outside the Victorian built school, standing as it always had with its terracotta bricks and surrounding wall that her brother Peter used to run a stick along. She had pictured him in his little buckled shoes and long socks. As a member of staff walked through an automatic door, Lottie looked disappointed. They took a moment to sit in the church next door to the school, nothing had changed, it was exactly as she had envisioned. Even the red hymn books at the end of each pew. There she told them about the weddings and the christenings and the boring Sunday visits she had to sit through, forcing herself at times not to fall asleep during mass. The community hall had been converted into a day nursery and the park had been replaced with a care home. She pondered the thought that some of her old friends may be within the walls before her.

"I do like to think that Molly and Carol left this place and had adventures of their own and if they are in there then I will let them be. For we are not the same girls who once walked these streets."

Behind the care home, they came to a lovely large grass area. Small council bungalows sat in a circle surrounding the green with a large tree in the middle of it. Lottie could barely get there fast enough, her elderly body overcome with sudden energy as she made her way to the tree. They all stopped and watched their mum walk around the trunk scanning it until she found what she was looking for. She traced the rough bark with her shaking fingers, and they were heartbroken to witness the strong woman crumble. They sat on the grass and let her stay there a while wondering why the tree was so special. All Lottie's stories had been brief, with not much meat to them, so none of them could come up with an explanation. When she finally pulled herself away the gang made a plan for Arthur to pretend he dropped his car keys so he could run back and inspect the tree, he later told them that the letters **H + C** had been carved into it in the middle of a heart with the word ***Forever*** underneath.

Lottie's greatest disappointment was the allotments, which had been replaced by a supermarket. She cried for the flowers planted, for the fallen, the beauty created by hands each year, the picnics and the company enjoyed well into the evenings, the sanctuary to run to when feeling fear and despair, the sheds where lovers hid, and life was brought into the world. Not far from the supermarket down a short lane stood a row of terrace houses all neat and tidy she pointed at number 17; it was a bright yellow door with double glazed windows. She said it was the home of Mr Flint, a man all the gang were familiar with. Henry and Lottie had told them many tales of their friend. Sarah's middle name Rufina was even given in honour of the gentleman.

"Despite the makeover and the new occupants, to me this house will always belong to the kindest man I knew," Lottie said, before moving on to her old lanes standing outside of number 29 and 31. Sarah remembered thinking what on earth must people have thought if they looked out their window to see five people stood staring at their houses.

"This street, this village, hold both the saddest memories of my life but also some of the most beautiful," Lottie sniffed.

They didn't stop for too long, they were all aware of the stories that had unfolded there, it had all got too much for Lottie and she called it a day. However, while driving towards Durham city centre, not far from the end of the village, Lottie asked Arthur to park his car at the bottom of a steep hill. Florence aided her mum as they made the trek up to the top where the view was breath-taking, they could see out for miles, hills, fields, and Durham. They sat down together, and Lottie told them that Joe had brought her up there a few times.

"We were so foolish," she said tearfully.

"You were both young, Mum," Arthur told her.

"And both grieving," Nancy added.

"Do you think he is still alive, still out there somewhere?" Sarah asked.

"If he is, then I like to think he's finally been able to stop running."

Joe wiped his eyes then filled them in on his journey in life and how he came to be with Betty.

"She was so desperate in the end to know what happened to you both and her brother Peter," Florence said, piling the empty mugs into a tray. "We tried searching for you all online but couldn't find anything."

"Oh, my Uncle Peter died in the Falkland War," Betty revealed sadly.

"That would have made Mum very sad to hear, but she would be so thrilled to see us all here now in her house, sat all together," Nancy smiled.

"Even if we arrived late to the party?" Betty questioned.

Nancy gripped her big sister's hand. "If there is one thing I know about our mum, it's that she believed it was never too late for anything."

One Last Bit

2020

Down in the basement Sarah was showing Joe and Betty some items she thought they might like to see. With upstairs always so spacious and tidy, the gang had never realised how much stuff their parents had stored away. Straight away, with some help down the stairs, Joe got excited.

"Look at that sign!" Pushed to the back wall was a large shop sign. "This is the original sign for my dad's shop, I remember sweating in that little workshop."

"They grew massively, we have a Walter and Sons in almost every city in the UK and Northern Ireland," Sarah said.

"It was the dream," he beamed.

They came across a cardboard box filled with old draft manuscripts of Lottie's books.

"I am so glad she achieved her dream, she was talented," Joe said.

"What is this?" Betty asked, picking up a delicate black book with thin yellowed pages. "Is this Charlotte's?"

"This is Lottie's Auntie Joy's book of poems; she actually got them published into a book. You should read it; it is called *Bloom: by Joy Anderson."*

"Wow, are these her journals?" Joe exclaimed picking up a fragile notebook. "She never went anywhere without these, when we ran away, she barely had any clothes at first because her journals took up all the space in her bag.

There are so many more it seems. So many more years I was never a part of. Have you read them?" Joe asked Sarah.

"Yes," she admitted. "We all have."

"Did she hate me?"

"No, she didn't hate you Uncle Joe. You gave her so much hope and happiness in that little flat above the bookshop," Sarah smiled.

"If it wasn't for me then she wouldn't have had to go through everything she did with that Danny guy," Joe said with gritted teeth.

"Dad, that was not you're doing. Charlotte had a haemorrhage after she had me, therefore her parents would have found out about me regardless. Sadly, Charlotte would have still ended up in London and perhaps still ended up in Danny's clutches," Betty said placing an arm around Joe. "It was the adults that failed her, I love my maman, I can't help that, but since knowing about Charlotte, you know I wasn't on great terms with my grandparents."

Joe nodded.

"The past can't be changed no matter how much you have at times wished it, but without all the paths everyone took, it could just be me and you standing in this room now," she added smiling at Sarah.

Ebb Tide played loudly above their heads followed with a loud laugh from Nancy.

"It was Dad's favourite," Sarah informed them.

Joe lifted an eyebrow. "Really?"

"Yes, there is a sentimental reason behind it that we found in Lottie's journals after years of having to endure it."

Next, they came to the box that Sarah really wanted Joe to see, the box of old photos that had been inherited when her Granda Walter had passed away. Joe shed more tears the moment Sarah showed him the first set.

"Gosh, I haven't seen my parent's faces in decades."

"You look like your dad," Betty cheerily said giving her dad a squeeze.

He flicked through birthdays and Christmas', school picture day and baby pictures. Then he came across a photo of Henry and Lottie's First Holy Communion. They were stood side by side outside St. Mary's door all dressed to the nines, their hands together as though in prayer and behind them stood Cathleen and Joe and they were all grinning from ear to ear.

"Did they have a wonderful life together?" Joe asked.

"They did, they gave us all a great example of what a great marriage should look like."

"I'm glad. That is all I hoped—for both of them."

"You know, she would be so pleased to know that you both have also had wonderful lives. She felt immense guilt that she had let you both down."

"We were impulsive, but I regret none of it, my time with her will always be looked on as nothing more than magical and it gave me my Betty, of course."

Betty smiled at her dad's words.

"I hope one day I will get to meet them both again, and I will introduce them to my late wife, Madeline, and together we might be able to start again in harmony. I hope the bad times can be healed and I can be forgiven."

Sarah placed her hand on her uncle's arm, feeling the very same jacket Lottie had many moons ago. "I believe you will be."

Fin.

Acknowledgement

Love Lottie was not a planned novel, it came to me during my third draft of Dear Lottie. I grieved for the end of my characters and wished to do more with them so Love Lottie was created.

Again I have to thank my partner, our girls, and my mam for being my biggest fans and cheering me on. Their love and enthusiasm has kept me pursuing my dreams.

To my editors, Jessica Runyard and Sophie Tate you take my story and wave your magic wands, thank you very much.

I thank Peter and Caroline at Bespoke Book Covers for another beautiful cover. As soon as I saw it, I knew all my ideas were taken into account and it looks gorgeous next to Dear Lottie.

Every author loves writing and loves the moment where they get to hold their book for the first time, but what I also love is the feedback and the excitement from my readers. So I thank YOU.

You didn't think I would just leave it like that did you?
What did Henry say to Lottie on the beach?
What was their life together like?
What did Walter think of it all?
What happened to Danny?

There will be a Lottie and Henry novella as well as a spin off novel featuring one of the characters from the books in the future.

In the meantime I am publishing a new novel next year with a brand new couple to fall in love with. To keep up to date with upcoming novels follow me on Instagram @melswritingjourney.

If you enjoyed Love Lottie don't forget to leave your review on Amazon, Goodreads, or Instagram.

Printed in Great Britain
by Amazon

44389842R00212